PRAISE FOR
THE DEADLY OPS SERIES

Bound to Danger

"Reus follows *Targeted* with a fast-paced, high-stakes romantic thriller. . . . Strong characterization and steadily mounting tension are powerful weapons in this talented author's arsenal." —*Publishers Weekly*

"Katie Reus has the amazing ability of pulling the reader onto the front lines of the action and drama. *Bound to Danger* is a fast-paced, intelligent, and spirited story of suspense, mystery, intrigue, and murder. . . . It is a story of heartbreak and grief; friendship and love; betrayal and revenge." —The Reading Cafe

"*Bound to Danger* is both romantic and suspenseful, a fast-paced, sexy book full of high-stakes action." —Heroes and Heartbreakers

"Loved. This. Book. *Bound to Danger* by Katie Reus is why I read romantic suspense. It is an emotional ride that will have you on the edge of your seat during the action scenes and your heart melting during the passionate ones. The plot engages you from the beginning and has you turning pages quickly." —Magical Musings

Targeted

"Fast-paced romantic suspense that will keep you on the edge of your seat!" —*New York Times* bestselling author Cynthia Eden

"Sexy suspense at its finest." —*New York Times* bestselling author Laura Wright

"Reus strikes just the right balance of steamy sexual tension and nail-biting action. . . . This romantic thriller reliably hits every note that fans of the genre will expect." —*Publishers Weekly*

"Nonstop action, a solid plot, good pacing, and riveting suspense." —*RT Book Reviews*

"Katie Reus pulls the reader into a story line of second chances, betrayal, and the truth about forgotten lives and hidden pasts." —The Reading Cafe

"If you are looking for a really good, new military romance series, pick up *Targeted*! The new Deadly Ops series stands to be a passionate and action-riddled read."
—That's What I'm Talking About

continued . . .

W9-CDI-418

PRAISE FOR
THE MOON SHIFTER SERIES

Mating Instinct

"Katie Reus creates a vivid world filled with sexy shifters, explosive danger, and enough sexual tension to set the pages on fire. A fabulous paranormal romance!"

—*New York Times* bestselling author Alexandra Ivy

"*Mating Instinct*'s romance is taut and passionate. Add to that a fast-paced suspense plot and a deftly built paranormal world, and Katie Reus's newest installment in her Moon Shifter series will leave readers breathless!"

—*New York Times* bestselling author Stephanie Tyler

"I could not put this book down. . . . Let me be clear that I am not saying that this was a good book *for* a paranormal genre; it was an excellent romance read, *period*."

—All About Romance

"A sexy, well-crafted paranormal romance that succeeds with smart characters and creative world building."

—*Kirkus Reviews*

"This series keeps getting better and better."

—Joyfully Reviewed

Primal Possession

"Reus has definitely hit a home run with this series. . . . This book has mystery, suspense, and a heart-pounding romance that will leave you wanting more."

—Nocturne Romance Reads

"Reus's world building is incredibly powerful as she seamlessly blends various elements of legend and myth. . . . But the romance between a shifter and human is the real highlight—it's lusty, heartfelt, and shows love can conquer all."

—*RT Book Reviews*

"[*Primal Possession*] has all the right ingredients: a hot couple, evil villains, and a killer action-filled plot. . . . [The] Moon Shifter series is what I call Grade-A entertainment!"

—Joyfully Reviewed

"If you like your romance hot with plenty of buildup and a plot that sucks you right in, *Primal Possession* is simply a must read."   —A Book Obsession

"Impossible to put down. . . . Ms. Reus bangs out a top-quality story."   —Fresh Fiction

Alpha Instinct

"Reus has an instinct for what wows in this perfect blend of shifter, suspense, and sexiness. Sexy alphas, kick-ass heroines, and twisted villains will keep you turning the pages in this new shifter series. *Alpha Instinct* is a winner."
           —*New York Times* bestselling author Caridad Piñeiro

"A wild, hot ride for readers. The story grabs you and doesn't let go."   —*New York Times* bestselling author Cynthia Eden

"Reus crafts a fast-paced action story. . . . *Alpha Instinct* is awesome: an engrossing page-turner that I enjoyed in one sitting. Reus offers all the ingredients I love in a paranormal romance."   —Book Lovers Inc.

"Prepare yourself for the start of a great new series! . . . I'm excited about reading more about this great group of characters."   —Fresh Fiction

"A strong book full of mystery, intrigue, and a new world to explore."   —Ramblings from a Chaotic Mind

"If you're looking for a new shifter romance to sink your teeth in, then look no further. *Alpha Instinct* is action-packed with a solid romance that will keep the reader on the edge of [her] toes! . . . Highly recommended for fans of Rachel Vincent's Werecat series."   —Nocturne Romance Reads

"A well-plotted, excellently delivered emotional and sensual ride that grabs hold and doesn't let go! . . . Ms. Reus delivers mystery, suspense, and a romance nothing short of heart pounding!"   —Night Owl Reviews

ALSO BY KATIE REUS

The Deadly Ops Novels
Targeted
Bound to Danger
Chasing Danger
(A Penguin Special from Signet Eclipse)

The Moon Shifter Novels
Alpha Instinct
Lover's Instinct
(A Penguin Special from Signet Eclipse)
Primal Possession
Mating Instinct
His Untamed Desire
(A Penguin Special from Signet Eclipse)
Avenger's Heat
Hunter Reborn

Enemy Mine
(A Penguin Special from Signet Eclipse)

SHATTERED DUTY

A DEADLY OPS NOVEL

KATIE REUS

A SIGNET ECLIPSE BOOK

SIGNET ECLIPSE
Published by the Penguin Group
Penguin Group (USA) LLC, 375 Hudson Street,
New York, New York 10014

USA | Canada | UK | Ireland | Australia | New Zealand | India | South Africa | China
penguin.com
A Penguin Random House Company

First published by Signet Eclipse, an imprint of New American Library,
a division of Penguin Group (USA) LLC

First Printing, June 2015

Copyright © Katie Reus, 2015

Penguin supports copyright. Copyright fuels creativity, encourages diverse voices,
promotes free speech, and creates a vibrant culture. Thank you for buying an
authorized edition of this book and for complying with copyright laws by not
reproducing, scanning, or distributing any part of it in any form without permission. You are supporting writers and allowing Penguin to continue to pub-
lish books for every reader.

SIGNET ECLIPSE and logo are trademarks of Penguin Group (USA) LLC.

ISBN 978-0-451-41923-1

Printed in the United States of America
10 9 8 7 6 5 4 3 2 1

PUBLISHER'S NOTE
This is a work of fiction. Names, characters, places, and incidents either are the
product of the author's imagination or are used fictitiously, and any resem-
blance to actual persons, living or dead, business establishments, events, or
locales is entirely coincidental.

If you purchased this book without a cover you should be aware that this book
is stolen property. It was reported as "unsold and destroyed" to the publisher
and neither the author nor the publisher has received any payment for this
"stripped book."

For my wonderful husband. Thank you for helping me brainstorm and for being so patient when I pepper you with a dozen seemingly random questions at once. You keep me sane.

Prologue

Tango: NATO Phonetic Alphabet representation of the letter T. In military and law enforcement operations, tango often means target/terrorist.

Seven years ago

Levi hated the fucking jungle. Give him the desert or mountains any day of the week over the wet, muddy, dangerous jungle. He eased out onto one of the branches of the tree he was currently hiding in, careful to ensure there weren't any snakes waiting to strike.

Nature in this Colombian hellhole was just as deadly as the men he was about to kill. Venomous snakes, insects the size of your face, deranged flying termites—which weren't actually deadly, just annoying as shit—and poisonous tree frogs were the tip of the spear for what he had to look out for. In addition to gun-toting assholes.

The branch was thick, sturdy, and because of Diego Jimenez's stupidity in not trimming the foliage around his mansion, it was the perfect way to gain entrance into the piece of garbage's house. Levi had very specific orders and for one of the few times in his career in the Marine Corps, he had authorization to kill on sight. Didn't have to worry about being fired on first or other rules of engagement. Every single person in this house and on the grounds was the enemy.

Since Levi knew Jimenez was into the skin trade, he didn't feel an ounce of guilt. Anyone working for the guy should die. No one had a right to own another human being, much less rape and degrade them.

It was close to three in the morning and even though there were guards on the twenty-acre property, Jimenez kept only a total of five outside and right around the exterior of the house. Since the skin trader had a secured wall around his property he thought he was safe. His arrogance would be one of the things that got him killed.

Somehow this guy had pissed off someone in the CIA; it was why Levi was here. All he knew at this point was that Jimenez had taken a teenage girl and was keeping her captive. No details about what she looked like or why she was important. Just that she was an asset to national security and he must retrieve her at all costs, killing whoever got in his way. A teenage girl was important to national security? He wasn't sure he bought that—more likely she was the daughter of someone important—but he didn't need a reason to help a female.

Below him one of the guards strolled by with an AK-47 held loosely at his side as he puffed on a cigarette. His laziness was offensive, making Levi want to drop down and kill the guy right now on principle.

Once the man had passed under him and rounded

the corner of the home, Levi continued inching his way along the branch until he hovered five feet above a small stone balustrade balcony. After another visual sweep of the surrounding land, he dropped down, his boots making a soft thud barely audible over the sound of monkeys and birds. Still, he crouched low, peering through the opening of the stone columns, waiting to see if he'd been discovered. There was a video camera by the top corner of the French door of the balcony, pointing right at him.

Jimenez had security cameras all over the compound and Levi had avoided most of them. It had been impossible to remain completely invisible though. He wasn't a ghost. He waited thirty seconds, counting down in anticipation of an alarm sounding.

Nothing.

Somehow, he was still undetected. He and the rest of his six-man team waiting in the jungle had been told that he'd have twenty minutes where the video feeds would fail. Until now he hadn't been positive it was true, but there was no way he'd have made it this far without those things being disabled.

It was go time.

Turning toward the doors, he quickly jimmied the lock and slipped inside. Again, no alarm, as promised. He'd also been given instructions and a crude map for how to rescue the principal. The French doors were the entry point in what appeared to be an unused guest room. He wouldn't be going out this way though. Hell, no. He'd be going right out the front gate.

Normally he had his M-4 carbine rifle for any mission, but not this one. It was too bulky for the close quarters and likely hand-to-hand combat he'd be facing. He was coming in with his silenced MP5 submachine gun, a KA-BAR knife for up close kills, grenades in case he had a hot exit, and enough Semtex to blow this place to the ground.

This job was too last minute and they didn't have enough intel. Less than twenty-four hours ago he'd been at Camp Pendleton, debriefing his commander on his most recent mission and dreaming about a cold beer when two men in black suits—like a fucking cliché—walked in and ordered him out. Barely a half hour later he was gearing up again and headed out on an unmarked cargo plane to a vague destination with a team of guys just as in the dark as he was about the mission.

His commander had demanded he be on point for this since he had more experience and more kills. Now he was about to put his skills to good use.

Scanning the plush room, he made his way to the far door. First, he placed a small brick of explosive under one of the dressers, pushing it up against a wall. It was undetectable to the eye in case anyone peeked in the room in the next few minutes. Once it was in place, he paused at the door and listened intently before slowly pulling it open.

One of his sidearms drawn, he swept out into the hall. Empty. His rubber-soled boots were silent as he hurried down the hall, mindful of the damn video cameras.

Even though they were turned off, their presence made him feel like he had a bull's-eye on his forehead. At the designated door he found the keypad entry system just as he'd been told. Levi typed in the code he'd memorized, wincing at the soft beeps each press of a button made. The door opened with a barely discernible click. The CIA must have a seriously deep mole in Jimenez's organization for this kind of intel.

His boots were silent as he descended the flight of stairs. According to his information there might or might not be a guard waiting. He slung his MP5 over his shoulder, then pulled out his KA-BAR as he reached the bottom stair.

The stairs opened up into another hallway with three doors. A guard was leaning against the wall next to the middle door—where Levi needed entrance—looking at his cell phone. Probably texting.

Without pause Levi hauled back and threw the blade at the man. It hit its mark, sinking into his throat.

Eyes wide, the guard's phone fell from his fingers, clattering against the wooden floor as he reached up for his neck, making choking sounds. Before the man's knees had even hit the ground, Levi had closed the distance between them. He withdrew the blade, then cut the man's throat. Quick and efficient. Unfortunately there was a shitload of blood.

Shoving the body to the side, he easily picked the lock. Adrenaline pumping, he withdrew one of his backup pistols. The back of his neck was tingling, his gut telling him the shit was about to hit the fan.

His instinct was never wrong.

Pushing out a slow breath, he eased the door open, weapon at the ready.

There was only one piece of furniture in the small room: a twin bed. A slim, hooded female was lying on her side on it. Her arms were bound in front of her with flex cuffs and she wore thin shorts and a tank top. Her breathing kicked up the slightest notch when he stepped into the room, so he knew she wasn't asleep, but she also wasn't calling attention to herself. Smart. She was tall and thin but he couldn't tell if she was the teenager or not. She was a little more developed than he expected a teenager to be. Still, even if she wasn't part of the mission he wasn't leaving any woman here like this. He didn't have the operational latitude to make that kind of decision but if the CIA didn't like it, they could suck his dick. No one was getting left behind tonight and if he had to improvise, so be it.

"Scorpion?" he whispered, the only code word he had to give her.

At that she jolted upright. "Yes." Her voice was raspy beneath the hood, as if she hadn't used it lately.

There was a metallic collar around her neck, holding the hood in place. "I'm going to cut your hands free, so don't move," he whispered, moving to kneel in front of her. "Is the collar rigged?"

"No, but it's impossible to take it off without tools. I can see well enough anyway. We need to leave," she whispered as he sliced through the cuffs, her body shaking with tension.

"Do I need to carry you or can you really see with that thing?" It was a mesh material that looked breathable, just uncomfortable.

"I can see your face paint," she said, standing. She reached out and touched his paint-covered cheek. She still sounded hoarse. He wondered if her throat had been injured but didn't ask. First he needed to get her to safety.

He was surprised she'd touched him, but didn't pull away. Poor kid, he hated imagining what she must have been through. He tapped his earpiece. "Scorpion acquired. Everyone in position?"

Once he received affirmations from the team, he pulled out another small explosive and placed it in a corner of the room. Then he nodded toward the door. "Your guard is dead. I'm going to carry you over him so you don't step in blood." There weren't any shoes or clothes in the room, so she'd be leaving like this. "Whatever I say, you do it. Don't question me and we'll get out of here alive. Understood?"

"Yes. Can I have one of your guns?"

She surprised him again by the question but considering how scared she had to be, he figured she wanted a way to protect herself. "You won't need it." Without waiting for a response, he lifted her into his arms and hurried toward the door. He hadn't heard anything, but he scanned the hallway before stepping over the body and back toward the stairs. At the foot of the stairs he placed her on her feet and glanced at his watch even though his internal clock told him how much time had passed since his infiltration. Keeping his voice low, he said, "We've got eleven minutes to get to the garage unseen. After that, we're going to come under heavy fire, but that's okay because we've got backup. You're going to stay down and out of range. No matter what happens, you keep your head down. If something happens to me, my team will get you out of here."

She nodded, the hood moving oddly over her face. "I promise. . . . Thank you."

That was all the affirmation he needed. Moving

swiftly, they ascended the stairs. The upper hallway was still empty. He was glad because he didn't want to have to kill someone in front of the girl. She was likely already traumatized enough.

Two doors down on the right side he stopped. There was another keypad. As he typed in the code, he felt her tentative hand at his back.

When he turned, she leaned in close. "There will be at least two guards in the garage." Her voice was barely above a whisper.

He held a finger to his lips.

She nodded and wrapped her arms around herself, clearly nervous, but at least she was keeping it together. He didn't have time for a hysterical principal. It would fuck up the entire op. When they reached the end of the stairs he glanced over his shoulder just to make sure she was still with him. Beyond the stairwell he could hear male voices. Multiple. More than two.

Shit.

He peered around the corner before quickly ducking back. There were four men, all clustered together as they joked about tag-teaming some woman. His mother had been born in the United States but her parents had emigrated from Spain and she'd taught him what she considered pure Spanish. But he understood these fuckers perfectly well even with some of the different pronunciations. Oh yeah, these guys were going to die tonight. Levi took out another explosive and placed it on one of the stairs.

He motioned for the girl to stay put, then handed her his KA-BAR. Under normal circumstances he'd never give up a weapon, but he wanted her to have a way to defend herself. When she just nodded and clutched the knife tightly in her grip, he readied his MP5.

Envisioning the scene, he knew he'd have one chance to take these guys out in a single sweep. Their close proximity gave him a huge advantage. Finger on the trigger, he stepped from his position and opened fire.

Only one of the men managed to reach for his weapon before they all hit the ground, covered in blood, dead or dying. The MP5 was truly a masterpiece of weaponry. Unlike other submachine guns with silencers this beauty used standard ammo and was one of the most accurate of its kind. And he loved it. He tapped his earpiece as he peered back around the corner of the stairwell. As he waved at the girl to move, he said, "Exiting now. Watch for movement."

"We've got eyes on the gate."

While the girl stepped cautiously into the four-car garage, he quickly scanned for some sort of key holder. A pegged board or—

"They're in the vehicles," she said, reading his mind, still clutching his knife like her life depended on it. Not that he blamed her. What he wouldn't give to kill Jimenez himself.

Nodding, Levi pointed at the biggest SUV. As she hurried toward the passenger side he placed Semtex under the other three vehicles: two cars that cost more than he made in a year and a custom-made ATV.

Moments later he was in the driver's seat, his adrenaline flashing through him like lightning even though he was rock steady. He wanted to order her into the back, but didn't bother. They wouldn't be in the SUV very long. Just as she'd said, the key was in the visor.

"Moving out now," he said as he started the engine. As it flared to life he pressed the garage door opener, barely waiting until it had cleared the SUV before reversing.

As he tore into the driveway he was surprised they weren't fired on. But as he whipped around in a one-eighty, he heard shouts then pings against the SUV. Like rain on a tin roof, it splattered over them, but he'd already known the SUV was bulletproof.

"Blow it now," he ordered as he raced down the long driveway. "And get down," he said to the girl.

She immediately complied, ducking in her seat.

Less than fifty yards in front of them a giant explosion rent the air, orange flames lighting up the night sky as the heavy gate blew off its hinges, carving them a direct path to freedom.

"Tangos are down, you have a clean exit," Ortiz, one of his teammates, said. "We'll cover you. Get Scorpion to safety."

Levi pulled out a detonator and pressed the button. A multitude of explosions rocked behind them as they flew through the gate.

"Holy crap," she murmured, sitting up and turning around in her seat. "Do you think Jimenez is dead?" she asked, the hope lacing her voice clawing at him.

What kind of fucker kidnapped a teenager and assaulted her? Unfortunately there were too many men in the world like that and not enough bullets. "If he's not now he will be in the next ten minutes. Trust me." An airstrike would be called in as soon as he and the rest of the team were cleared.

A glance in the rearview mirror told him they

weren't being followed as they sped down the quiet road in the jungle. Jimenez's place was out in the middle of nowhere but according to Levi's exit plan, they were barely twenty minutes from what had to be the coast of Cartagena.

"All tangos are down and the main target has been eliminated," Ortiz said.

"The principal is secure. We'll be at the meet point in less than twenty. Going dark," Levi responded.

"See you back home. Watch your six," his teammate said before cutting off communication.

Levi glanced at the girl. "Jimenez and everyone in that compound are dead. You're safe."

She swallowed loud enough for him to hear as a shudder racked her entire body. "I wish I could have seen him die."

Her statement wasn't surprising. "From here we're going to get on a small boat." They'd be piggybacking on a naval special operations craft. Those on board wouldn't know anything about this op other than he and the girl were to be taken to a drop point and the girl was top priority. "About a mile out to sea, you'll be getting on a yacht and taken to safety."

"You're not coming with me?" she asked quietly.

"No, but you'll be okay. They used a lot of fucking manpower to save you, so don't worry." The words were meaningless considering what she'd likely been through but he wanted to say something to soothe her.

She didn't respond and by the time they reached the pick-up point, she was full-on trembling. He parked the SUV in a deserted parking lot right off a small public beach. When she nearly stumbled getting out of the SUV, he picked her up, holding her close. "Hang in there—we don't have much longer," he murmured.

Curling into him, she wrapped an arm around his shoulder, but didn't respond. For all he knew she was going into shock. Waves crashed in the distance, the salty scent of the ocean tingeing the air. With sweat rolling down his face, he stuck to the shadows as he passed through a cluster of foliage and onto the soft sand. The beaches here weren't like back in California. There weren't any homes or shops around for miles.

The bright moon illuminated the waiting SOC, but he paused, scanning the beach. Two shadows moved near the coastline. When he saw the burst of a blue handheld flare light up, he finally allowed himself a sliver of relief. Holding up one hand, he silently hurried toward the two men as fast as he could move through the sand carrying the girl.

Less than sixty seconds later they were seated on the back of the vessel and though he'd tried to put the girl down, she wouldn't let go of him. Sitting against the side of the boat, they hummed through the water at an impressive speed.

He held the young woman in his arms, hating how frail she felt. "Did they hurt you?" he murmured loud enough for only her to hear. The hum of the engine drowned out everything in a two-foot radius and the other men—SEALS, he guessed—were standing guard around the perimeter of the boat and armed to the teeth.

"I've got a hood over my head—what do you think?" she snapped, her voice shaky and watery sounding. As if she was crying under the hood.

But at least she was talking. He held back a curse, hating that he couldn't take the thing off her. It just felt so wrong to sit there with her, taking her to safety and not being able to show her that freedom was close. She might be able to see a little, but it was likely difficult on the boat. "I mean . . . do you need special medical attention? Maybe a female doctor?" He wasn't even sure how he'd get one for her, but he'd be damned if he didn't try.

"They didn't rape me if that's what you mean," she said so quietly he barely heard her. "Jimenez threatened me with it, but I'm way too valuable for that."

He didn't have much experience with fragile females, but he rubbed her back lightly, up and down, hoping the soothing action calmed her.

"What are you doing?" she shouted, sounding panicked as she tensed in his arms.

He immediately stilled but didn't let go of her, not wanting her to lose her balance if they hit a rough wave. "I was trying to help you calm down."

"As long as you don't rub any lower."

Despite the situation he laughed. "Shit, kid. Not everyone's a fucking pervert."

"In my experience they are. You sure like the F word."

He chuckled again. "Sorry. Comes with the job." Being a Marine meant he had a degree in cursing.

"What is your job exactly? Do you work for the CIA or NSA?"

He paused, surprised by the question. "Can't tell you that."

"Oh. What about your name?"

"Can't tell you that either."

She was silent for a long moment and he thought the conversation was over until she said, "Well, thank you for saving me. I wasn't sure if my message got out."

He had no clue what she meant by message and he wasn't going to ask. Sometimes the less he knew, the better. He grunted and to his surprise, she laid her head on his shoulder and finally relaxed enough that his KA-BAR loosened in her grip. He grasped it, not wanting her to hurt herself, and sheathed it.

When the boat started to slow, she jerked against him with a short cry.

"You're okay. Can you stand or do you need help?" he asked gently. He still couldn't pinpoint her age with the hood on but he guessed fifteen or sixteen.

"I'm good, I think." She placed a hand on his shoulder and pushed up, her legs shaky.

Looping an arm around her shoulders, he pulled her close as he took in the two waiting vessels: a huge yacht and a Donzi speedboat. He knew which one he was getting on.

She tensed beside him, so he looked down at her hooded face. "You're safe now, I promise. They don't send in guys like me unless the rescue is important, okay?"

She nodded, but didn't respond.

"Come on, kid. Give me something. You're going to be okay, right?" He wanted to hear her say it.

She nodded again. "Maybe I'll feel better if I can have your knife."

His KA-BAR? His first instinct was to say hell no, but he had no clue what this kid had been through and if it would make her feel safe, he'd do it. He unclipped the sheath and gave the whole thing to her, handle first. "Be careful with it."

"I will." Taking him off guard she lunged at him, pulling him into a big hug and sobbing against his chest as she murmured what sounded like "thank you."

Embarrassed, he glanced around at the other men on the craft. They were looking anywhere but at them. Thank God.

Ah, hell, he tightened his grip around her and kissed the top of her hooded head. Something told him this was one op he'd never forget. He knew it'd be impossible to find out what happened to her after tonight but he really hoped she was going to be okay.

Eighteen hours later Levi rolled out of his warm bed, thankful to be back home on base. He'd gotten only a few hours of sleep but his schedule was all screwed up and he didn't want to sleep the entire day. He scrubbed a hand over his face and decided not to bother shaving. His stubble was long enough that it was against regulations but, until a few hours ago, he hadn't slept in almost three days and grooming wasn't a priority now. He had a week's leave coming and he planned to take full advantage. Already dreaming of a cold beer and a warm, willing woman, he made his way to the bathroom of his two-bedroom home.

A loud knock at his front door made him pause. He wasn't expecting anyone, but he headed to the front and didn't bother asking who it was. Probably a neighbor needing help with a broken lawn mower or something.

His heart rate kicked up a notch when he opened the

door to find his commander, Colonel Harkin, standing there with a man in a suit who looked vaguely familiar. It took all of two seconds for him to recognize the other man: Lieutenant General Wesley Burkhart, new head of the NSA.

What. The. Hell.

Levi started to stand at attention until the colonel shook his head. "Lazaro, this is—"

"Lieutenant General Wesley Burkhart, I know. Am I in trouble?" Might as well get to the point. There was no good reason for these two highly decorated men to be standing on his front porch.

The colonel grunted in that dismissive way of his and shook his head. "No. And since you know who this is, I'm going to leave you two alone to talk. You already know he's got the highest clearance in the country, so you can discuss anything with him." Taking Levi by surprise, he reached out and shook his hand. "Good luck, son."

Still waking up, Levi didn't respond as his commander headed back down the walkway. He nodded inside his home. "I was just about to make some coffee."

"Sounds good." Burkhart stepped in after him, shutting the door behind them. The man was maybe fifty, with gray hair and in good shape for any age. And the man moved like a damn predator, each step calculated and efficient as he scanned the interior of Levi's sparsely furnished home.

After he pulled down two mugs from the cabinet above his coffeemaker, he started filling the glass pot with water. "You might as well start since I have no clue why you're here," Levi said. Behind him he heard the slight scraping of one of the kitchen table chairs being moved.

"You did a good job on that last op. Why'd you give the girl your blade?"

The question and tone made him pause. It didn't surprise him that Burkhart knew about the op, not since he was the new director of the NSA. Levi imagined the man carried more secrets than anyone had a right to know.

Levi finished preparing the pot before turning around and answering. "She was a scared kid and she wanted something to feel safe. Is she all right?"

Burkhart's mouth curved up the tiniest fraction, almost a micro-expression, as he nodded. "Yeah, she's good, thanks to you and your team."

Levi just nodded, not certain if he should respond.

After a long moment, in which Burkhart was almost preternaturally still, watching him like a lion watches its prey, the man spoke. "How'd you know who I was at the door?"

"I read a couple of articles you wrote a few years ago when you were in the Navy."

His head tilted to the side a fraction, as if he was surprised. "You read the *Navy Times*?"

Levi nodded. He read most military newspapers online.

"I'm going to cut to the chase then. I'm putting together a team of men and women for black ops stuff. Similar to what the CIA has, but not. Less rules, less bureaucratic tape, and more funding. You're the first man I'm approaching about this and if you say no, I'll expect you to forget we ever had this conversation—but I don't think you're going to say no. I could give you the whole spiel about how this country needs men like you, but you already know it. I'm asking you to help your country because you have a certain skill set and you're highly intelligent. You won't be able to jump out of planes forever and you'll be doing a lot of good if you work for me."

Levi watched the man, looking for telltale signs of bullshit, but Burkhart was impossible to read. Which was good considering his job. Levi had read enough on the man to understand his politics—which were middle-of-the-road, thank God; extremists on either side were dangerous—and he'd be lying if he said he wasn't interested so far.

The coffeemaker whirred quietly behind him as he digested what Burkhart was offering. "I'm skilled and highly trained." He wasn't being arrogant, it was just a fact. He wouldn't be part of MARSOC if he wasn't good. "But there are a lot of men like me. Why am I your first?"

"I could give you a long answer about your ridiculous number of medals or the fact that you take top honors for every class or training exercise or that every individual who's ever worked with you has nothing but praise, but . . . you asked how the girl was doing. It was your first question. And you gave her your fucking KA-BAR because she needed to feel safe. You care, Levi."

Levi rubbed the back of his neck, uncomfortable with the praise, hoping he wasn't supposed to respond.

Burkhart continued, "I need men and women who

give a shit about the people we're going to help. I will almost always look at the big picture, about what's best for the country as a whole. I need people working for me who will question my decisions and will remind me that the individual person helps make up our country." Reaching into his jacket, he pulled out a thin manila folder and laid it on the kitchen table. "If you read this and you're not interested, we part ways and you never speak of this meeting. But if you are interested, you get an honorable discharge and start your training tomorrow."

Beyond curious, Levi picked up the file and started reading. By the second paragraph, his decision was made. He'd miss the Marine Corps more than anything, but he couldn't pass up this opportunity.

Chapter 1

Terrorist: a person who uses extreme violence (terror or terrorism), as a weapon to send a message or for his own gain. Often a political weapon.

Tasev gave a brief nod to the guard standing by the reinforced metal door. Immediately the man moved, quickly averting his gaze to a spot over Tasev's shoulder as he slid a foot to the side. He was smart not to meet his gaze. No one wanted to appear as if they were challenging him.

Ignoring the man, Tasev put his hand over the biometric scanner, then leaned forward so the retinal scanner could register his left eye. Out of the corner of his right eye he kept focus on the guard, ready for an attack, even though that was unlikely. He paid his men very well and rewarded them with other perks, including willing prostitutes, on a daily basis, but that didn't mean he could buy their loyalty. No one was truly loyal and it was something he always remembered. A few moments later, the door opened with a soft *snick*.

As he stepped onto the metal walkway Tasev looked at the floor below where Dr. Claus Schmidt was busy writing letters and symbols on a giant dry-erase board at warp speed. The man used computers when it suited him but for the most part the eccentric genius preferred to write things out by hand.

Tasev didn't care how the man worked as long as he provided results. For the past two years Schmidt had been making steady progress, using the live subjects Paul Hill—an international businessman who'd been involved in all sorts of illegal activities, including the skin trade—had been providing for him to test different toxins. Now that Hill was in prison for crimes unrelated to Tasev, he had lost his source of live human test subjects.

It was frustrating but at this point not much of a setback. Schmidt was zeroing in on the necessary antitoxin. Tasev could feel it in his bones how close they were. Now, after two years of tireless work, it was almost time to unleash hell on the United States.

Over five years ago he'd retired, knowing it was time to get out of the gun and slave trades. He'd made more than enough money and had two sons who'd stepped up to take over the family business. But after they'd been killed in Afghanistan by American troops, Tasev had come out of retirement with a slow burning rage building inside him every second of every day. His sons had simply been doing business and gotten caught up in the crossfire of a war that hadn't concerned them.

He didn't have time for politics or religion, though he found them useful for business. If fools wanted to kill one another in the name of their gods, he'd been happy to provide them with the weapons to do it. But the skin trade had proved much more lucrative. Unfortunately more and more governments had started cracking down. It was why his sons had gone back to reliable weapons trading.

His jaw clenched as he thought of them, of his loss, of the fact that his line wouldn't continue. Finding the perfect female had been difficult too. Their mother had been British, cultured and while stupid, she hadn't been a whore. He might fuck prostitutes but he would never procreate with any of them.

He'd wanted his children to be proud of where they came from and his sons' mother had been good to them, though he'd gotten rid of her influence by the time his boys turned ten. They'd been turning too soft but he'd drilled it out of them by the time they were eleven. After a freak skiing "accident" had killed their mother, it had been easy to guide them.

No distractions made all the difference in the world. He'd thought the same would be true for Dr. Schmidt but the brilliant scientist seemed to be dragging his feet the last couple of weeks. It was nothing Tasev could prove—he barely understood when the man spoke— but he always trusted his gut. Now it was telling him that Schmidt was stalling.

Though he couldn't figure out why. Tasev paid him well and while he didn't let him leave the grounds of his Miami home, every need he requested was granted. He lived in opulence and was allowed to use live human subjects, something he would never have been allowed to do in his civilized scientific community. It should have been a dream for the doctor.

Heading down the walkway to the stairs, Tasev was

aware of the moment Schmidt finally registered his presence. The man had absolutely no situational awareness. But he wasn't a soldier so that was to be expected.

Schmidt jerked upright from his crouched position at the bottom of the dry-erase board. He had shadows under his eyes, his plaid button-down shirt was wrinkled under his lab coat, and he smelled as if he hadn't bathed in days. According to his guards' reports, the doctor hadn't. He also hadn't been eating enough.

"How is your progress?" he asked in English, keeping his voice neutral. Tasev couldn't yell or make demands with a man like Schmidt. It worked him into such a frenzy that he couldn't work. Sometimes for days. He'd learned that early on in their working relationship. Luckily Tasev had found the man's weakness. So far mere threats had worked against the genius but something told Tasev that it would take more than simple words now.

"One month," he said, not looking at Tasev. Not because he was frightened in the way that his guards were, but because Schmidt didn't look anyone in the eye. Whether it was a quirk or habit, Tasev wasn't certain.

And he didn't care.

"That's what you told me four and a half weeks ago." His jaw tightened, but he kept a lid on his rage. He had to play this the right way.

"You want results, you give me one more month." It was said with absoluteness. And a little arrogance. The doctor knew he was irreplaceable.

"Seven days."

The doctor shook his head before turning his back on Tasev. A death sentence should anyone else do that to him. Muttering to himself, Schmidt crouched in front of the board again and started back with his scribbling.

Sighing, Tasev pulled out his cell phone and sent off a text. "You leave me with no choice, Doctor."

The man paused for only a second in his writing, but it was enough to let Tasev know he'd heard. Good.

A moment later the door above opened. Tasev didn't have to look to see who was entering. Other than himself, only his second in command had the code. Vasily was a beast of a man with a scarred face and body. With tattoos covering the majority of his upper body, he terrified most people. Right now the trembling woman he held by the throat should be scared.

"I told you what would happen if you displeased me," Tasev said quietly.

Something about his tone must have registered in that giant brain of Schmidt's because he turned around. When he looked upward, the man paled. It was the second time Tasev had ever seen real fear in his gaze. The first had been when he'd simply threatened to do what he was doing now.

Tasev looked up at Vasily and nodded. The man released the woman's throat then pinned her to the edge of the metal balcony, bending her over. Eyes wild, the dark-haired beauty screamed and fruitlessly struggled as he tore the back of her skirt from the hem to the top, ripping it completely apart and tossing it away. Her black panties were the only thing covering her bottom half.

"Enough!" Schmidt shouted, rage reverberating through that one word.

Vasily didn't move until Tasev nodded. The woman

continued sobbing and begging them to stop even after
Vasily just held her in place. Tasev tuned her out and
glanced back at the doctor.

He froze. The man was holding a pen to his carotid
artery, the placement perfect for killing himself if he
applied enough pressure.

Tasev had killed a man once by ripping into his carotid using his teeth, so he knew how deadly an injury
there would be. And he couldn't let the doctor die.
He'd put too much time and money in the man to start
over again.

There was a sharp gleam in Schmidt's eyes as he
held Tasev's gaze for the first time. The intense way he
stared was almost jarring. "You do this, I kill myself.
Then you lose two years of work. Worse, you have no
record of my notes." He tapped his head with his free
hand, a reminder that most of Schmidt's work resided
there, not on paper.

"I'm not letting her go," Tasev said with resolve.

"I know. I will finish in seven days, but she stays
with me the entire time in the lab. Never out of my
sight. You or your men will not harm her. She will be
fed and taken care of and you will bring her a soft bed
to sleep in. And a television and books for her entertainment. One of those e-readers so she can purchase
what she wants. If you agree, I do not kill myself and
will give you the antitoxin." As he spoke he glanced
away again, as if losing the ability to hold eye contact.
But his hand never wavered, the pen placed directly
over his artery.

Tasev would never admit it, but the man's resolve
was impressive. He hadn't thought Schmidt had it in

him. He was too far away to stop the doctor and it didn't matter anyway. Tasev's threat had worked. Now he would gain what he wanted in the necessary time frame. "We have a deal. If you'd agreed to my time line initially I never would have needed to kidnap your sweet daughter."

The girl gasped, clearly confused, but didn't respond.

"Send her down. If you go back on our deal or try to stop me from killing myself it won't matter. I won't finish the work if she's hurt."

Gritting his teeth, Tasev nodded. He hated anyone ordering him around. It reminded him too much of his youth. But he was backed into a corner. As soon as Schmidt was done he'd be killing the doctor anyway. But first he'd make him watch as Vasily raped his daughter. Feeling better about the situation, he nodded at Vasily and gave a sharp command.

His second in command shoved the girl toward the stairs, grinning as he stared at her barely covered ass. He knew Tasev would give her to him soon. On trembling legs, the girl made her way to the stairs, most of her sobbing subsiding as she clutched the railing. When she was at the bottom of the stairs, Schmidt spoke again, his words so low that Tasev almost didn't hear them.

"If you kill Vasily right now, I will make it five days." A promise.

Excitement leaped inside him followed by a thin thread of regret. Vasily was a good commander, but like all of Tasev's men, he was replaceable. The doctor was not. Withdrawing his gun, he aimed and shot Vasily between the eyes, dropping him on the spot.

"Why did you ask that man to kill the scarred one?" Aliyah asked Claus, the first words she'd spoken since he'd given her one of his lab coats and some of Tasev's men had come to take away Vasily's body and clean up the blood. There had been surprisingly little of it.

He looked at his daughter, trying to drink in every inch of her lovely face. He'd seen her only in pictures, her American mother telling him of Aliyah's existence six years ago. And only because she'd needed to see if his kidney would be a match for Aliyah's. He'd had a brief affair with Chaya, but she'd been married and had lied to her husband about Aliyah being his. The husband had been dead for a decade, though, so she could have come to Claus before that. She'd chosen not to until their daughter had needed something.

"Because he deserved it," Claus said, realizing he needed to respond and stop staring at her. "Is that the only question you have?"

She shook her head, her pale green eyes a match to his own glimmering with tears. "You are my father," she said.

He raised his eyebrows. "Yes."

"Did you give me your kidney?"

Again he was surprised but perhaps he shouldn't be. "How did you know?"

"My mother said it was a miracle that we found a donor but I knew she was lying. There was no way we'd gotten such a perfect match and moved up the list so quickly. And the mysterious money she left me when she died—I knew it wasn't from her. And . . . I knew it was unlikely that my dad was my biological father from a young age."

Claus frowned, but didn't ask how she'd known.

She answered anyway and pointed to herself. "Simple genetics. If you'd ever seen him you'd understand. He was very fair-skinned and fair-haired. I'm not stupid and neither was my father. Besides, he said something once, when I was about ten . . ." She shrugged, trailing off. "It doesn't matter. Why am I here? And what are you doing working for that monster, whoever he is?"

"I'm here because I'm an arrogant fool." He'd written multiple papers on what could happen if certain toxins were altered. It had been interesting to speculate but he'd just been theorizing. He hadn't actually planned to test his theories. No one outside his scientific circles paid attention to his ramblings anyway. Or so he'd thought. "I have altered what's known as foodborne botulism into a stronger, deadlier strain." And that in itself was a feat considering how deadly it already was. "Right now I'm working to create an antitoxin." He already knew the formula but hadn't put it into practice. Or on paper.

She stared at him as if he was a monster, something he'd expected. And something he deserved. But he wouldn't be less than honest. Before he could continue the door opened again. Instinctively Claus stepped in front of Aliyah, knowing there was little he could do to protect her if Tasev decided Claus's life wasn't worth anything anymore.

Two men strode in carrying a mattress. Behind them

another of the guards carried two bags. Claus was still as they strode down the stairs and placed the bed in the darker shadowed area underneath the stairs. His lab was huge and he tended to dim the lights only when he dozed on his cot, but he'd have to see about getting his daughter more privacy.

The guard carrying the bags tossed them onto the bed, then looked at Claus. In Russian he told him there were clothes for Aliyah and bedding. Tasev had also given her an iPad loaded with books, but it wasn't connected to the Internet. When the guard looked past Claus, his gaze heated as he looked at Claus's daughter. All the rage Claus had been bottling up for two years boiled to the surface.

"Maybe I ask Tasev to kill you too," he murmured in Russian, not wanting his daughter to understand what he was saying. She was already horrified enough by him, he didn't need to give her more reasons to hate him.

That snapped the man's attention back to Claus for a moment. He gave him a look that promised death before turning on his heel and striding after the others.

Once they were gone, he turned to Aliyah to find her standing next to one of his many tables, her arms wrapped around herself. She looked so lost and vulnerable and though Claus had always thought himself a nonviolent man, he knew in that moment he would have no problem putting a bullet in Tasev's head to save his daughter. For the past two years he'd done nothing but dream of killing the man who held him hostage and forced him to do unspeakable things.

He cleared his throat. "They brought you clothes,

bedding, and an iPad. But you won't have any Internet." Or so that fool Tasev thought. Claus would have only one chance to contact outside help. For two long years he'd waited for something like this. He'd gotten a message to one of his friends—who worked for the NSA—two years ago but he'd been taken before they could meet up. She was smart but there was no way for anyone to track him when he'd been unable to communicate with the outside world.

Until now.

He was going to have to try again even with the risk. At this point he would risk death if he could just get a message to his friend Meghan Lazaro. If she knew he was still alive she'd help him. He had no doubt.

Chapter 2

FFP: final firing position (sniper term).

Selene Wolfe chewed on a piece of teriyaki beef jerky as she lay flat on her belly, looking through the glass of her Leupold Mark 4 scope. She'd been in position for only five hours waiting for her target to show his face. Ramsey Jurden, a freaking white supremacist terrorist. She hated these guys. Especially ones with a predilection for kids. Yeah, this job wasn't going to sit heavy on her soul. Not like some of the others.

Normally Wesley didn't give her anything he didn't think she could handle anyway. Her specialty was computers, which made her a valuable asset to the NSA. It was the sole reason they'd recruited her at the age of sixteen. But when he'd hired her she'd insisted that he give her any training she asked for. After years spent living on her own she knew what it was to be helpless, and she'd sworn to herself that it would never happen again. Since she couldn't very well train herself and anyone she hired wouldn't have been nearly as good as someone Wesley could have recommended, she'd been quite insistent on her terms of employment. So he'd given her everything she wanted—because he'd have done pretty much anything to ensure she worked for him— which meant she'd gotten to train with the very best.

Her weapons mentor, as she liked to think of him, was a retired USMC sniper school instructor. He'd been a hard-ass and hadn't cared that she was a woman. If anything, she guessed he pushed her harder than normal because of her gender. Which was fine with her. He'd given her a valuable gift, one nobody could ever take away from her.

Knowledge was the ultimate power. Something she never took for granted.

She understood computers and, thanks to her instructor, she understood what it was to protect herself and her country. Considering that roughly fifty percent of the decisions she made at work ended up setting black ops missions into motion, she was thankful that she had an understanding of what the field people had to do all the time. Taking a life wasn't something she did lightly and she knew they didn't either. It would have felt hypocritical to know that her decisions sent people into the field to kill when she had no concept of what they were doing or the impact of carrying out those ops.

Slight movement to her left had her shifting her Remington 700 a fraction. Two horses trotted out of the barn, shaking their heads and tails, clearly happy to have freedom.

Without looking at her watch she knew the time was near. If her target didn't show up today at two, she'd have to come back next Wednesday. It had been impossible to get the man's schedule since those in his growing organization were loyal.

Had to give the guy that. He inspired loyalty, even if it was misplaced. She wondered how loyal they'd be if they knew he was a freaking pervert of the worst kind.

After some on-the-ground recon—which meant she'd flirted shamelessly with the delivery guy at the local feed store—she'd discovered that the target insisted on being at his family's ranch when the horse and other animal feed was delivered every Wednesday.

She figured he liked to micromanage or maybe it was just a weird quirk. She didn't know and she didn't care.

Another flash of movement caught her eye and anticipation started to build inside her, a steady hum that sharpened all her focus as she readied herself for what she was about to do. The delivery truck was making its way down the dusty country road. One of the guards at the gate talked to the driver before checking the back of the truck. No surprise, the guard then had the driver get out and frisked him for weapons. Once he was waved through, Selene slowly shifted her weapon toward the house and sure enough her target exited with two guards, one on either side. She'd expected more personal guards but Jurden clearly felt safe enough on his family's ranch. Which she understood. His perimeter security was good.

She was better.

A doable shot, but not good enough. His guards might not be innocent, but that wasn't her decision to make. She had very specific orders. *One shot, one kill.*

Which would cut the head off this burgeoning organization before it grew too big. A couple of well-respected think tanks at the NSA had run scenario after scenario with Jurden, and if he was allowed to grow more powerful, he would cause irreparable damage. He'd already bombed three schools in inner-city neighborhoods, making it look like gang violence. Hundreds of children and teachers had died. And he thought he'd gotten away with it. But bombs leave a unique signature and the man he hired to make the bombs had flipped on him a few months ago to the FBI.

Before that Jurden hadn't been on anyone's radar. Now the FBI, NSA, CIA, and a whole lot of other three-letter organizations were currently working to take apart his terrorist cells. It was insane how he'd managed to avoid detection. Insane and scary. They'd have eventually figured out who he was but by then it would have been too late—well, later than it was, considering the loss of life.

His cause would have been bigger and his followers more radical. For once her people had a chance to stop a terrorist organization before it grew unstoppable.

• Looking through her scope, she tracked his movements, watching as he talked to the delivery guy, smiling and laughing as if he was just a normal guy, before he headed to the barn. He ran a hand through his blond hair, his blue eyes clear through her scope. She carefully watched his movements and deducted that he wasn't wearing a vest under his shirt. It wasn't always possible to tell but Jurden's movements were too relaxed and his shirt was unbuttoned enough that she was almost positive. So she wouldn't have to take a head shot. It was almost time.

Her heart rate kicked up the slightest notch but did nothing to alter her concentration. If anything, she was hyperaware of her surroundings. It had taken her a solid two hours to get into position and the past five that she'd been sitting on the property had been mundane, but now the familiar hum of adrenaline coursed through her.

She'd chosen this specific hillside for her final firing position because it was the only area where she could make a rapid escape. The reverse slope of the hillside gave her perfect cover and concealment for her escape and evasion route. No one would even know where she'd set up. Not when she was in her homemade ghillie suit and had camouflaged herself with vegetation from the surrounding area. They might figure it out later, but it would be way too late to serve any purpose and she'd be in another state by then.

Everything else around her ceased to exist as she watched him ride out of the barn on a beautiful stallion. His two guards were with him, but riding far enough behind that they wouldn't be an issue.

Focusing, she made wind calculations using the grass and mirage at the halfway point to her target. That was something Hollywood got wrong a lot in movies. When snipers calculate wind they don't do it off where the target is. They do it at the halfway point because that's where the bullet is at its highest point of trajectory and the wind has the most effect upon it.

Based on the calculations from her range card, she used one of her favorite tactics, the ambush method. She placed the crosshairs of the scope at the point where she knew her target would ride.

She pushed out a deep breath. Steady mind, steady hand.

Three, two . . . She stopped breathing and pulled the trigger.

She hit him center mass. Because of the high caliber, he tumbled backward off the horse, a red stain blooming across the front of his shirt. From there, panic ensued with the two guards and others running from the house and barn, weapons drawn.

That was her cue to get the hell out of Dodge.

An hour later as Selene cruised down the highway in a fifteen-year-old Ford truck with a bad paint job—but a pristine engine—and dressed in a button-down flannel shirt and worn jeans, she put the battery into her burner phone and made the call. Her weapon and ghillie suit were hidden in a secret compartment underneath the toolbox in the back, so even if someone decided to search it, they'd never find it.

Her boss and friend, Wesley Burkhart, answered on the first ring. "Well done."

"It's confirmed?"

"Yep. Already hit the news stations." Burkhart was hard to read, but Selene had known him long enough that, even though his tone was muted, she could tell he was happy with the results. "And eighty percent of his cells have already been dismantled. We'll be leaking the truth of his perversions to the media in a few days."

Maybe she shouldn't have been surprised his death had already hit the news, considering Jurden's family was richer than some small countries. His parents had died five years before, under suspicious circumstances, leaving their massive fortune to their sole heir. Even if he'd been found guilty of his terrorist crimes and ended up in prison, according to the analysts, he would have been able to gain an even bigger following. Selene shuddered as she ran over the potential casualties in her head. "Soon I'm going to switch vehicles but I'll be back at base in about two hours."

"Good. Listen, I know you were planning to take a vacation after this but I've got a job for you. It involves Tasev."

Selene's eyebrows rose at the name. Tasev—first or last name, no one knew for certain—was a true monster. With no allegiance to any country, the man had gouged a huge path of destruction for about a decade, selling weapons to the highest bidder and funneling eastern European women all over the world for the right price. No one had ever been able to get a mole inside his organization either. Then about five years ago it seemed as if he'd fallen off the face of the earth. Some thought he was dead. She'd guessed so too. "He's still alive?"

"We don't have visual confirmation but it appears so. You'll understand why when you read the files. Tasev is planning something huge and we've got five days to stop him. But . . . Tasev might be involved with Meghan Lazaro's murder."

Bile rose in Selene's throat and she clenched her fingers tight around the steering wheel. Meghan Lazaro had been a good agent, a good woman, and when she'd been tortured and killed she'd left behind a broken husband. A man who by all accounts had been a freaking Boy Scout before her death. At least according to his files and everything Wesley had ever said about the man. Now he'd gone off the reservation and was on a dark path of vengeance. Selene shook her head, suddenly weighed down with sadness. "Does Lazaro know of his involvement?" If Levi found out about this, he'd do everything in his power to take out Tasev himself.

"I don't know but I'm sending you all relevant files. You can be on the ground or not. It's your choice. You'll be a valuable asset either way." She knew he was giving her the option because of her unique training. For a job like this she'd be a strong asset whether in the field or in the comm center.

"Ground," she said instantly, not even having to think about her decision. And it wasn't because she wanted to bring down Tasev, though she definitely did. She wanted to help Levi Lazaro. The man had gotten a raw deal and she knew how easily he could get caught in the crossfire if there wasn't at least one person looking out for him. "See you soon."

Chapter 3

Off the reservation: when an agent has left the fold of their Agency and no longer recognizes anyone's authority but his or her own.

Levi held the tumbler Alexander Lopez had just given him loosely in his hand. It was filled with top shelf scotch, neat. He sat on the same chesterfield he'd lounged on mere days ago talking to Lopez about Paul Hill. Hill was a piece of garbage who'd been busted running one of the biggest sex slave rings the world had ever seen. And he'd been doing it right out of Miami. He wouldn't last long in prison though; there were already multiple hits out on him. Levi hoped the fucker suffered when he died.

Unfortunately his capture meant Levi lost a possible source in his hunt against whoever had killed his wife.

He couldn't risk going to prison to visit the man either because there would be recordings of the man's daily visitors and he knew that a lot of the agencies were closely watching Hill right now. They wanted to see what else he was holding back, if anything. Since Levi had left the NSA under less than ideal circumstances and they likely wanted him arrested, he couldn't get caught on any official radar. Not until he'd avenged his wife's death. That goal was what made him get up in the morning.

Then he didn't give a shit what happened to him.

Alexander sat across from him, watching him warily. Or maybe he was just nervous in general. Normally the gunrunner was the epitome of laid back. He tended to wear cargo pants and bright button-down Hawaiian shirts. A little gaudy, but they worked for him. Even though he was in his standard "uniform," now he was wound tight and none of his normal guards were in the office.

Sighing, Levi set the glass down. They both knew he wouldn't drink it anyway. He never did. "What's going on?"

The gunrunner shrugged and rubbed a hand over his face. But he still didn't respond.

"The beard's new," Levi said, just trying to make conversation. His internal radar wasn't pinging and whether it was stupid or not, he more or less trusted Alexander to be straight with him and not shoot him in the back. They'd done enough business and even though Alexander knew Levi as Isaiah Moore, he trusted the guy more than most criminals.

"Yeah, trying something out. You didn't bring Jasmine with you today," he said suddenly, stating the obvious.

Levi straightened at the mention of the escort he'd used as part of his cover on multiple occasions over the past few months. The background he'd built for his current cover ID was a man who loved hiring prostitutes. It had helped establish the type of man he was for his new criminal contacts, and even the smallest details were important when building a background. Something he'd learned with the NSA. He didn't sleep with any of them, and he liked Jasmine in a nonsexual way. She was real, self-deprecating, and just sweet. No one deserved to get stuck in that life. As of a couple of days ago he'd convinced her to get out of the escort business completely. "Why the fuck are you asking about her?" He hadn't thought Alexander used prostitutes. It was one of the reasons Levi liked the guy. He had a weird sort of code about stuff like that and it made him different from his criminal counterparts.

To Levi's surprise, Alexander flushed a dark shade of red and looked down at his own glass. "I heard she's not in the business anymore. I was just curious about her," he muttered, the complete lack of confidence out of character.

It took a moment for it to register why Alexander was acting this way. Levi leaned back against the seat, some of the tension in his shoulders loosening. "You like her?" When Jasmine—real name Allison—had accompanied him to meet Alexander on multiple occasions they'd talked a few times. She'd never said about what but maybe she'd made an impression on the arms dealer.

Alexander looked up again but his gaze was shuttered. "I've got the information you requested."

Levi realized he was changing the subject and left the Jasmine topic alone. It wasn't his business anyway. "Why do I get the feeling there's a 'but' in there somewhere?"

Alexander half smiled, looking like the predator Levi knew him to be. He might hide behind his low-key attitude but the man hadn't lasted in this business for decades by being stupid. "I'll give you the morgue files for our normal fee, but . . . I've also come across something I think you'll find interesting. The man who engages in that fucked-up killing style you're hunting was found dead too."

All the blood rushed to Levi's ears, the roar so deafening it took him a moment to find his voice. He tried to appear as if he was unimpressed when in reality he'd sell his soul to find the man. For almost two years he'd jumped from cover to cover, working deep off the grid in various criminal organizations as he tried to hunt down the man who'd tortured and killed his pregnant wife. He knew the man was Russian and he had his name. That was it. "You're sure it's the same man?"

Alexander nodded. "His name's Vasily and he's linked to almost fifty murders across the globe. All murder for hire. It's him."

Levi had never told anyone the name Vasily. "And you have confirmation?" That bastard was dead? Levi should feel relief but instead he felt rage that he hadn't been the one who'd killed him. Even if Vasily had been behind Meghan's murder, he'd been hired to do it. Which meant Vasily wasn't the final target. Levi wanted the man who'd given the order.

"I have more than that—I know who his boss is."

Levi didn't bother hiding his eagerness now. He couldn't if he tried. His heart rate kicked into overdrive and his damn palms actually grew damp. "What do you want for this information?" Because he didn't doubt it was good. Alexander wouldn't have come to him with it otherwise.

"Our normal fee plus you set me up with Jasmine. On a date. A real one. You'll tell her what a good guy I am and make it happen."

Levi blinked, watching Alexander to see if he was messing with him. He didn't respond though, a tactic he used when he wanted his opponent to keep talking.

Alexander's jaw clenched. "I'm just asking for a setup. That's it. I would ask her out myself but I can't find her," he muttered.

That was because she'd gotten out of the business and was using her real name instead of Jasmine. "You know she's not for hire—that a real date would be just that. A *real* date."

"I know. I want to take her out, not pay for . . . You want the information or not?" Alexander snapped, his face flushing again.

"You know I do. I give you my word I'll set something up with you two. Other than a date, I can't guarantee anything though." He wasn't a freaking pimp. And even if he'd sell his own soul to get the information he desperately wanted, he'd never sell another human. He might have crossed some lines in the past couple of years but he'd never cross that one.

The arms dealer nodded. "I also have one more condition. After I give you the information on Vasily's boss, I know you're going to want to meet him. I also know you take escorts with you for whatever reason, and we both know you're not sleeping with them. My only other condition is that you don't take Jasmine—or any hired woman—with you when you meet the man. He's worse than Paul Hill."

It took a lot to surprise Levi, and right now, he was stunned that Alexander knew he wasn't sleeping with the escorts and by the man's odd request. There could be a multitude of reasons for the request, but the mention of Hill made him think there was only one: Alexander didn't want any women to get hurt. "Deal."

Alexander nodded once, then picked up two manila envelopes sitting next to him on the couch and handed them to Levi. "These are the known victims, and this"— he slid another, thicker, envelope over to him—"is all the information I was able to gather on Vasily. Looks as if he was killed by a single shot to the head. Whoever dumped the body did a piss-poor job of weighting him down. He was dropped in the Everglades but a driver for one of those airboat tours found him tangled up in some tree roots."

Though Levi was eager to devour the contents of the files, he held off opening them. He'd do that once he was alone and wouldn't have any interruptions. "Who linked all the murders?" Because there had been no fingerprints or DNA left with his wife's . . . body parts. Her killer, or killers, hadn't even left him her whole body to bury. Hadn't left them their unborn child . . . *Fuck*, he shook his head as that dark abyss he struggled with every day threatened to swallow him. They'd left pictures of what they'd done, of her being raped, before they'd killed her. He'd burned them all, unwilling to let them go into evidence. No one would ever see Meghan like that. He closed his eyes for a moment, trying to banish the horrific images but that just made it worse.

Levi clenched his jaw, a sharp slice of rage threatening to overwhelm him.

Alexander shifted in his seat, that wariness back in his gaze, and Levi realized he probably looked as if he wanted to murder someone. "Ah . . . Interpol. I'm sure there are other agencies that linked them as well, but my contact is with Interpol."

That was certainly interesting, but maybe it shouldn't be. Alexander had managed to avoid prison for a long time so it stood to reason he had an interesting array of contacts. Ones who found him too useful to bring in. "Who's his boss?" Because whoever that was, he would be the man who'd ordered Meghan's execution. And once Levi had that name, he'd rain hell down on the man and he didn't care who got in his way as long as the animal wound up dead.

Alexander glanced over his shoulder at the door, even though Levi already knew the room was secure. The man had anti-surveillance hardware in place that basically blocked the government from eavesdropping on anything said in this room. When he looked back at Levi, for the briefest moment there was a flicker of fear in his eyes. For himself, or Levi, he wasn't sure. But then it was gone. "Tasev."

Levi shook his head, every muscle in his body going rigid. "He's dead." Otherwise he would have been at the top of Levi's list of suspects. Levi knew Vasily had worked for him at one time but Tasev had died about five years ago and Levi had assumed the man he was hunting had found a new boss. A Russian for sure; they tended to stick together. About a year ago Levi had embedded himself with a group of them working in

Odessa but had quickly realized they knew nothing about Vasily and weren't as violent as he'd originally thought. So he'd moved on.

Alexander shook his head. "No he's not. And he's in Miami."

Too many emotions bombarded Levi at once as he realized Alexander wasn't bullshitting him. Vasily, the man who'd tortured his precious wife beyond comprehension was dead and the man who'd likely ordered it was in the same city—if Tasev was actually alive. It was like kismet if he believed in that shit. "Tasev, you're sure?"

Expression grim, Alexander nodded. "I make it my business to know what goes on in my city."

His pulse thudded hard in his throat. "I want an introduction." *I'm gonna kill him, Meghan. I swear it.*

Alexander shook his head.

Before he could say anything Levi continued, "Whatever the cost."

The arms dealer sighed and waited, watching him as if he was trying to read his mind. "Are you on a suicide mission? If you get in bed with him, he'll eventually kill you. He kills almost everyone he does business with."

Levi knew all about Tasev, a monster who'd created far too much havoc for a decade. No one even knew if Tasev was his first or last name. Or even his real name. It was simply his moniker in the criminal underworld. "Not if I kill him first." And it didn't really matter as long as Tasev died by his hand. If Levi died in the process, so be it. It would be a kindness.

Alexander's eyebrows rose a fraction but he nodded. "Fine. I won't introduce you but I'll set up a meet with someone who will. His name's Gregor; he's a middleman."

"Gregor 'the German'?" Levi knew him by reputation but their paths had never crossed. If someone wanted something—priceless antiquities, an organ from the black market, whatever—Gregor Winkler was supposed to be able to get it or introduce you to the person who could.

"Yes. But—"

"Make it happen." He didn't need Alexander trying to talk him out of this. Levi was so close to vengeance he could taste it.

"Fine, but don't say I didn't warn you. I'm attending a party tonight. Black tie. The German will be there." A knock at the door made him frown.

Levi had noticed that Alexander's guards never interrupted him and they had serious respect for him. That said a lot in his world. Anyone could instigate fear, but respect was a different and rare beast.

"What?" he snapped.

A moment later, one of the men Levi knew was named Meza stepped in. He glanced at Levi, then strode toward Alexander. Leaning down he quietly whispered something to the arms dealer.

The change in Alexander's body language was subtle as he nodded and straightened, effectively dismissing Meza, who left the room but didn't close the door, leaving a clear message for Levi that it was time to leave. Alexander seemed pleased as he turned back to Levi. "I have business to attend to but I'll send you the information about tonight. It starts at eight and the

German will be prompt. He has other meetings lined up but I'll work you in, even if I think it's a mistake."

"Thank you." Levi let himself out, his shoes silent against the marble-tiled hallway as he made his way to the entryway.

His body hummed with an anticipation he could barely contain inside him. If Tasev was the man behind Meghan's death, Levi was going to find him, hunt him down, and make him regret he'd ever taken his first breath.

Selene smiled warmly at Alexander Lopez as he greeted her on his well-guarded lanai. The Olympic-sized pool glistened behind him as he stood and kissed her on both cheeks. For a criminal, she actually liked Lopez. He was honorable in his own way, with a code he kept to. He didn't hurt women, didn't hurt children, was picky about who he sold weapons to, and, surprisingly, donated a lot of money to various charities. The man was a walking contradiction.

"To what do I owe this pleasure, Selene?" he asked as he sat across from her.

He knew her as Selene Silva, a cover ID she'd been building for five years. She was supposedly an efficient assassin who worked for hire and her street name was The Wolf. It amused her that her real last name was almost the same as part of one of her many aliases. She wasn't even sure how her cover ID had gotten the nickname but it had spread after one of her supposed kills and Wesley liked the idea that her ID was intimidating enough to garner a signature.

"I'm in town on business and calling in one of my

favors," she said pleasantly as she sat next to him on one of the cushioned outdoor couches. Turning toward him, she crossed her legs, making sure she kept her body language relaxed. She might adore Alexander but she never forgot they were on opposite sides of the law. It was a beautiful sunny Miami day and cool enough that she could get away with wearing loose cargo pants. Luckily his guards had missed one of the blades strapped to her inner thigh. She always felt naked without her weapons. Sometimes they used a metal wand to detect weapons but she'd been here enough times and they'd opted not to.

His dark eyebrows rose. "I'm scared to ask what you want," he said wryly.

"It's an easy favor. I need an introduction to the German. I know he's going to be at Shah's party tonight. And I already have an invite." She just didn't want to have to do a cold introduction. It would look much better if a third party did the introductions and she knew Alexander would have no problem setting up the meeting considering he often acted as a go-between for these types of things. Wesley thought there was a one percent chance Tasev himself might be at the party but they and the analysts running this op doubted it. Still, the German should be there and he was a piece of shit who would give her a meet with Tasev if the price was right. Or perhaps just give her Tasev's location. She preferred that to a meeting. She wanted to infiltrate where he was staying and see if the intel on an antibiotic-resistant toxin they'd received was indeed true. If it was . . . she mentally shook herself. She couldn't even think of the devastation Tasev could wreak on the country and eventually the world.

Lopez watched her for a long moment, his expression unreadable. "Why do you need the introduction? I can get you what you want."

No, Lopez couldn't. Because she knew him well enough that he wouldn't introduce her to Tasev for a multitude of reasons. He might not even know the man was a) alive and b) in Miami and she didn't plan to tell him. Even if he knew, Lopez had a strange code and he wouldn't introduce a female to someone like Tasev. Honorable but annoying. "I'm not explaining myself." Her voice was light but had a slight edge to it. He'd never asked her to explain herself before and she didn't like that he was now.

His jaw tightened but he nodded. "Fine, I'll introduce you. But you're going with me and leaving with me."

Now she raised her eyebrows. "Putting stipulations on this? That's not how favors work."

"Then humor me. I need a date anyway."

She eyed his gaudy shirt. "I hope you plan on changing."

The tension in his shoulders loosened as he leaned back against the chair. "Fucking Shah. I should show up wearing this just to piss him off. I hate black tie stuff."

"I don't know why. I bet you clean up good." She hid her smile when he flushed. For a badass arms dealer he sometimes got flustered around women. It was charming. "But what's up with all this?" she asked, motioning to her face.

"Some women like beards," he said almost defensively.

"I never said I didn't. I was just asking about the

change." He shrugged, not giving her an answer. "Well, it looks good. Very rugged. What time should I meet you?"

"I can pick you up."

She snorted and stood. There was no way she'd tell him where she was staying and he knew it. "Nice try. I'll be here at seven if that works."

He nodded, amusement making his eyes twinkle. "It works."

They made small talk as he walked her to the front door. Once she'd left his exclusive neighborhood she'd have to pull over and scan her vehicle for tracking bugs. Lopez was decent enough but if he could get info on anyone, he would. It was the nature of his business and probably why he was so successful.

She didn't care if Lopez had planted a tracker. If she could meet with the elusive man known as the German—and hopefully keep Levi Lazaro from finding out about Tasev at all—their team might stop what could be one of the worst terrorist attacks the country had ever seen. The bombing that had happened weeks ago at the Westwood mansion would be nothing in comparison to what Tasev wanted to unleash. They had to stop him at any cost. And killing the man who'd likely murdered Meghan Lazaro was a bonus.

Chapter 4

Agent: a person officially employed by an intelligence service.

Claus stared at his dry-erase board, his heart thumping erratically in his chest. He'd done it.

He'd finally figured out the rest of the coding sequence. He was positive.

But he couldn't let anyone know. It was way too soon. He wasn't even sure if he'd managed to get his message out. He was ninety percent sure he had by using the iPad Tasev had given his daughter to use, but until he knew without a doubt, Claus had to keep this to himself. That fool Tasev thought he was so smart but it didn't matter that he'd disconnected the wireless system on the iPad. Claus had easily bypassed the block. He nearly snorted at Tasev's arrogance.

As Claus stood there staring at his work, he felt Aliyah's hand gently touch his forearm. He almost jumped, but steadied himself and turned. She hadn't cried today at all so that was good at least. This was the wrong time and wrong place for him to start being a father. It was his fault she'd been dragged into this. Somehow she didn't seem angry at him. Or maybe she was putting on a front. If she was angry he wouldn't blame her. He almost wished she was. Maybe it would give her an outlet for the pain he knew she must be feeling right now.

"Come eat with me?" she asked.

Eat? He glanced at his watch and frowned. It was well past his normal lunch time. "I'd like that." That was when he noticed she'd cleared off space and set up plates and food for them on one of his metal lab tables.

A guard must have brought food down and Claus hadn't even noticed. He inwardly chastised himself. He knew he needed to pay more attention to stuff like that, but he often got so caught up in his own world that everything else funneled out. But with Aliyah here he needed to be sharper.

"I'm sorry you were taken because of me," he said as he sat.

"You don't have to keep apologizing." She wore a pair of light blue scrubs Tasev had provided. They were loose fitting and she seemed comfortable enough. Her face was pale and it was clear she was distressed but was putting on a brave face since there was nothing they could do to escape. "How's your project coming?"

He grunted, not wanting to answer. He wasn't sure if Tasev had video cameras watching him, but he knew the man had placed audible recorders in the room. He'd found one early this morning and it was new, so clearly Tasev thought he'd confide something of use to his daughter. "Tell me about your work, your life, everything." After the shock of last night she'd fallen into a deep sleep so he'd left her alone and continued his work. This morning they'd had breakfast together but she'd mainly picked at her food, still confused and terrified.

"Um, well, I'm sure you know some of it, but I'm an advisor at a financial consulting firm. Our captor made me call in with a family emergency so no one would know I was missing. He's very thorough," she muttered.

"Yes, he is." Claus wanted to reassure her that help was on the way but since he didn't know if that was true, and he would tip his hand if he said anything, he said nothing about it. "Do you like your job?" he asked.

She nodded, half smiling as she picked up one of her fish tacos. It was mahimahi with ceviche, something he ordered all the time. He was glad she seemed to like it too.

For a few brief moments he was going to pretend that he wasn't in a prison and his daughter wasn't alive only because a monster had decided Claus was necessary. He was going to pretend that he was merely having lunch with his daughter for the first time—and hope that the NSA got his SOS message. Whatever happened, he just wanted her safe. If he had to sacrifice himself to get her to freedom, he'd do it.

Levi jerked out of his reading when his watch beeped. Blinking, he glanced at the face and turned off the alarm. He couldn't believe it was time to get ready for the Shah party. Since returning to the abandoned mansion he'd been hiding out in, he'd been devouring the files Alexander had given him and cross-referencing what he knew about Vasily and Tasev. What the hell was up with no last names?

At least Vasily was dead. And now that Levi had an actual name, *Tasev*, he'd reached out to some old contacts. So far no one had gotten back to him, but with the time differences it wasn't a surprise.

Before he killed Tasev he had to figure out why the hell he'd gone after Meghan. Nothing she'd been working on at the time would have warranted what happened to her. A year and a half ago his old boss had discovered a mole at the NSA. The guy had been killed by the very man he'd been leaking information to. From what Levi had gathered, that mole had had nothing to do with Meghan. Some days he wondered if the problem had even originated within the NSA or if it had come from somewhere else.

Meghan had been quirky and highly intelligent. A supernerd, as she'd liked to call herself. She'd kept a journal and even that had been in her own personal code. She'd loved numbers, codes, and figuring out puzzles and while she'd been deadly in her own right, she'd preferred working behind a computer to being in the field. They'd been different in so many ways but they'd fit. It hadn't been a love-at-first-sight thing, but a slow build that had developed over years of friendship. Hell, she'd been his best friend so he'd lost his wife and closest friend at once.

After her death he'd figured out the key to her journal because he'd known her better than anyone else had. From it he'd discovered that the week she died she'd had a meeting scheduled with one of her old friends, Dr. Claus Schmidt. Schmidt had been a low-level asset for the NSA for Meghan's recruiter, Louis Bachman, years ago. Bachman had introduced Meghan and Schmidt at a conference, but they'd never worked together in an official capacity. Despite their age difference, the two had become friends. They'd loved talking science and numbers together. Unfortunately Bachman had died of a heart attack so Levi had been unable to question him further.

And Schmidt had been missing for two years.

Ever since Meghan was killed. The timing wasn't a coincidence but Levi couldn't figure out how the two events were related or where the hell Schmidt was. But he knew the doctor was somehow connected.

Hurrying, he showered and dressed in the tuxedo he'd bought on the way back to his hideout. It wasn't custom but the fit was decent. He didn't care, as long as he blended in well enough to do the meet tonight. He'd already contacted Jasmine/Allison about the party and planned to knock out two birds with one stone. When he'd mentioned that Alexander wanted to talk to her she'd seemed stunned but also pleased. The two couldn't be more different but what the hell did Levi know.

The drive to Allison's place took him less than five minutes. Even though he was staying in an abandoned mansion, it was still in a prime part of town close to her high-rise penthouse suite. Luckily he didn't have to park; she was waiting inside the lobby. When she waved at him through the glass door, her doorman opened it and escorted her to Levi's SUV. He would have normally opened the door for her but the doorman was determined to, fawning all over her and practically drooling as he helped her in.

He understood why. The woman was exquisitely

beautiful. She was like one of those pinup models from half a century ago with a perfect hourglass figure. Not that his dick seemed to notice. Beautiful women just didn't do it for him these days. Nothing did. Deep down, he knew it was because he was dead inside. When he'd lost Meghan and their unborn child—without even the chance to bury their daughter—something inside him had cracked wide open and not just broken, but shattered.

The only good thing about that was that he didn't care if he died. Death might even be a mercy. It made this mission easier than any he'd ever done. As long as he took out everyone guilty with him, Levi didn't give a shit if he burned too.

"You look beautiful," he murmured to Allison, flicking her a quick glance as she strapped in.

"Thank you. You look pretty good yourself."

He grunted as he looked in the rearview mirror, checking for a tail. So far he didn't see one but that didn't mean anything. "Thanks for coming with me to this." He'd offered to pay her but she said she didn't want his money, that she didn't want any man's money even if he hadn't been offering to pay for her body. He was glad to hear that and he wasn't sure why. His dead wife's ghost would probably tell him it was because he still had a conscience somewhere in his hollow chest, but that couldn't be it. He didn't care about anything other than avenging her.

"Does Alexander know I'm going to be there?" Her breathing rate kicked up a notch when she asked and even though she was perfectly still, seeming at ease, he saw the pulse point in her throat fluttering faster than normal.

"No, but he'll be pleased." That being an understatement.

She didn't say anything, just turned to look out the window.

The drive to Shah's mansion in Coral Gables was quiet, which was just as well. Levi had already pulled the building records to get the layout of the place and used Google Earth to scan the area so he was familiar enough with the place to be comfortable about heading in relatively blind. If he'd still been with the NSA he'd have had better intel, but fewer resources was part of the price of going off the grid. The ten-bedroom, ten-bath place was around thirty thousand square feet of livable space, lavishly furnished, had a private beach, and was located in the gated Tahiti Beach neighborhood. Levi wondered if Shah's neighbors knew he was a highly sought-after thief.

Tonight was just an excuse for Shah to make contacts and show off some of his newly acquired art. He'd be watching everyone as much as they watched one another.

"Have you been to Shah's place before?" he asked Allison as he steered up to the gated neighborhood.

He gave the guard his alias, Isaiah Moore, then waited for him to check the list of guests. The gate opened and let them through, but he knew they'd be searched before being allowed entrance. Standard procedure.

"No, but I've heard it's stunning."

"How do you want me to introduce you tonight?" he asked, shooting her a quick glance. Even though she'd told him that she was done with the escort business she hadn't given him any more details about what her plans were or how she'd be assimilating back into a normal life. Or if she even planned to. He hadn't wanted to pry.

"Jasmine to everyone else but Allison to Alexander," she said softly.

"You're going to break that man's heart," Levi murmured as he pulled behind a luxury sedan slowly turning into Shah's long driveway.

She laughed, the sound delicate and feminine as she shook her head. "I doubt it. The man . . . I don't even know why I'm attracted to him. He's so gaudy and brash but I like the way he looks at me."

"There's no explanation for attraction." If it was something that could be forced or made sense of, he'd be attracted to her instead of feeling this deadness inside.

He hated it and that rage was the only thing that reminded him he was actually alive. He couldn't even jerk off without losing his erection. He'd think of what had happened to Meghan and lose it. For two fucking years he'd been living in this fucked-up state and couldn't shake it no matter how hard he tried. Because the only thing that would make a difference was his vengeance.

"You all right?" Allison asked, her voice soft, a slight trace of concern lacing her words.

He realized he was gripping the wheel tight and his expression probably matched his black mood. "I'm good." He tried to smile, though he was pretty sure he failed when she didn't seem any more at ease. Then he felt like a douche for making her feel uncomfortable. She'd probably gotten good at reading people over the years, especially in her former profession, and an angry client could be a bad thing. "Sorry—just have a lot on my mind. Stick close to me tonight. I need Alexander to introduce me to someone. Then I'm leaving."

She nodded.

After being scanned with a metal-detecting wand, then walking under an actual metal detector, they were both allowed access to the party. Levi didn't mind not having a standard weapon for tonight because anything could be deadly. He could use the broken-off stem of a champagne glass or even one of Allison's stilettos to stab someone. Or if necessary he could use his hands.

"You might want to smile or something. You look like a rabid beast about to attack anyone. Even the servers are avoiding us," Allison murmured next to him, her arm loosely linked with his, her fingers resting lightly on his forearm.

They'd already lapped the interior of the main room that Levi knew was Shah's living room, but he'd cleared out all the furniture so that it looked like an art gallery. Hell, he could fit a house in this room. Female servers walked around carrying trays of champagne and hors d'oeuvres. They wore black and silver belly dancer costumes and they were indeed cutting a wide berth for him and Allison. He tried to force himself to relax. He needed to tone down his mood and get it together. Considering how close he was to meeting the man who could introduce him to Tasev he couldn't afford to lose it now.

He looked around at the well-dressed people—most criminals, but some not—talking and laughing under the sparkling chandeliers. The marble floors were polished and many guests were admiring the priceless art on the walls and in display cases.

Levi didn't care about any of that. The tension and anticipation slamming through him was almost too much to contain. But he knew better than to get his hopes up. He'd been hunting for two long years. This could be another dead end. Still, a small thread of hope spooled through him, telling him that this was it. "Let's head to the pool area."

He scanned faces as they went, looking for Alexander or the German. He didn't think Alexander would bail on Shah's party but as they stepped outside and he still didn't see him, another surge of irrational annoyance started to rise. Even though Levi knew the arms dealer would be here, impatience was making him edgy.

"Alexander's there," Allison said, a strange note in her voice.

He followed her line of sight and spotted Alexander striding outside with a woman on his arm. They were about fifteen feet away, in one of the open glass doorways.

But she wasn't arm candy. This woman wasn't some piece of fluff. Tall, sleek, strong, she was an operator. No doubt about it, just from the way she moved. She scanned the enormous pool area, looking at faces and taking mental notes. He could see it in every tight line of that hot body.

She was drop-dead gorgeous, though that description fell way too short of reality. She had to be at least five feet ten, but it was hard to tell with her heels. Her white blond hair had been pulled into a twist type of thing, falling over one of her breasts like a long rope. Her dark blue dress was long and fitted but not skin-tight and the asymmetrical one-shoulder look was sexy as hell. Since when had shoulders become sexy? The dress accentuated all her curves, making his mouth water. The reaction stunned him as much as it pissed him off. Unlike practically everyone here tonight wearing black her dress was blue. He wondered if it matched her eyes. Immediately he hated himself for his curiosity. He didn't give a shit about some woman Alexander had arrived with.

Liar.

Then she turned fully toward him and all the breath left his lungs in one whoosh as their gazes collided. Something flared in her pale blue eyes. Something he couldn't read as she looked him over from head to toe, unabashed in her perusal. He couldn't tell if she was checking him out with sexual interest or sizing him up. Did she know who he was? Truly was . . . He wasn't sure why the thought crossed his mind. He didn't know all of Wesley's operators but this woman was looking at him as if she knew him. Or maybe she just wanted to get to know him. Hell if he knew. It'd been too long since he'd paid attention to a woman and he hated that he couldn't tell if that was feminine interest in her gaze.

And now, after two years, his cock decided wake up.

Fuck.

Striding forward he practically dragged Allison with him, ignoring her little yelp of surprise as he barreled toward them. By the time he'd reached Alexander and the woman, Alexander had pulled two champagne glasses from one of the passing server's trays.

The arms dealer's eyes widened a fraction as he turned to find Levi and Allison standing there. He completely ignored Levi and his date and smiled at Allison. He held out a glass to her, a hell of a lot more polite than Levi had been tonight. "I didn't know you'd be here," Alexander said, clearly pleased to see her.

"Thank you," she murmured, taking it. "I like the beard. It suits you."

"I remember what you said and thought I'd try it," Alexander said, staring at Allison as if mesmerized. The blonde was still watching Levi.

Gritting his teeth, Levi cleared his throat. "Allison, you already know Alexander." He turned to the man's date then. "But we haven't met."

The blonde continued to watch him curiously as Alexander handed her the other glass. "Of course. Selene, this is Isaiah Moore, an associate. And this is the lovely Allison."

The blonde nodded politely at Allison, then turned that pale gaze on Levi. "Isaiah?" Her voice was throaty, sexy, and sent another pulse of need to his cock. She seemed almost amused by his name. As if she didn't believe it. And fuck it, he wanted to hear his real name on those lips. Damn it, what the hell was wrong with him? He resisted the urge to tug at his collar. It was cool outside but a slow-building heat had started deep inside him, making him question his sanity.

Levi nodded. "Selene what?" He wanted to know her last name, wanted to know everything about her. Which just pissed him off. His skin felt too tight for his body as his gaze strayed to those bee-stung lips. A woman didn't have a right to be so damn beautiful. And he shouldn't want her. He shouldn't want *anyone*. Something dark settled in his chest and for a moment he wanted to drag up the horrific images that lingered on the edges of his consciousness practically twenty-four/seven, but he shoved them back.

For once, he didn't want to tumble into that deep abyss. He wanted to feel something other than the clawing pain, wearing down his insides every second of every day. That realization sent a sharp stab of guilt into his chest.

The woman started to answer but Alexander spoke. "My apologies, this is Selene Silva. She's an old *friend* of mine," he said, stressing the word "friend" as he looked at Allison.

It took Levi all of two seconds to register that name. Silva. Yeah, he recognized it and it pissed him off more than his attraction to the woman. "Alexander, will you please keep Allison company? I need to speak to your *friend* privately."

Levi heard Alexander murmur his acquiescence as he and Allison stepped away. Without pause, Levi grabbed Selene's elbow. Her eyes narrowed to slits at the unexpected touch. She started to pull away but he leaned in close so that their noses were almost touching. He wanted to see her eyes up close, to gauge if she was lying. "You're working for Wesley? And don't fucking lie. I *know* that name."

She paused, but eventually nodded. "Yes." He figured the only reason she was being honest was because she had no choice. Lying to him would serve no purpose.

"You think you can fucking take me down? Or maybe you thought I'd leave with you because of that hot body? I didn't realize Wesley had gotten so desperate." Levi glanced around, looking for other NSA agents, wondering how big of a team his old boss had sent in, as he mentally calculated his escape. He'd been beyond careful for so long but a few weeks ago he'd broken his own rules and reached out to Wesley because Levi had needed to give him the location of a terrorist group. Now he wanted to kick his own ass for his weakness. He'd probably led Wesley right to him.

To his surprise, the woman laughed, the throaty sound having the most annoying effect on his cock. He inwardly cursed himself as he met her gaze again. Those pale eyes filled with humor. "I'd heard you were arrogant. I didn't know you'd be here and you're the least of my worries," she murmured as she pulled her elbow from his grasp.

"What?"

"I know who you are and I don't care. Levi," she whispered his name so low he barely heard. Then to his surprise, she turned and walked away, the sway of that tight ass making him positively stupid for a moment.

As his gaze trailed up and over her sleek lines his gaze narrowed on a tattoo peeking out at the top of her dress. It was just the tip of what looked like wings, but he couldn't be sure. His fingers itched to pull it down, to expose what she was hiding, to trace his fingers over her soft skin.

Let her go, he ordered himself. She wasn't important. Nothing but his mission was. But she could report him to Wesley. Hell, she'd probably do it as soon as she left the party. Shah didn't allow any electronics in so it was unlikely she'd be able to contact Wesley now. But Levi needed to find out her endgame and why the hell she was in town. If it had anything to do with him or Tasev, there was no way in hell he'd let the NSA or anyone get in his way.

Chapter 5

Clandestine operation: an intelligence operation intended to be secret.

Selene knew Levi would come after her. He'd be stupid not to. She needed to somehow gain the upper hand and regain her composure. He might not even be able to tell she was ruffled but right now her heart was racing out of control. He shouldn't know that she worked for Wesley. Obviously it was because of her cover ID, but no one was supposed to know that that ID wasn't legit. She'd contemplated denying it, but if she needed him, she hadn't wanted to start off with a lie. It would have set the wrong tone immediately.

That wasn't the only reason she was off her game. It was the man himself affecting her. She'd seen his pictures before and once she'd seen him in person. But that had been different. She'd certainly never been attracted to him. Now . . . well, now she was very aware of him as a man. A very desirable one. It was beyond jarring because she hadn't expected the attraction to him.

And he'd felt it too. She was sure of it. She'd been on

the receiving end of a lot of appreciative male and female looks, but the way he'd stared at her had been so
raw, so . . . primal. And he'd seemed angry as he'd
watched her. But that was before they'd been introduced so she didn't understand the anger part of his
reaction. Unless he'd already known who she was.

Out of the corner of her eye she saw Alexander
talking to the woman Levi had arrived with. Alexander
had spotted them a few minutes before the other couple had gone outside and subtly tried to make his way
to them—because he'd wanted to talk to the woman—
and he'd told Selene the oddest thing about Levi. He
hired escorts but didn't sleep with them. The arms
dealer had also made an offhand comment that Levi—
whom Alexander knew as Isaiah Moore—had a meeting with the German tonight. That knowledge made all
Selene's alarm bells go off.

She'd barely taken three strides before Levi fell in
step with her. Taking her by surprise, he placed his
large hand at the small of her back. Even though she
knew he meant nothing by it, it felt possessive. "Walk
with me to the beach. We need privacy," he said quietly,
his voice a seductive whisper against her ear.

She knew he was trying to make it appear as if they
were lovers looking for privacy. He wasn't asking so
much as ordering her and while she bristled at the
command, she knew they needed to talk. She had questions and if she found out that Levi was interested in
Tasev, then she had her orders to follow.

As they walked around the pool her heels clicked
against the stone patio. The only thing she hated about
getting dressed up was the footwear. Heels were im-

possible to run in and completely impractical. Give her boots any day. Or flip-flops. Also impractical but at least they were comfortable.

She spotted a half dozen guards in the shadows around Shah's property as she and Levi made their way down the long stone walk to the private beach and dock. Shah had multiple boats including one worth over a million. And according to her file on him, he took it out only once a year. What a waste.

Instead of heading down the path that would take them to the beach, Levi guided her toward the dock. There weren't any guards around here that she could see, but she was still cautious, scanning the water and secured boats. The dock spread out into a cross-shape with a couple of built-in benches.

Without waiting for him to tell her what to do, she sat on a bench and crossed her legs. As soon as she did, the split on the right side opened up, revealing skin all the way to her thigh. She'd used the sight of her body as a distraction before but she hadn't meant to now. When his gaze raked over her, she felt as exposed as if she was sitting there naked.

Surprising her, he sat directly next to her, invading all her personal space. He had a warm, spicy masculine scent that made her think of the forest. She tried to pull back but he wrapped his hand around the back of her neck, holding her in place.

His grip wasn't hard and she was ninety percent sure he wouldn't hurt her. Not the Levi she'd read about, anyway. He'd been a protector, a man dedicated to helping his country, not caring that he never received any public recognition. He'd been the best kind of warrior. But then his wife had died and Wesley said something inside him had broken. So there was a slim chance he could attempt to hurt her. But she hoped he hadn't gone that far over the line. While she was trained, she wasn't stupid enough to think she could take on a man like Levi one on one. She could defend herself enough to get away, but if it came down to a fight to the death, he had more training.

Selene hated what had happened to him and his wife and while she knew it wasn't technically her problem, she owed Levi. He didn't know it, but she did. So when it came down to it she wasn't even sure if she could pull off her complete mission. Taking down Tasev she knew she could do but the other thing . . . Levi's thumb rubbed gently against her pulse point, his eyes a midnight black, so dark she could barely discern the iris.

She fought the shiver that slid through her, not wanting him to know he was affecting her. And she didn't like that he actually was affecting her.

"So you know who I am," he murmured, his gaze straying to her lips.

She ran her tongue over her bottom lip, trying to find her voice and hating the way her nipples tightened as his gaze darkened with lust. "Yep. How did you figure out who I work for?" According to her intel there weren't any listening devices on the dock—it would be a stupid place to keep them with all the water—but she didn't want to come out and say Wesley or the NSA.

"The name Silva. I recognize it."

"Bullshit." Wesley and a small handful of people knew The Wolf was an NSA creation.

His jaw clenched, those eyes darkening, even if that seemed impossible. "I'm not lying."

It struck her that there was a small chance he did know Selene Silva's cover ID details. Meghan Lazaro had helped build the alias. It was against every regulation to tell her spouse or anyone else, but that didn't mean the woman hadn't. Married agents talked. Period. Selene eyed him cautiously. "Meghan told you."

He jerked back as if Selene had slapped him. She regretted the effect her words had but gauged his reaction.

Jaw tight, his mouth pinched, he didn't respond one way or another.

And even though she knew it might be a mistake, she continued, "I'm . . . sorry about what happened to her. I know words are meaningless from a stranger, but I truly am. She was a good woman," Selene whispered. "I didn't really know her, but she guided me on a couple of really tough missions early in my career." God, it had been only a little over three years ago though it seemed longer. "She had an easy way with people." She'd saved Selene's life once because of a last-minute find and Selene would never, ever, forget that. She'd been stuck in the field, young and alone, with no backup and Meghan had been the voice on the other end of her comm, keeping Selene sane.

He seemed frozen, staring at her as if he didn't know how to respond. He didn't drop his hand from the back of her neck but he let out a ragged breath, keeping his gaze pinned to hers. "I haven't talked about her with anyone in years."

In that moment the stark loneliness in his dark eyes

clawed at Selene like razor wire. He looked completely adrift for just a fraction of a moment before that hard expression returned. And so did the pressure around the back of her neck.

"Why are you at this party?" he asked.

She shook her head. "You know how this works. I don't have the authority to tell you that. And unless you plan on . . ." Shit, where was her head? She couldn't say "unless you plan on torturing the information out of me" all casually. What the hell was wrong with her? "You know I can't tell you," she murmured.

"Now I call bullshit. You have situational discretion. You here to meet the German?"

She didn't respond but he must have read the increase in her heart rate. Damn it, that's why he was holding on to her neck; he was reading her. It was difficult to do and wasn't exactly scientific, but she had no doubt he was gauging the changes in her pulse. She could attempt to get out of his grip, but wasn't sure it would be worth it. Part of her mission concerned Levi, and making an enemy of him wasn't something she or the NSA wanted. "So what if I am?"

"Concerning what?" Levi bit out.

"You expect me to just tell you this as if you still have the clearance, as if you *didn't* go off the reservation, and as if you haven't crossed too many lines to count?" She didn't actually blame him for going rogue, but she needed his hand off her and she needed some space. He was wreaking havoc on her senses, making it difficult for her to think straight. She was trained in weapons and had been hacking pretty much since she was old enough to use a computer—which was why

Wesley had brought her into the fold to begin with—but with men, she had a terrible track record. She pretty much had no experience or training. Especially not enough against a man like Levi Lazaro. He exuded so much raw sexual appeal and danger it was practically pouring off him in waves and it was having a strange effect on her. She wished she'd been at least a little prepared for this attraction, but it was taking her completely by storm.

That grip tightened again but this time he started rubbing his first two fingers against her neck in a soft little rhythm. The action was almost erotic. Or maybe that was just the effect he was having on her. She could feel his gentle stroking all the way to the pulsing point between her legs. Maybe she had mental issues that this man was turning her on.

He leaned closer, skimming his mouth against her jawline and she froze. Just completely, utterly froze. "Are you meeting Tasev?" he whispered.

She'd told herself to be prepared for this question, to keep her reaction under wraps, but he came to his own conclusion if his savage curse was anything to go by. Damn it, Wesley was going to be pissed at her, but Levi had been right. She had operational latitude right now and she needed to keep Levi close. They needed to know what he knew and what he was planning. Trying to shut him out now, when he was at the party specifically to meet the German, would be stupid. Levi had stayed off their radar for two years because he was good. Of course Wesley hadn't exactly sent out a worldwide manhunt for him either. About a year ago he'd decided to more or less let him go.

Now . . . "I met with the German earlier tonight. He squeezed me in before some of his other meetings."

Levi snorted, his gaze dipping to her lips once more, that hungry look in place again. It was so raw and in her face it was hard to ignore that kind of desire and what it was doing to her. "I can understand why."

Even though Levi didn't ask she decided to use the latitude she had and bring him in on this. They had similar goals. She needed to bring Tasev down and rescue a very important scientist—if he was even the man who'd sent out an emergency message to Meghan/Wesley—but that didn't mean she couldn't let Levi have Tasev once she'd gotten what she needed. "I'm meeting with Tasev tomorrow night."

At her words every muscle in Levi's lean, fit body stilled.

Before he could respond, she continued, "I'll make you a deal. You can come with me to the meeting—if we can work out an agreeable plan—but you don't kill him until I get what I want. I have less than a week. Can you live with that time line?" She was allowed to bring one person with her to the meeting, so it would be Levi—if he could be a professional and if Wesley went for it. And of course, if Tasev did. They had a lot to discuss before she was on board one hundred percent, but bringing along a seasoned agent—former agent—like Levi could be beneficial.

Levi watched her carefully again, his gaze roaming over her face, as if he was trying to see into her mind. "You're not lying. Why are you doing this?"

"Because if I try to shut you out you'll cause me

more problems than I want to deal with. And I don't want to kill you."

Those dark eyes narrowed a fraction with just a hint of amusement—as if he knew she couldn't take him on physically. "And?"

"And . . . I owe you." Selene didn't explain because she knew he'd think she was referring to when Meghan saved her life. That was fine with her. Telling him exactly how she owed him would strip her open too bare and she wasn't willing to let anyone see that vulnerable side of her.

"Telling the truth again." He frowned now, true confusion in his gaze. Whether from her words or the fact that she was letting him in on this op. "You plan to try to bring me in after the op?"

"No." That was actually the truth. Wesley, however, was a different story. But she refused to let her mind go there, knowing Levi would pick up on it.

Levi started to respond when a burst of gunfire from the pool area made them both turn at the noise. Selene automatically moved off the bench, crouching down behind it and to her surprise Levi moved in front of her, blocking her even though they were too far away to be in any danger from what she could hear.

"This is what happens when you get a bunch of criminals under the same roof," he muttered.

She snorted in agreement. "I'm leaving using the beach. You're free to join me." There hadn't been any more gunfire so likely the guards had the situation under control but she wasn't heading back up there. She'd already had her meeting so she had no reason to return.

Now he snorted as he turned to face her, still crouching low. He slid his long, callused hands down her bare arms. This time she couldn't hide the shiver. "Oh, I'm joining you," he murmured, a seductive note in his voice.

But the timing was all wrong. For once she wished she understood the opposite sex more. What was he doing? She'd already told him he could come on the op with her. Her nipples tightened and her body hummed with a strange anticipation as he lightly held her wrists in both hands, his thumbs rubbing her inner wrist in small circles. She started to pull back and he let go of one of her wrists. As she pushed out a sigh of relief, the feel of cold steel skimmed her skin just as the soft snick of handcuffs clicked into place.

If it had been flex cuffs she would have gone into panic mode, but she retained her cool as she looked down at her hands. While she internally cursed herself for letting her guard down, she could get out of these whenever she wanted. "Really? I already said you can come with me. And what kind of pervert carries handcuffs around?"

"If you think I trust you, you're out of your damn mind. You're coming with me and I'm not letting you out of my sight until we meet with Tasev. For all I know you're going to call Wesley." He grabbed her forearm, surprisingly gently, and tugged so that she had to stand with him.

In the distance she could see and hear people still at the party. Apparently a little gunfire was no big deal to this crowd. "Of course I'm going to call him, but not about you."

Levi just grunted and motioned toward the beach. Since she could get out of the cuffs anytime she wanted, she let him think he had the upper hand and allowed him to lead her. If anything, her compliance might lull him into feeling secure around her. The NSA knew Levi was in Miami since he'd helped them locate a nasty group of terrorists just a couple of weeks ago but they had no idea where he was staying.

As they reached the beach she tugged against his grip. "Unless you want me stumbling every few feet, let me take my shoes off," she demanded.

He turned to look at her, his expression unreadable. "Try to take me out and you'll regret it." There was a dark note in his voice that should have scared her but instead did strange things to her insides.

He bent down in front of her, the moonlight playing off his inky hair. She lifted one foot and again, to her utter surprise, he was incredibly gentle as he took her ankle. Her silver shoes were strappy and delicate with a small buckle on her inner ankle. Even after he'd unstrapped it, his fingers lingered as he rubbed that same soft pattern over the top of her foot as he'd done to her wrist.

It was weird and erotic at the same time. She felt his touch all the way to her core. Just as quickly as he started he jerked to a stop, shaking his head slightly. When he took off her other shoe he did it in seconds, barely grazing her skin. For some strange reason she was disappointed. Selene shouldn't care whether this man touched her or not but she couldn't help the new burst of desire that had erupted inside her.

She was so good at compartmentalizing her emotions. It was something she'd been doing since she was a teenager. She'd had to in order to survive and it was part of the reason she was such a valuable asset to the NSA. Unfortunately just being in Levi's presence was jeopardizing everything she'd worked for.

Wesley looked through the glass pane of his temporary office in the NSA's covert Miami location at his team of agents and analysts busy working their asses off as he waited for Jack Stone to pick up his damn phone. The former Black Death 9 agent was one of the best Wesley had ever trained. It was a tie between Levi and Jack for who'd been the most lethally efficient. And they'd been tight, closer than any other agents Wesley had known.

Until Levi left the fold.

Jack picked up on the third ring with a quiet, "Hey."

Wesley could hear a rustling in the background. "Bad time?"

"Nah, just give me a sec." Jack said something Wesley couldn't make out, as if he'd covered his phone. A few seconds later he was back on the line. "What's up? Everything all right?"

"Yeah. How's everything with you and Sophie?" The woman Jack had left the NSA to marry. His childhood sweetheart and one of the nicest people Wesley had ever known. He rubbed the back of his neck, trying to ease the growing tension there.

"Good, but that's not why you're calling. You just dragged me from bed with my beautiful wife so come on, what's going on?"

"You think any more about my offer?" he asked, still not ready to tell Jack what he needed to.

A long pause. "Yeah, Soph and I talked about it and I'm interested."

After the Westwood bombing a couple of weeks ago Wesley had used Jack in a very unofficial capacity to guard a witness. When shit had gone haywire Jack had stepped up and helped save the witness alongside a team of highly trained men. Wesley had used him as a contractor of sorts and after the op he'd seen that gleam in Jack's eyes that said he'd missed the adrenaline rush of his old job. Not enough to work for Wesley full-time but he'd offered Jack the option of taking contract work for jobs in the Southeast. The man owned a successful boat and Jet Ski rental business in Key West but Wesley had figured it couldn't hurt to ask. "Good. That's good."

"Shit, whatever this is must be bad for you to stall. Just tell me. Is there a hit out on me or something?" he asked, only half joking.

"No." After he pressed one of the buttons on the wall, the window frosted over as he turned from it. "Is your line secure?"

Jack just snorted in response. As in, Wesley was stupid for even asking.

"I got an emergency message from one of Meghan Lazaro's old e-mail accounts." He'd had all her accounts forwarded to him after she was killed. "I haven't received anything in over a year and a half and this one . . . Hell, I don't even know if it's true but my gut says it is. Dr. Claus Schmidt says he's being forced to work for the infamous Tasev."

"I thought Tasev was dead."

"So did I. Maybe he still is. Supposedly he's been

working on a vicious new antibiotic-resistant toxin for the last couple of years. He doesn't know what Tasev's endgame is but he knows that the man wants to infiltrate various water supplies all over the United States. Then he can blackmail the government into paying for the antibiotic that only he has. Without being able to isolate the toxin it'll be damn near impossible to develop an antibiotic in enough time to save people so we would have no choice but to comply. This isn't one of those cases where we wouldn't negotiate with terrorists." The man would have them over a barrel and they'd have no choice—which would set a really bad precedent. "Schmidt is working on it but as soon as he gives it to Tasev, he's a dead man. He says his daughter—and I didn't even know he had one until his message—is being held with him at an undisclosed location in Miami."

"Schmidt's name is vaguely familiar."

"He was a small-time asset for Bachman. Remember him?"

"Shit, yeah. He's dead, right?"

"Yep. Heart attack." Which hadn't been a surprise considering the man's diet. "Schmidt occasionally passed Bachman information he overheard at medical conferences if he thought it'd be of any use to us, but his relationship with Meghan wasn't professional. They were good friends. And he fell off the radar around the same time she was killed."

"That doesn't sound like a coincidence. Is Tasev or Schmidt somehow connected to her death?"

"I think so. Tasev at least."

"Not Schmidt?"

"My gut says no." The CIA had helped get some of Schmidt's family out of East Berlin back in the eighties, for one. And it didn't fit his profile.

"So just Tasev."

And Wesley wanted to rip Tasev apart limb from limb if that was the case. He'd never gotten over what had been done to Meghan. Those in the know about her death had been horrified and it took a lot to rattle the people he worked with.

Jack was quiet a moment. "Levi know?"

"I don't know. But he's in town, somewhere, and I think he's close to discovering the connection." His sources told him that Levi had been ready to meet with Paul Hill before that fucker had been arrested. And according to Schmidt, Hill had been providing him with live test subjects. So Levi was close.

"What are you gonna do?"

Wesley rubbed a hand over his face. "I don't know." Levi deserved his revenge and Wesley wanted him brought in, but not to arrest him. If this terrorist threat was real he might have to make an impossible decision and bring Levi down. Because if he had to choose the safety of the country and countless innocent lives, and Levi decided to get in the way—there might not be another choice. Some days he hated his job.

Chapter 6

Operational latitude: on a mission an agent has a broad scope of flexibility when making mission decisions.

"If you think you're going to put a hood over my head you're out of your freaking mind," Selene said quietly, her stance defensive as they stood next to Levi's SUV.

The majority of the partygoers had decided to stay so most of the vehicles at Shah's place were still there. He and Selene had avoided the guards as they used the beach, then a neighbor's property, to make their way to the parked cars.

Before he could respond, she continued, her stilettos held tightly in her cuffed hands. "You'd better be prepared to fight me to the death, because you're not putting that thing on me."

In that moment Levi felt like the monster he knew he was slowly turning into every passing day. The blackness spreading across his insides was like a cancer and even though he knew it, he couldn't stop it. It ate away at him day in and day out until he could barely look in the mirror. And he didn't like the way Selene was look-ing at him now.

A person could bottle up rage and hate only so long before it started to kill him. Normally he shoved all that shit back down, but as Selene warily watched him, he felt a glimmer of the man he'd once been start to sur-face and guilt washed over him.

He needed her hooded so she wouldn't see where he was staying, but more than anger, there was a stark kind of fear in her pale blue eyes. It fled quickly but it had been unmistakable. For some reason the thought of making her feel vulnerable made him feel like shit. He had no idea how trained she was—though he knew she had to be a decent fighter to work for Wesley—and a fight with her wouldn't be worth it, even if he did win in the end. He'd lose all semblance of trust between them. Not that he was even sure that they had any, but starting things that way after she'd agreed to take him to meet Tasev would be monumentally stupid—and guarantee that Wesley would come after him hard. Jaw tight, he yanked open the passenger door. "Get in," he ordered.

"Only because you asked so nicely." Her voice was saccharine sweet and her expression deadly as she slid in. When her long dress shifted, the right side splitting and revealing one of her long, toned, tan legs his entire body reacted, his cock flaring to life at just a peek of her damn skin.

Angry, he looked up at her but realized she hadn't done it intentionally. She wasn't even paying attention to him, just surveying the interior of the SUV. Which he'd have to ditch soon. He'd been switching vehicles regularly and after coming to Shah's party knew this one wouldn't be safe anymore. Shah might have put a tracker on it or any government agency with an interest in the man could have been surveying the party and taking note of all the attendees.

He resisted the childish urge to slam the door, shutting it quietly instead. After scanning the interior and underneath the SUV for trackers he slid into the driver's seat.

"We're going to have to come up with a reason we're both meeting with Tasev," she said, her expression hard. "Or you coming with me will never fly."

"What's your meet about?" he asked as he steered out of his spot.

"I'm using my cover to offer my services as a freelancer. The German said I had good timing. Not sure what that meant but . . ." She trailed off, shrugging.

Levi thought about the files Alexander had given him and decided to information-share. It was small but he knew he needed to show he was a team player. Even if he wasn't. "His right-hand man, Vasily, was found dead. If his resident assassin is gone he'll need someone else soon."

Her pretty mouth pulled down. "Huh."

"You guys kill him?" he asked.

She shook her head. "No. Or, not that I know of."

He frowned as another thought occurred to him. "What's your real name?"

"My name *is* Selene. Not Silva though. And no, I'm not telling you my real last name." She glanced in the side view mirror, either looking for a tail or hoping her team—if she had one—had followed. "We need to check in with Lopez and your date, make sure they're okay."

Levi shot her a sideways glance as he pulled up to a stoplight. "You care what happens to Alexander or some random woman?"

She shrugged. "He's a good asset."

Right. She wouldn't have mentioned Allison if she didn't care. He found that interesting—and a little annoying. He didn't want to like Selene, didn't want to know that she could be a decent person. Not when she was just an asset to him. And that was all he could afford to let her be. He would just ignore this bullshit attraction he felt. "When we were on the beach he texted me that he and Allison are safe and he'll be getting her home. The gunfire was from a stupid argument and the two men in question have been escorted from the property for smuggling in weapons. He also wanted to make sure you were safe."

Selene didn't respond, but a soft smile touched her lips. Yeah, she liked Alexander more than she'd let on. Clearing her throat, she said, "So what's your cover, *Isaiah*? I'm going to need to know everything about your alias's background and why you'd want to meet with Tasev. It's gotta be strong if you're coming with me."

"We'll go over it tomorrow before we meet with him." He wasn't taking the chance that she'd run back to Wesley and tell the man everything about his current ID. Wesley might already have Levi's alias but he wasn't risking it. He'd covered his tracks well over the past couple of years but he didn't want the NSA knowing any more about him than necessary.

To his surprise she didn't argue or even respond. She just laid her head back against the headrest and semi-relaxed. To an untrained observer she looked at ease, but her posture was just a little too stiff, her body tense, as if waiting for an attack. And he hated that she felt that way because of him, hated that any female was afraid of him. But there was nothing to do about it. He'd made his decisions and he was seeing this thing through. He couldn't live with himself if he didn't.

The rest of the drive was quiet. Selene straightened as he pulled down a quiet street in an upper-class neighborhood under construction. Most of the homes were half-built and that wasn't changing anytime soon. The house he'd been staying in was a little over five thousand square feet. The previous owners had run out of money during the building phase and when the construction market crashed, this neighborhood was one of the casualties. He'd done his homework and most of the homes were bank owned now and just sitting there. The house he was in was basically done, with just a few small cosmetic finishes that needed to be completed.

"You're squatting?" Selene asked incredulously.

He shrugged as he pulled into the garage and shut it. It was the best way to stay off the grid. Thanks to contacts he'd been able to steal electricity, water, and even Internet. He used the electricity only when necessary though, not wanting anyone to see lights and get curious about them. "Come on," he said as he opened his door.

She followed, her feet silent against the concrete floor of the garage. There were two windows that let in enough moonlight for him to make out her graceful movements. Her pale hair seemed to almost glow against the backdrop of the windows, giving her an ethereal quality that just added to her beauty.

Something he didn't want to be noticing. He rolled his shoulders once, trying to ease out the tension building inside him. Why the hell was he even aware of her?

There weren't any coverings on most of the windows so the moonlight was a good enough guide as he took her through the kitchen and up a curved staircase to the master bedroom. He'd found a mattress and had the most basic needs covered so he could sleep and shower when necessary. Since there wasn't a bed frame he couldn't hook her to it so he headed for the bathroom with her in tow.

"What are you doing?" she demanded as he cuffed her to the rail in the walk-in shower, but she didn't struggle.

That surprised him, but he was betting on her not wanting to throw down with him either. "I'll be back in a few minutes." He had to check all his traps to make sure no one had infiltrated the place while he'd been out. They were all small and wouldn't alert anyone breaking in, but he'd know if they'd been triggered and that was what mattered.

Ten minutes later he was striding up the stairs—far too eager to see his captive—but froze at the top step. The sound of running water greeted his ears, making him go cold. What the hell?

Weapon drawn, he eased into the bedroom and was immediately struck by two things. The bathroom light was on and he hadn't left it that way. And Selene had been too far away to have turned it on. The second thing made his entire body heat up with a fire he'd never imagined.

Selene's blue dress was folded neatly and placed on the edge of the mattress.

Steam billowed out of the shower as he stepped inside. The frosted glass made it impossible to see her naked body, but he could make out her shadow.

"What the hell are you doing?" he asked louder than he'd intended.

"What does it look like, dumbass? I'm tired and since I don't know when I'm going to get another chance, I'm showering now. Do you have anything to eat here? I didn't get to try anything at the party and I'm starving."

He stood there, feeling like an idiot as she casually showered, as if he hadn't taken her captive. Or clearly, she'd just let him. "How'd you get out of the cuffs?" Because contrary to what television showed, it wasn't as easy as it looked. Currently they hung on the shower rail, mocking him.

Hell, she'd probably had a hairpin tucked in her hair. And that was the kind of thing he should have searched for. But the thought of getting too close to her, of running his hands over her body, made him ache in the best and worst way. She was walking, talking temptation. He didn't like it. It made him feel guilty, even if it shouldn't.

She peeked her head around the corner of the shower, her long blond hair dripping water. She held out her hands and bent one of her thumbs back completely to her wrist and grinned. "Double-jointed thumbs." Giving him what he could describe only as a cheeky grin, she disappeared behind the glass.

He started to respond when he spotted his bottle of vodka next to the sink, empty. It had been half-full before. "What the fuck? You dumped out my vodka?"

She peeked her head out again, her hair soapy from shampoo. Her pale eyes narrowed at him. "Yep. If we're working together, you're sober. I won't work any other way."

"It's not like I'm drinking on the job." He hadn't touched it before he'd left for Shah's party. But he drank at night. It was the only way he could get to sleep. Vodka took that edge off.

She raised one of her perfect eyebrows. "I don't care. You either deal with my rules or don't work with me. I don't *have* to take you with me tomorrow."

Which brought up another interesting point. "You think you owe me because of something . . . Meghan did for you?" It felt weird and a little therapeutic to say his dead wife's name. For so long he'd just thought about her but he hadn't been able to talk about her to anyone. Even if it was pathetic, he was starved to talk to someone who knew who he was. The real him.

Selene moved back behind the glass and he could see a blurred outline of her rinsing her hair out. "You did a lot for your country, Levi."

Okay, that wasn't an answer, but he wasn't going to push. Instead he went to the toilet seat, sat on the closed lid, and leaned back. "You could have left."

"Are you going to keep saying obvious things all night?" she asked, her voice light and teasing.

A rusty laugh escaped, the sound shocking him as it rattled in his chest. "Fine. Why didn't you leave?"

"I think you'll be a valuable asset and you've been

off the reservation for two years. Considering the people you've worked with—and yes, we know about some of them, but probably not all—your cover will be solid, which means you'll give me more credibility. My ID might be solid but I haven't done many meets. But if you give me a reason, I'll cut you out of this op and not lose any sleep over it."

Setting his weapon on the counter, he put his hands behind his head and leaned back. For the first time in years he felt like his old self. Not completely because he'd never be that man again, but he felt almost . . . normal. He grasped the illusion, knowing he'd have it for only a few minutes or maybe even hours. "How'd you get involved with Wesley? You look too young."

"How does anyone get recruited?" she asked vaguely.

He snorted. "Fair enough. How old were you when he recruited you?"

A long silence stretched between them and he eventually realized she wasn't going to answer. When the water shut off, he jerked upright and stood. Sitting here, he'd been trying to convince himself he didn't care that she was naked behind the frosted glass. The thought of what color her nipples might be or . . . damn it, what was wrong with him? It had been so long since he'd felt real attraction to a woman, not just noticed her in the physical sense. It wasn't as if he was blind because his wife had died, but his dick hadn't cared about any woman, period. Now it decided to wake up—with a woman he was going to be working with. Unless of course she decided to betray him to Wesley. That made him frown even more. "I'll give you privacy," he muttered, and strode from the room unsteadily. He shut the door behind him with more force than necessary, then cringed at himself.

As he stripped off his jacket he realized his laptop had been moved. It was only a half inch or so, but he was particular about the way he left his things. That kind of training had been ingrained into him long ago. Turning around, he whipped open the door and froze.

Selene was bent over drying her legs but she jerked up at his entrance. Taking him by surprise, she turned toward him, covering her breasts with one arm and snapped her towel at him lightning quick, hitting him right in the eye.

"Shit," he yelled, jumping back holding one hand up defensively while covering his stinging eye. "I wasn't—"

"I knew you were a pervert," she shouted, and before he was able to fully retreat something hard hit him in the middle of the chest. A bar of soap.

"Selene—"

She slammed the door in his face.

He could hear her moving around in the bathroom and while he tried not to think about the fact that her mound had been completely bare—and wondered if she shaved or waxed—he leaned against the wall by the door. His eye freaking hurt and wouldn't stop watering, but he ignored it. "Were you on my computer?" he asked through the door, already knowing the answer.

As the door flew open, he stepped back, ready for another attack, but she stood there with her hair wrapped in a towel above her head and another towel wrapped snuggly around her body, tucked perfectly between her breasts. "Of course. I was snooping, what else?"

He stared at her, forcing his gaze to remain on her face. "And you're just . . . admitting it?"

"Why would I lie? I'd be stupid not to take a peek at your computer. You shouldn't have left it out if you didn't want me to go through it. Your encryption is pretty good, but I'm better. And your playlist sucks, by the way."

"My playlist is awesome," he said without thinking. He shouldn't be arguing with her about his damn music, he should be yelling at her for going through his computer. Even if she was right. He shouldn't have left the damn thing out. There was nothing of particular value on it so he wasn't concerned about that. He used it mainly for communication but he always deleted his tracks no matter what.

Snorting, she sidestepped him and headed for the closet. Moments later she came back out wearing one of his T-shirts and jogging pants—and no bra. He swallowed hard, trying not to notice how full her breasts were or imagine how they'd feel cupped in his hands. *Fuck him.* He closed his eyes, trying to shove away the image of her lean, smooth body but it was impossible. He could easily envision those sexy tan lines and fantasize how her bare mound would feel against his mouth and tongue.

"'Awesome' is not the word that comes to mind. More like, wrist-slitting depressing. And you don't even have any good country music on there."

His eyes snapped open and he watched as she sauntered over to the mattress and collapsed on it as if she totally belonged there. The fact that he liked seeing her there made something shift inside his chest—and the guilt was back. She pulled the towel off her head and dropped it on the floor in a messy heap.

"You like country?" he asked before yanking up her towel. He wondered if she was messy in general, then cursed his curiosity. He should not care what kind of habits she had. She was just going to be an asset to him, nothing more. *Right*.

"Uh, yeah. Jason Aldean, Florida Georgia Line, come on—who doesn't love those guys?"

It was too weird to be having this conversation with her, but he shook his head and hung that towel and the one she'd left haphazardly in the closet back in the bathroom. As he finished stripping off his shirt, shoes, and socks he said, "That's not real country."

"Really? Because I'm pretty sure they're topping the Billboard country charts," she said, finger-combing her damp hair.

"You know what I mean," he muttered, sitting on the opposite side of the mattress. When he thought of country it was Hank or Autry. "You're sleeping here?" He'd originally planned to just cuff her to him but now she'd proved the cuffs were useless and she didn't seem to be going anywhere.

"Well, I'm not sleeping on the floor. Unless you're worried about me killing you in your sleep?" The light note in her voice took away what could have been a deadly question.

Rolling his eyes, he turned off the only lamp in the

room and lay down next to her. He noticed that she'd slid under the sheet he'd thrown on the mattress, giving them a little separation.

It was beyond surreal sleeping next to a woman who worked for his old boss—and who'd just mocked his taste in music as if they were friends—and it was made worse by the fact that he wanted her. Desperately.

He didn't trust many people and he didn't trust her, but he also didn't think she was going to stab him in the back either. At least not literally. She might still sell him out to Wesley. Only time would tell. Stretching out next to her, he shut his eyes and tried to find sleep but his mind was racing with too many thoughts. Tomorrow he could meet Tasev. The thought alone made a punch of adrenaline jolt through him. He still had to figure out if Tasev had been involved with Meghan's death, and if he was, he was dead.

"You asleep?" Levi asked after a few minutes even though he was certain she wasn't. Selene's breathing was steady enough, but there was a certain stillness to people when they slept and she kept shifting around, fidgety.

She softly sighed. "No."

"So . . . country music?" It couldn't hurt to talk. If anything it might make him more tired. He wasn't opening dialogue because he wanted to get to know Selene.

Keep telling yourself that.

"Yeah. But that's not all I like. I'm a little eclectic when it comes to music."

"You from the South?" It was hard to tell. She didn't have a discernible accent, which had likely been trained out of her. He was from Georgia but didn't have an accent either.

"What do you think?" she asked quietly.

"Forget it," he muttered. She wouldn't give him any personal details.

After a long moment she spoke again, surprising him. "I'm from Alabama."

He frowned in the darkness. There was no way he'd know if she was lying. But he was surprised they both had Southern roots. "Why are you telling me?"

"I've read your file, it only seems fair you know a little about me too."

When she didn't continue, he didn't either. He was beyond mentally exhausted and even with the knowledge that he was closing in on Meghan's killer racing through his mind, he knew he needed sleep if he was going to stay on his game.

For the first time in a long time he decided to trust that the woman next to him, who smelled like peaches and cream and made him think of nothing but sex, wasn't going to kill him in his sleep.

Chapter 7

Black Death 9 Agent: member of an elite group of men and women employed by the NSA for covert, off-the-books operations. A member's purpose is to gain the trust of targeted individuals in order to gather information or evidence by any means necessary.

Wesley shut the door to his office and pressed the button to frost the glass window again. He'd been going over reports and scanning all of his analysts' findings on mentions of Tasev over the past five years, but he was running on no sleep and had to catch an hour or two if he wanted to be functional and an asset to his team.

He slid his shoes off and dimmed the lights. He wouldn't bother heading to his hotel now. It was already three in the morning so he'd just grab a few hours of sleep on his couch. It was why he had the thing in his office. As he loosened his tie, there was a sharp knock at the door.

"Come in," he called out, trying not to let his annoyance show. This was part of the job.

Nathan Ortiz stepped inside, his dark hair military

short even though he hadn't been in the Marines for years. "Hey, boss. I know you're snagging some sleep but I wanted to let you know that Selene's tracker is back at Alexander Lopez's house, but she's not with him. He arrived back at his place with a dark-haired woman instead."

Wesley scrubbed a hand over his face. Selene had gone to Shah's party tonight to gain a meet with the German so she'd have an intro to Tasev. They hadn't tailed her because she needed to appear as if she was working alone, but they'd kept eyes on Lopez's house. About an hour ago Wesley had received a brief e-mail from her telling him that she was fine but that plans had changed. She'd told him that she wasn't with Lopez anymore and not to worry, she'd check in when she could. Under certain circumstances he would have sent a team in with her, but they hadn't been able to risk it at Shah's party. "Shit, sorry. I should have told you. She's gone dark for now." This was exactly why he needed to rest. He wasn't a robot and if he made mistakes because of lack of sleep, the consequences could be huge.

Ortiz nodded and stepped back toward the door. "Get some sleep. No one will bother you unless there's an emergency."

"Thanks." He stripped down to his slacks before stretching out on the couch. Outside the office there was a quiet hum of everyone working.

As he lay there he started mentally cataloging his day as he always did. Normally it put him to sleep but now he couldn't focus. He knew why. Thoughts of Selene worried him as they always did. It didn't matter how trained or talented she was.

She was more than just an agent to him. He'd more or less recruited her when she was a kid, though it hadn't been an official recruitment until she'd finished college—which he'd insisted on and the government had paid for. Not that it had taken her long; she'd graduated with honors at the age of eighteen. When it came to computers the woman was a genius. She'd hacked the CIA when she was fifteen.

That was when she'd first gotten on the government's radar, but he'd snapped her up before any other branch could. He'd watched her grow into the woman she was. Some days it was hard to remember that she was only twenty-three, but then he reminded himself that he'd seen combat earlier than that. Some people just didn't get a chance to grow up normally. What the hell was normal anyway?

Lying there in the semi-darkness, with his eyes closed, he couldn't help but remember the first real mission Selene had gone on by herself. It played out in his head as if he was right there.

As the driver slowed, not fully stopping in the alley behind the five-star hotel, Wesley shoved the SUV door open. As he did, a door that led to one of the kitchens flew open. Selene, wearing a dark wig and a server's uniform for one of the restaurants inside, strode out, her pace steady but not hurried.

She glanced around the alley before hurrying to the creeping SUV. Once inside she shut the door and took off her square-framed glasses and pulled the cotton rolls out of her cheeks. The windows were too darkly tinted for anyone to see inside, including any CCTVs to catch a glimpse of her. Not to mention this vehicle had untraceable plates. And his group of analysts with the NSA had made sure there would be a complete blackout with the security at the hotel for an hour.

"Are you okay?" he asked when she still hadn't spoken after a solid minute. This was her first official field mission by herself. Under normal circumstances he wouldn't be here but Selene was different, special to him. And if he was being honest, he knew that she had what it took to eventually become a Black Death 9 agent. It wasn't her age holding her back, though she was young at only twenty, but she was still too untried despite all her training.

Selene nodded, her jaw clenched tight as she looked out the window of the SUV, away from him. That was when it hit him. She was upset. It looked as if tears glistened in her eyes. Oh, fuck.

After everything that had happened to her parents and then the shit that had gone down afterward, before he'd taken her under his wing, he'd gotten her counseling. She'd balked at it, but he'd been insistent. It had been part of his hiring requirements. Only a small percentage of the population had the mental fortitude to do what his Black Ops people did long-term. She was one of them. He wasn't certain if he believed in the nature or nurture theories for how people turned out, but Selene had an amazing ability to compartmentalize things and years of therapy had proved what he'd always known about her—she was made of titanium. But hell, maybe he'd screwed up. Maybe all her psychological tests were wrong. Shit, shit, shit.

He reached out a hand and placed it reassuringly on her shoulder. "Honey, the first kill is always hard."

Her head whipped around, her contact-colored brown eyes widening in surprise. "What . . ." She shook her head, a frown pulling her eyebrows together. "I'm not upset because that guy is dead. I'm pissed at myself because I almost screwed up." She punched the cushioned leather seat next to her thigh. "Son of a bitch! I was so focused on making sure his drink was the one poisoned that I almost knocked over a tray of drinks one of the servers was carrying." She cursed again, her self-loathing clear.

Wesley and his team had eyes on the inside, though nothing was being recorded—no evidence of this op would ever surface—so he'd seen her the whole time. "I saw you. You were perfect."

Jaw clenched tight, she shook her head. "I got too into my head, was too focused on the target. I could've made a mistake that got me noticed."

Relief hit him square in the chest. Selene was always hard on herself, no matter the situation. So this wasn't out of the ordinary and he hadn't been wrong about her capabilities. He let out a low laugh.

She punched him the shoulder, though not very hard. "This is funny?"

"No, I just . . . thought you felt guilty."

Snorting, she tugged the wig off and let out a sigh. "That POS doesn't deserve my guilt. He doesn't deserve anything but what he got. Actually, he deserves way worse but . . ." She shrugged, not continuing and seemingly less angry at herself.

People handled their first missions differently. He'd seen all the reactions, including this one, before. He was just thankful he and the various psychologists had been right about Selene. He had a feeling she'd do extremely well in this world and he was almost never wrong.

Sighing, he rolled on his side and attempted to get comfortable. He needed to stay sharp and this wasn't helping. Focusing on the office sounds he let the steadiness lull him to sleep.

Tasev looked down at the architectural plans for the first water plant his team planned to hit. Every second that passed he grew more exhilarated at the thought of so many people dying, of making it clear to the United States government that they would suffer for taking away his sons. Even ordinary citizens would feel his wrath, his pain.

He glanced up as the door to his private office opened. Grisha took a step inside, as quiet as a ghost. The man kept his brown hair cut so close to his head that his scalp was visible and his dark blue eyes were shrewd. He'd been with Tasev only a very short time, mere months, but had proved himself valuable. So far he didn't seem to have any vices. He didn't even indulge in the prostitutes Tasev hired for his men. It was odd that he turned down free pussy but some men didn't like to pay for it or accept paid women. Tasev could actually respect that. Grisha nodded once at Tasev. "The men are here as you requested."

It was three in the morning and he'd been holding off telling anyone about this until the last minute. All his men knew that Schmidt was his prisoner but that he was not to be harmed under any circumstances. However, they didn't know the full details of Tasev's plans. Only Vasily had known everything.

Grisha knew a little, but only about his plans to poison various water supplies. He'd been helpful in getting some of the blueprints, solidifying his role in Tasev's organization. Soon Tasev would tell Grisha about his goal to blackmail the US into paying for the antitoxin to Schmidt's toxin—when the doctor finally figured it out— but for now no one needed to know about Tasev's ultimate goal of revenge and becoming even richer.

"Send them in. You remain too," Tasev said.

With a flick of Grisha's hand, two men appeared behind him. Abram and Kolya. They would each lead a four-man team. Both had experience in the ground forces of the Russian military and were well trained.

Tasev stepped back from the table and motioned for both of them to approach. Abram rubbed a hand over his face, but he could tell neither of them had drunk last night, per his orders. Good. "You know the drills we've been running?" He'd been conducting simulated drills at various warehouses he owned around Miami with the sole purpose of getting them ready for this mission.

They both nodded, with Grisha remaining silent about a foot away from them.

"All your practice will now be put to good use. In less than thirty minutes you will each be heading to different destinations, each running your own four-man team. I've already selected the others but you two will be point. Just as in the simulations, everyone is expendable." It was much easier to just kill on missions. He nodded at the plans on the table. For missions he never used phones or computers to convey his orders. Everything was a hard copy. "These are the designs for two different water plants you will be infiltrating. The layouts should look familiar."

Both men scanned the blueprints and nodded, not asking questions until he was done. They knew better.

"I've compiled a file for each of you containing smaller

versions and with all the relevant information you'll need. Abram, you will arrive at your destination around eleven. Kolya, at noon. You will infiltrate, then meet up with your contacts. All their information is in the files. You will transport the containers that are already waiting in your vehicles. They'll know what to do with the contents. Once they've completed their part of the mission, you kill them." He'd paid off one employee and threatened the family of another to help with the breach of the water supply. That was the tricky part, which is why he'd chosen smaller towns to start. This was his testing ground. "When you leave, destroy the semitrucks and find alternate transportation."

He would soon reveal what he'd done to Schmidt, hoping to make him work faster. He knew enough about the doctor that his guilt would eat at him for being responsible for the deaths of so many people. He'd be driven to provide an antitoxin even faster.

"Any questions?" he asked.

They both shook their heads and left like the good soldiers they were. He paid them well, gave them women, and they got to kill as part of their job description. It was the perfect setup and why his men stayed even when many were fearful of him.

But Grisha wasn't fearful. Tasev had realized that from the first moment he'd come to work for him. He also met Tasev's gaze, though never in challenge, so Tasev allowed it. "I have something else for you to do. I need you to meet with the German. He's set up an appointment for me but you will meet with him now."

Grisha's eyebrows rose slightly. "It's three in the morning."

Tasev frowned. It wasn't exactly a question but he couldn't tell if Grisha was questioning his authority. "He will still be awake."

Grisha nodded and Tasev relaxed.

"He met with The Wolf in person. I want his personal take on the hitter." The assassin, who was surprisingly a female. "Gauge his speech, everything." That was something else about Grisha, he was very good at evaluating people and Tasev planned to utilize that to the fullest extent.

The German had never set him up with anyone who turned out not to be who they said they were, but Tasev always did his homework before any meeting.

"I'll report back as soon as I have anything," Grisha said before leaving.

Once the door shut behind him Tasev smiled, pleased with the way things were turning out. He went to the minibar near the window and poured himself a shot of vodka. He rarely indulged in alcohol but today called for it.

By this evening, his plan would be in motion and panic would be spreading across the southeast. A mere hint of the devastation he would unleash in the weeks ahead.

Chapter 8

Mole: an agent that has embedded himself into an organization.

Selene was surrounded by the most amazing sense of warmth and security. Sinking into the blissful sensation, she cuddled against her pillow, but it was hard. That was wrong though. Forcing herself to wake up she realized a few things all at once. One, she was cuddled up against Levi like he was her freaking pillow. Two, his bare chest felt amazing beneath her fingertips and for some reason she was stroking his skin like she had every right in the world. Finally, he was definitely awake and there was no mistaking the erection she felt against the leg she'd thrown over him in her apparent attempt to hump him in her sleep. Worse, she was actually turned on. She was damp between her thighs. Had she been making noises in her sleep?

How mortifying. She immediately stilled her fingers and his breathing kicked up the slightest notch. Taking a chance, she shifted her head and looked up at him to find him watching her intently.

Faint morning light was streaming through one of

the windows and even in the dimness of the room she could see his expression clearly. And he wanted her.

Badly.

His dark eyes gleamed with such a potent lust that the apology she'd had all ready for molesting him in her sleep died on her lips.

When his gaze landed on her mouth she knew what he was about to do before he did it. His mouth crushed over hers and moving lightning fast, he'd rolled over, pinning her to the mattress underneath him. He was so hot and hard that the sharpest punch of hunger slammed through her at the feel of him covering her with that deliciously muscular body.

Selene knew she should stop this. It was beyond stupid to be intimate with someone on a mission, but this wasn't just anyone. This was Levi Lazaro, a man likely still in love with his dead wife and walking a deadly edge between right and wrong. Not to mention he'd gone completely off the reservation and she couldn't trust his motivations.

And to top it off, her past experiences with men weren't the greatest. Her ex-boyfriend, if she could even call him that, had tried to sabotage her job because of his own insecurities. Clearly she couldn't trust her judgment when it came to men. But . . . damn, Levi felt amazing.

She quickly shut down that annoying voice in her head when his tongue dipped inside her mouth, teasing against hers in the most delicious way. It was frenzied yet somehow sweet. She wrapped her arms around him, tracing her fingers down the hard, muscular lines of his back.

It was like the man was carved from stone. He'd left his pants on but it didn't matter. She could feel his hard length pressing against the juncture between her thighs, their clothes blocking nothing.

Unable to stop herself, she continued downward, stopping only to grab onto his firm ass. She wanted to feel him without any barriers but wasn't brave enough to do that just yet. Maybe she'd never be.

Her touch changed something in him because he groaned into her mouth, his kisses becoming hotter. When he slid a hand under her shirt, his fingers skimming her bare stomach, she jerked against him as if he'd singed her. His callused fingers created a scorching path straight to one of her breasts.

She should be shocked by his bold move, but she wanted this, wanted him in a way that scared her. She knew it wasn't just physical. The man was so broken it killed her when she knew how different he'd been before. This wasn't about owing him or any bullshit like that; she wanted to see him smile, to regain some of the man he'd been.

Not that she thought sleeping with her would do any of that for him, but they both deserved some relief and for some reason she trusted him with her body. He was safe in a way others weren't because he knew what she did for a living and when all this was over, they'd be going their separate ways. That made him safe to . . . use in a sense. She felt bad even thinking that but it was true. Because this type of attraction was rare, that much she knew. When he lightly rubbed a thumb over her nipple he moaned as if the sound had been torn from him.

Selene rolled her hips against him, feeling almost mindless with need, excited about what might happen between them, when he suddenly stopped. Pulling back, he stared down at her, his chest rising and falling erratically in tune with her own breathing.

She wasn't sure what to say so she started to withdraw her hands from him when he suddenly blurted, "I'm sorry."

She blinked, unsure why he was sorry. "I was . . . willing." Which he had to know.

His jaw tightened for a long moment, his eyes never leaving her face. "I know. I feel . . . guilty."

Hurt and anger erupted inside her, but she didn't outwardly respond, not wanting him to know his words affected her. "About me?" she asked carefully, inwardly cursing when her voice shook.

"Yes. No. Not about you. About how I feel about you. When I saw you at Shah's party my reaction was . . . intense." He looked away when he said the last part, as if in shame. His profile was hard and unforgiving.

Understanding set in and she wasn't sure what to feel. She knew she didn't like the sick sensation in the pit of her stomach, but she liked that she affected him as much as he did her. "So you feel like maybe you're being unfaithful in a way?" Even though all they'd done was kiss. She wasn't even sure why she'd asked. She should just let this drop, but couldn't seem to help herself.

Swallowing hard, he looked back at her and nodded. "Sort of. I keep thinking, what if I'd met you when I'd been married. Would I have reacted the same? I don't know. I just can't turn my head off."

"You wouldn't have reacted to me if you'd been married." Of that she had no doubt. It wasn't the way Levi was hardwired.

His expression darkened. "How can you know that?" he asked, his voice savage.

"Because you're not a douche. That's how I know. When you were married you were faithful, committed, and in *love* with your wife. You wouldn't have been *looking*. And you can't play the 'what-if' game because it'll only drive you insane. Trust me. Things happen and our futures change and there are no what-ifs anymore. The path we're on is the one we're supposed to be on. And I'm not saying stuff happens for a reason. I hate that saying because it's total bullshit. I'm just making the point that you're not doing anything wrong by wanting me. But if you feel guilt or shame, then this stops right now." Because she wasn't going to take any man's scraps. Selene pushed at his chest, wanting to get up from the bed, but he kept her pinned beneath him, an immovable force.

"I don't . . . *fuck*," he growled, the self-loathing in his voice pretty damn clear. His breathing had grown even more erratic, his chest rising and falling against hers. For a long moment he just watched her with those dark, penetrating eyes.

Right about now she wished she understood the opposite sex more. She understood men, or at least that their dicks seemed to motivate them more often than not, but Levi was too damn complicated. Everything she'd read about him, not to mention his ability to stay off the NSA's radar for two years, told her that he was a man not used to showing any emotions, to doing whatever it took to get the job done. She'd already agreed to take him to the meeting with Tasev so she didn't think this kissing episode and little confession was about him manipulating her. She didn't have much experience with men so she couldn't be totally sure. God, what the hell was she thinking though? She *couldn't* trust him. She shoved at him again, this time harder.

Thankfully he moved off her, his expression dark and full of too many emotions for her to sift through.

"We've got to prepare for tonight and stop by my place. I've also got to call Wesley," she muttered.

She mentally shook herself for this stupid lapse in sanity—and self-control. No matter what, Levi was a man on a mission and she wasn't stupid enough to think that because he desired her that it would mean anything if she got in the way of that mission. She needed to remember that. She knew exactly how men could be when it came to their own self-interests.

Sitting on the edge of the bed, turned away from her, he finally spoke, his voice guttural. "This isn't over between us." Without waiting for a response, he shoved up and stood.

She should have said something witty to make it clear that this was never happening again. Unfortunately her body flared to life at those heated words. She wanted to know what it was like to be completely possessed by this man. Instead of scaring her, the thought sent the most erotic thrill racing through her.

If she was stupid enough to sleep with him, she knew that things between them would end badly, but she wanted Levi in a way that defied logic, and probably her sanity, and she wanted everything he had to offer. Even if she got burned in the end.

Wesley cracked open his eyes at the hard knock on his door. He glanced at his watch. Barely a couple of hours had passed. "Come in," he barked out, already sitting up. If someone was interrupting him, he knew it was an emergency and he wasn't going back to sleep.

Ortiz walked in, his expression tense and even though Wesley knew he hadn't gotten any sleep the man still looked sharp. Fucking youth. "Sorry—"

Wesley shook his head, picking up his button-down shirt as he stood. "It's fine."

"Max Southers is on the phone. Line one. Said it's an emergency."

A jolt of energy shot through Wesley. He'd turned the volume on his cell down so that's likely why the man had called his office. He nodded at Ortiz as he fished his phone out and swiped his finger across the screen. Sure enough he had a few missed calls from Max. "Thanks. I know it's not your job but—"

"I've already got a fresh pot of coffee brewing and I'm having bagels and other breakfast stuff picked up for the entire staff." Ortiz was a relatively new Black Death 9 agent but Wesley liked working with him and had kept him in Miami for this job after the last op they'd run because he'd wanted Ortiz to see how ops ran from the tech side. The man was one of the toughest Wesley had worked with, a fast learner and surprisingly good in an office situation as well as the field.

"Thanks, Marine." Even though Ortiz hadn't been in

the Marines for years Wesley still called him that sometimes.

The man grinned and stepped back for the door. Before he left, Wesley pinned him with a stare. "Call Bell,
Freeman, and Dax and wake them up. Are you good for
an op?" he asked even though he knew Ortiz would be.
A few weeks ago he'd been hit with a direct round and
thanks to a vest had been protected. Still bruised and
battered, he'd been ready to go hours later on another
mission.

"Yeah." Not even a pause.

"Good." Wesley dismissed him by picking up the
office phone. Everything here ran through so many layers of encryption he never worried about privacy. "Hey,
Max. What's the problem?" he asked as Ortiz shut the
door behind him. Considering the early hour he knew
that the Deputy Director of the Drug Enforcement Administration wouldn't be calling him unless it was an
emergency.

"You still in Miami?" Southers asked, his voice humming with unusual intensity.

Wesley sat up straighter in his chair. "Yeah."

"I've got a tip for you. Anonymous. No one can know
this came from me, but there's a player in Miami who
just sent out two teams of armed men to infiltrate two
cities' water supplies with an unknown toxin. One
right outside Tallahassee. The other outside of Albany,
Georgia. And they've got a two-hour head start on you
but if you send teams now you can cut them off." He
quickly rattled off the names of the two water companies.

Wesley's blood ran cold at Southers's words, already

retrieving his cell again so he could call in his people. "Who's the operator?"

"I can't—"

"Tasev?" Wesley took a shot in the dark. This was no coincidence, especially with what Schmidt's message had relayed.

"Shit. How'd you know?"

"I'm working an op right now involving him." And now the question of whether the man was indeed alive had been answered. Not that Wesley had doubted it. "You have an inside man?" Because there was no way Max could have gotten the tip otherwise. When he was met with silence Wesley gritted his teeth. How the hell had Southers even gotten someone inside Tasev's organization? "Fine, I get it. Why are you contacting me instead of another branch?"

"It was either you or HRT and I don't have a contact there who'll listen without more info. You're one of the only men I know who won't have to wade through red tape to get this op off the ground. Good luck. And if you leak that this came from me, we're no longer friends." Max ended the call before Wesley could respond.

Which was out of character for him. So was the threat at the end. Because that's exactly what that had been. If they weren't friends, they were enemies. Wesley would never betray his friend's confidence. After calling Ortiz and ordering him to get another team together, he headed out to the comm center for this op.

The team of analysts had switched shifts for the night with the night crew smaller than the day one. Right now one of his favorite people was working,

Karen Stafford. He swore the woman never slept. Knowing he'd have roughly twenty minutes before the two teams gathered here, he grabbed a chair and sat next to Karen at her computer station.

The redhead continued typing and raised her eyebrows without looking at him. "What's up, boss?"

He could be wrong, but going with his gut, he thought about what he would do if he was in an undercover situation. He wouldn't make a phone call from any cell phone, no matter how encrypted. No, he'd go old-school and use a pay phone. Making contact with a handler or anyone on the outside during the middle of an op was one of the riskiest things an agent could do, which told him this tip had to be real.

Wesley wanted to know if he could find out who Southers's inside guy was. He wouldn't betray his friend, but information was power. And if they could track the inside guy back to Tasev's place they could bring the terrorist down without Selene ever needing to meet him. If he could keep her out of harm's way, he'd do it. "I need you to look into something for me. Off the books and erase your tracks when you're done." They erased so damn much of what they did that this wasn't an odd request.

She nodded and instantly cleared her screen before looking at him. "What do you need?"

"Check all the CCTVs in the area starting with two and a half hours ago and locate anyone using a pay phone in a one-hour period after that. Eliminate any locals." Which would be easy enough using facial recognition software. He'd go back and look at locals later if they didn't pull anything from the search, but if

Southers had an inside guy working with Tasev it was unlikely the man was a local.

Without asking questions Karen got to work, her fingers flying across her keyboard. He sat patiently waiting, knowing it would take her less than five minutes to get what he needed. Sure enough, minutes later she pulled up a list of names and faces along with their DMV records. "I'm surprised by how many people use pay phones," she muttered more to herself, still typing away. "All right, it's early so there weren't as many people out around that time. Of the twenty people, seventeen are locals, two are known prostitutes, and this guy . . ." She frowned, pulling up another screen.

Her frown deepened as she zoomed in on a man wearing a hoodie. "I can't get a scan of his face. Even when he leaves the phone, watch this . . ." She trailed off, pulling up screen after screen, showing him in different parts of the city and his face was always hidden from any CCTVs. Eventually he disappeared into a public parking garage with no cameras inside. At least none they had access to.

Oh yeah, this was their guy. Someone didn't conveniently manage to avoid every single camera. It was statistically impossible. That was some damn fine work to be able to do that. He'd have had to memorize the whole damn layout of the city in advance to pull that off. "Who'd he call from the pay phone?"

She pulled up another screen and worked her magic as she located that individual pay phone, then accessed the list of outgoing calls. Karen highlighted a number, then ran it through multiple programs. Eventually she stopped typing and shot him a surprised glance. "It's gotta be a burner phone. I can't even figure out where it was bought from."

Wesley nodded, taking what he needed from this. "Track all vehicles leaving that parking garage and make a list of their final destinations if you can. If not, track them as far as you can and note the area." He had no clue if it would yield anything but he had to try to locate Tasev any way he could.

"Good work," he said to Karen, standing as he started to make another call.

He needed the choppers ready to leave in five minutes and to check in with Ortiz to make sure his guys were ready to go. Because Wesley was going on this op. He wouldn't be part of the infiltration but he was going to be there to bring in whoever was trying to poison and kill American people.

Chapter 9

Tactical team: a small law enforcement unit that uses military-grade weapons and engages in high-risk operations including hostage rescue and counter-terrorism maneuvers.

Nathan Ortiz stayed hidden in the shadows of the second floor of the water plant. He was inside on a metal balcony walkway, using it as a perch to watch anyone coming through the warehouse-type roll-up door. If anyone was going to poison the water supply, this was where they'd ultimately have to do it.

"I've got a visual. Unmarked white van heading your way. Two subjects visible. Could be more in the back. Not sure if they're civilians," Dax said quietly over his earpiece.

Ortiz tensed, readying for an assault. Dax was outside as the lookout and the rest of the team was waiting inside to take down the threat if one materialized. According to their contact at the water plant, no one should be coming back here this time of day and with the van being unmarked . . . Ortiz prepared for the worst.

He'd ended up calling in a bigger team for this op since they hadn't known how large of a force they'd be up against. Seven of his guys plus himself against whoever was in that van—those were odds he liked.

M-4 in hand, he watched through his scope as a man wearing an employee uniform hurried out of the lone office on the first floor. He made his way to the roll-up door and pressed a large red button. He looked around nervously, as if he knew he was being watched, though he could have no clue how many eyes were on him now. Ortiz could see the gleam of sweat across his brow before he wiped it with a shaking hand. Immediately the door started to open. The moment the van was through, the man closed it again.

Ortiz tapped his earpiece. "I've got a visual. Everyone confirm."

As the other six team members inside confirmed, he watched as two men slid from the front of the vehicle: the driver and the passenger. Ortiz scanned them quickly and noted one had a bulge under the back of his shirt and the other in the front of his shirt. Keeping a weapon tucked in the front of your pants was stupid, but some people did it anyway.

Immediately the back door opened and another man stepped out. The butt of his weapon stuck out from the back of his shirt.

The man in the uniform seemed nervous and shaky as he started talking to the driver. Though Ortiz was only about a hundred or so yards above them he couldn't hear what was being said. They were speaking too low. When the employee shook his head, starting to protest something, the driver pulled out a pistol and held it to the man's head.

"Move in. Now," Ortiz ordered, remaining in position as a sniper. Normally he was on the ground for any operation but they mixed it up for ops so no one got comfortable. That way if something happened to one of them, anyone could take on any role. It was standard for their units to be cross-trained.

As if they'd choreographed it, Bell, Freeman, and two others moved in on the suspects, surrounding them as they shouted for everyone to hit the ground and keep their hands up. There were still two other teammates in different perches just like Ortiz.

They were keeping these guys locked down tight in case anyone tried to flee. When the side door of the van slid open and a man jumped out with an automatic rifle in his hands, Ortiz shook his head.

"We've got a runner," he said into his earpiece before firing at the man's thigh. Shouting in agony, the man dropped to his knees, letting go of his weapon with one hand.

As the rifle dangled from his right hand and he tried to stanch his wound with his left, Ortiz shot again, hitting the hand holding the rifle. The weapon immediately fell and before it had hit the ground Bell had moved around the van, his M-4 aimed at the fallen man as he ordered him to stay down.

"All tangos are secure. Nice fucking shot," Bell said as he kicked the man's weapon away and began binding his wrists behind his back.

Ortiz tapped his earpiece, clicking over to another

secure channel. "It's clear to move in," he said to Burkhart, even though his boss had a visual.

They'd managed to get here almost an hour and a half ahead of time. Only two trusted employees had known about the NSA's infiltration of the plant in case Tasev had an inside man at the water plant. From the looks of it, he'd had at least one. Soon enough the NSA would know why he'd helped terrorists attempt to poison his own city's water supply

Ortiz didn't care about the whys though. That wasn't his deal. He just wanted Tasev stopped. They all did.

Levi was on edge in a way he hadn't been in a long time. Selene's presence was the main reason, but being in her temporary condo as she changed clothes and packed up her things had him tensing at every little sound.

For all he knew she'd called in backup and an assault team was currently gearing up to rappel in from the roof and infiltrate through the windows like something out of a bad movie. That was unlikely considering she could have called a team on him anytime over the last few hours, but the knowledge didn't stop his imagination from working overtime. She'd told him this place was secure and wasn't bugged, but he wasn't certain he believed her that there weren't listening devices in place.

After that kiss earlier he was all sorts of fucked up and off his game. She'd seemed so surprised by the kiss but also so willing to take it to the next level. And there had been nothing calculating in that pretty face of hers.

She'd been turned on, breathless, and ready for more. She could have been acting. Some agents had no problem using their bodies to get the job done, but he didn't think that was the case with Selene.

He'd had this strange compulsion to confess his damn guilt to her. What had he been thinking? That was just it; he *hadn't* been thinking. He lost the ability to around Selene. She'd gotten under his skin without trying. At least he'd managed some sort of fucking control.

"What are you thinking?" Selene's soft voice cut through his thoughts.

Blinking, he realized he'd been staring at the bed as she packed. Staring and trying not to imagine what Selene would look like splayed out for him. That little peek of her naked body in the bathroom hadn't been nearly enough. He wanted to savor every inch of her until they were both breathless and sated.

Lust. Simple lust, he reminded himself. That was all this was.

She stood near a simple four-drawer dresser in the small room of the condo. She hadn't said but he knew the NSA had gotten this as part of her cover. It was sparse and set up like an impersonal hotel. He'd stayed in places like this more than once.

"Just wondering if you called in a team to pick me up," he said dryly.

She snorted and turned back to the top drawer. "You seem to think very highly of yourself, Mr. Lazaro."

The way she said his name made him grin, even though nothing in the world should be able to make him do that now. "Don't deny Wesley wants me."

"He does, but not for the reasons you think. He's worried about you." The note of truth in her voice as she pulled out a pair of panties shook him. He ignored the black scrap of material and pretended he wasn't affected by thoughts of what she'd look like wearing it. Or nothing at all.

Levi didn't want to hear that Wesley cared about him. His wife had been murdered and Wesley had done nothing. Okay, that wasn't true, but he hadn't done enough. Until everyone involved with Meghan's murder was dead, Levi would never rest.

Before he could respond, she continued, "Besides, we've got a lot more important things to worry about than you." She pinned him with that pale stare, her expression fierce. "Do you know how many innocent people will die if we don't stop Tasev?"

He shook his head because he didn't know shit about Tasev other than he might have been involved in Meghan's death. "You know I don't."

She watched him for a long moment, as if trying to read his mind. "Would you give up revenge if you could save hundreds of thousands of lives?"

"Yes." The word was out before he could think to censor himself. The truth of his statement shocked the hell out of him. Would he give up revenge for innocent people? He'd thought his answer would be no, but saying that to Selene felt too wrong.

"You seem surprised by that answer."

He frowned. What the hell was happening to him? He shouldn't care about anyone or anything other than giving Meghan justice, but at the end of the day if he let people die, Meghan would have hated the man he'd become. She'd been so damn patriotic. Just like the woman in front of him watching him with curiosity at the moment. "I am," he muttered.

"Glad you haven't lost yourself completely." She paused again, watching him with those pale eyes he swore could see straight to his soul. He was under the impression she didn't quite believe him either—and that annoyed him. "We got a message from a man named Dr. Claus Schmidt that he's being held captive by Tasev."

Levi nearly jerked at the name. *Dr. Claus Schmidt.* This was the connection, the verification he'd been looking for. Meghan and Schmidt had been friends and she'd been going to meet Schmidt the day she'd disappeared. And the man was being held captive by Tasev? Forcing himself to remain still and seemingly unaffected, Levi stood there and listened as Selene continued.

"Tasev is forcing him to create a toxin—well, he's created the toxin already, just not the antitoxin. He plans to attack American water supplies. There would be no way to contain it once it's out there. Unfortunately we don't know where or when he's planning his first strike. Even though Schmidt didn't say it, the only reason Tasev would want the antitoxin would be for blackmail purposes so he not only wants to kill thousands of people, he wants our government to pay for the cure."

A toxin like that could cripple the country in more ways than one. The ripple effect could be catastrophic. And this could be the monster who'd had Meghan murdered. Levi held on to his rage, but he couldn't ignore something like this in the face of his own needs. How many people, mothers, fathers, children could die? Looked like he wasn't a complete monster yet because he just couldn't turn his back anymore. If he did, he'd be no better than Tasev. *Damn it.* He scrubbed a hand over his face. "So why are they sending you in, apart from what you've already told me?"

Holding on to a change of clothes, she sat on the bed. "Basically I just need to see where his base of operations is. I don't know that I'll even get to go there the first meet, but if I can see him face-to-face, I can plant a tracker on him. Or at least get a better handle on what we're dealing with. Maybe even narrow down his whereabouts if I can't plant a tracker."

"That's a big risk." And Tasev would no doubt be wary of that. Levi didn't like the idea of her putting herself out there like that. Which was fucking stupid. He shouldn't care one way or another. And he didn't. *Yeah, keep telling yourself that.*

She shrugged. "It's worth it. Once we know where he's operating I can likely hack his system and we can get a team in to save Schmidt and eliminate Tasev."

It all sounded straightforward—on paper. But they both knew things rarely went that smoothly. "Who's your backup?"

"Tasev is very particular. I'll only be able to bring one guard with me."

"You're taking me."

She didn't even blink at the bald declaration. "Tell me the details of your ID."

He paused and he knew she realized he was weighing the pros and cons of telling her. There weren't many pros, but if he told her, she would bring him in. Otherwise, he wasn't going to the meeting. "Isaiah Moore. Legitimate businessman with shady partners. I've supposedly helped launder money and used various companies I own as front businesses. I keep myself diversified and there's no one I won't work with if the price is right. One of my businesses is a pharmaceutical company. I'd planned to approach him to partner with me using a different angle, but after what you told me about Schmidt and this toxin, we can use it to our benefit." Before, all Levi had really needed was to get close enough to the guy to discover if he'd been the man to order Meghan's rape and murder. Because Levi hadn't cared if he died then. Now . . . he still wasn't sure he cared about his own life but he sure as hell couldn't let hundreds of thousands of others die because of his own need for vengeance.

Her eyes narrowed. "How?"

Levi shook his head. "No way. You bring me and we play things a little differently. Once we're in we'll make it clear that the meet was supposed to be with me from the start. Tasev will be pissed at first, but he won't be surprised that someone like me used a decoy to meet him."

"So I supposedly procured the meeting and I'm what, your backup?"

He nodded. "And my lover." It would be easy enough to play the part and the plan that had started to form in his head was perfection—if Tasev went for it. The lover part wasn't necessary but it would make their story more believable and Levi wanted an excuse to keep his hands on Selene. "You'll need to start calling me Isaiah."

"That won't be a problem, but I'm going to need all the details before I agree to this. Otherwise I won't know how to act or could say the wrong thing."

Though he didn't want to reveal all his cards in case she decided to run with his idea and use it as her own—and cut him out in the process—he knew he'd have to trust her with at least that much.

Trust.

Still a foreign concept but one he would have to risk because the payoff could be everything he'd been working toward for two years. "With my plan we'll both get what we want." He crossed the short distance between them and sat next to her, invading all her personal space as he inhaled that sweet peaches and cream scent that drove him mad with desire. Reaching out, he cupped the back of her neck as he'd done last night. Her eyes narrowed as she realized what he was doing. Clearly she didn't understand he just wanted to touch her. He could read her expressions well enough now that he'd know if she was lying.

Using his forefinger, he felt her pulse on one side of her neck, but gently stroked the other side with his thumb. He had no reason to other than he wanted to touch her. He kept his gaze on hers, watching the way her pupils dilated. "Swear you won't fuck me over," he said softly, needing her to be real with him.

"I won't." The truth. It was in her beautiful eyes and the steady beat of her pulse. Yeah, it wasn't scientific but he'd been dealing with truth and lies for so damn long he knew when someone was fucking with him.

"Tell me something real about yourself." The words

were out before he could stop himself. It annoyed him, but he wanted to know more about her.

She blinked, clearly surprised by the change in topic. "Why?"

"Why the fuck not?" The question came out harsher than he'd intended.

Her jaw tightened the tiniest fraction, probably because of his tone. "You first. Something not in your file."

He paused, thinking. It was clear she had trust issues, which was just as well because he did too. "I never planned to work for the NSA or any other government agency after I got out of the Marines."

Surprise flickered across her face. "Really?"

He nodded. "Yep. When Wesley approached me I couldn't turn him down, but that had never been part of my life plan."

"What did you plan on doing, then?"

He shrugged. "I hadn't figured it out but I knew I couldn't be in SF forever and I wasn't going to sit behind a desk later. I . . . always loved horses." His grandparents and parents had had them and he'd planned to raise them, breed them, maybe even have a farm. Truthfully he'd never thought too far ahead, had been so damn focused when he'd been in the Corps but settling down like that had always been in his periphery.

She paused, watching him, as if debating what she was going to tell him. "My first field op for Wesley was when I was twenty."

He didn't think she was that much older now so the fact that she was running an op alone only a few years later—unless he was wrong about her age—was impressive. It wasn't exactly a surprise though. It would have been if she'd been male. Levi knew that men tended to be recruited later—usually after military service. Not that women in the military weren't recruited, because they definitely were, but most agencies scooped up their female agents right out of college. But twenty was fucking young. "What type of op?"

"Elimination." She looked at him almost defiantly as she said it and he could tell she wasn't apologetic about it at all. And that was way hotter than it should be.

"How'd you do?"

She seemed surprised by his question, but relaxed a fraction, letting out a self-deprecating laugh. "Well enough, but nothing really prepares you for the real-world situations other than being thrown into the deep end. I seriously thought I was going to pee my pants."

He snorted at her words. "You must have done better than 'well enough' for Wesley to send you on this op by yourself." He was fishing for more information, something she probably knew.

"Yeah." She didn't take the bait though, just dropped her gaze to his mouth. She swallowed hard and that awareness between them took on a life of its own.

The air seemed to crackle with intensity for a long, heated moment. Her blond hair was rumpled and hanging free around her face, making her look like she'd just come from the beach. Or a long night of raw fucking.

The images that thought evoked made him go hard all over. Against his will, he started to lean forward. The need to possess and taste this woman was like an addiction. She was too likable, too . . . something. He didn't understand what it was, wanted to convince himself that this was just physical. At first it had been, which made him feel shitty and guilty for reasons he didn't want to think about, but now . . . he found that he just plain liked this woman. She'd unabashedly snooped through his computer, made fun of his taste in music, was self-deprecating, and—

When she moistened her lips his cock jumped against his zipper. God, he hadn't been with anyone since Meghan. That had to be the only reason he was so insane for Selene right now.

Sure it is, liar.

He could tell himself whatever he wanted, but he knew the truth. He hadn't wanted any woman, not the professional Jasmine who looked like a pinup model, no one. Until Selene.

A buzzing sound hummed through the air, making them both freeze. They'd been at her place only a few minutes and she hadn't checked a cell phone but he guessed that's what it was. Sighing, her expression filled with regret and maybe a little bit of relief, she pulled away from him. Instantly he missed the simple feel of her skin against his hand and resisted the urge to draw her back to him.

When she opened her nightstand drawer he saw multiple cell phones. She pulled out one and her expression went deadly. "Looks like we might be too late to stop Tasev," she said with a savage curse.

Chapter 10

Interrogation: questioning/interviewing suspects, victims, or witnesses with the purpose of gaining information or a confession.

Selene's heart was an erratic beat in her chest as she scanned the previous texts from Wesley. She should have grabbed her phone as soon as she'd stepped inside the door but she'd wanted to put on clothes that didn't smell like Levi.

9-1-1. Call me. Target sent out teams.

That was all the last text said. Since Wesley wasn't prone to exaggerating she knew something was seriously wrong. Tasev was their target and if he'd sent out teams that was pretty much the worst-case scenario. Without giving Levi a chance to protest, she called her boss. She knew Levi would be annoyed but she didn't care. Just because she was bringing him in on this op didn't mean she was going to lie to her boss.

"You okay?" Wesley asked, picking up on the first ring.

"Yeah."

"Where are you?"

"The safe house."

"Good. We got an anonymous tip that Tasev was planning to poison two water supplies with that toxin. We stopped him before that happened."

"You have him in custody?" Hope blossomed in her chest for a moment. This could all be over and if Tasev had been behind Meghan Lazaro's murder he'd pay for what he'd done in addition to all his other crimes. Levi might not get the revenge he wanted but he'd be safe while Tasev was punished.

"No, just some of his men. None of them are talking. Yet." There was a dark note in Wesley's voice that he rarely used.

If anyone could get those men to talk it would be Wesley, but some people just never cracked. Especially if they were more scared of their boss than anyone else. "My meet's still in place tonight." She hadn't heard otherwise from the German so she was going on the assumption that it was. If Tasev's men had been arrested though, she knew the man would be on edge. Which could make him unpredictable.

"I'm sending Ortiz with you."

Selene shot a look at Levi, who was leaning against the doorframe. His stance was relaxed and casual but he looked like a lion, ready to strike. He was going to be pissed at her, but . . . "I've already got someone going with me."

Levi straightened, crossing his arms over his chest as Wesley said, "What?"

"Levi's with me now and if his cover ID is as good as he says, I think we should go with him." She held up a hand to Levi when he took a step toward her, his body rigid. If he was coming with her, they were doing things her way.

"Are you under duress?" Wesley asked quietly, the tension in his voice palpable.

"No." They had a code word for that if she ever was. All agents did.

Wesley was silent for a long moment, likely weighing if she was being honest or not. "Put me on speaker."

Levi was glaring at her, but she ignored him and pressed the speaker button. "We all want the same thing," she said to both of them. "Well, mostly. Now talk," she told Levi.

His jaw clenched and he never took his eyes off her. "Burkhart," he said tightly.

Selene resisted the urge to roll her eyes. Using Wesley's last name as a way to distance himself from the man. So transparent.

"Levi." Wesley's greeting was just as short and she could practically see the wheels turning in both their heads.

Levi was likely calculating how long it would take Wesley to send a team to the safe house to bring Levi in—and Wesley was likely calculating the same thing.

"I know what you're both thinking so stop it. Wesley, do you think you're going to crack Tasev's guys before my meeting tonight?"

"No." The word seemed to be torn from him, as if he didn't want to admit it.

But there it was and the only answer she needed. "Okay then. So we're operating as if this meet is still going through. Multiple people saw me and Levi leave Shah's party last night. I don't think we were tailed, but it's clear we know each other and if Tasev had eyes at the party—and I'm sure he did—Tasev will know that The Wolf left with someone."

"What's your ID?" Wesley asked, his question clearly for Levi.

Levi didn't want to answer, that much was clear, but he said, "Isaiah Moore. From Chicago."

Wesley wouldn't need more than that. Selene could have run all the information herself, but she wanted a third party at the NSA to do it. Wesley needed to feel secure in this decision too. "Hold on." Wesley put them on hold and Selene knew it was to have someone start running the alias's records. Probably Karen. That woman was a genius. Moments later Wesley was back. "Convince me why I should send you on this op instead of someone else."

"First, I'm better trained than anyone you've got, except maybe Jack—and he doesn't work for you anymore." From there Levi repeated what he'd told her about Isaiah's business dealings, ending with, "I'll approach him with an unrelated business opportunity, but I'll mention the pharmaceutical company I own in the conversation. Almost as an afterthought."

Selene frowned as she started to comprehend what Levi was saying. Or at least guess the direction. When dangling bait, you had to make sure your target thought he was the one who was targeting or using you. That he'd come up with the idea on his own, not been manipulated into making the decision you'd wanted all along. It was a fine line playing that game, especially with someone as smart and vicious as Tasev.

Wesley was silent so Levi continued, "If his plan is

to poison water supplies, then blackmail the government into buying the antitoxin, if he's smart, he'll go one step further and forget the blackmail."

Selene nodded, realizing she'd been thinking along the same track. Theoretically Tasev could do any number of things with the knowledge that Isaiah Moore owned a pharmaceutical company but if she was a criminal, she'd want to make millions off the very people she'd targeted. And doing it legally would be a giant kick in the teeth. It was kinda poetic in a fucked-up way.

"Instead of blackmailing the government, he might think bigger and opt to want to mass-produce the antitoxin," Wesley said, his voice thoughtful.

Because if the toxin made it into any water supply, everyone would be scrambling to find an antitoxin. And if Tasev got in bed with Isaiah, they could be heroes and make a fortune.

"Either way it won't matter because it'll never get that far," Selene said. "But after our first meet it'll give him an incentive to bring us onto his home turf and introduce us to the creator of the toxin. I just need inside his base of operations." Something Wesley already knew. It was the whole basis for her going on this op.

"Take me off speaker," Wesley said.

Though Selene could tell it annoyed Levi, she did it. "It's just me."

"How do you know he won't hang you out to dry? Selene, you don't owe him this much. He was just doing his damn job when—"

"I know and that's not what this is about." Not completely. "Have his credentials come back yet?" she asked, knowing that Wesley would already have a partial file on Moore pulled up on his computer. It would take hours to do a deeper investigation into Levi's alias, to make sure that it would stand up to Tasev's scrutiny, but Wesley would have enough now to make a decision.

"You know they have."

"And?"

"And, I don't like this at all."

She closed her eyes and looked away from Levi. "During our meet I'll plant a tracker on Tasev." With the micro-technology they had at their disposal, it would be easy enough to get it on him unseen. Well, depending on Tasev. He wasn't one to let a pretty face sway him so flirting was out. Especially if she was posing as Levi's lover. And the problem with the trackers was that they eventually disintegrated. So if Tasev didn't return immediately to his base, then it might not work anyway.

"You should just let me bring him in," Wesley said, changing topics, clearly talking about Levi now.

Standing, Selene moved away from Levi and strode to one of the bullet-resistant windows. She looked down at the beach, stories below. "You're free to do whatever you want," she murmured. Because no one *let* Wesley Burkhart do anything. He did whatever he damn well pleased. Something they both knew.

"You're putting me in a tough situation."

She snorted, but didn't respond. It didn't matter what she said, he'd go with his gut in the end. He always did.

"Damn it, Selene." Now he was really in a snit,

though he'd curse again if he heard her use the word "snit" in relation to him. After a long pause in which they both attempted to wait each other out, he finally sighed. "If his ID is solid he can go with you but this changes nothing."

"I know." Even though Wesley had decided to let Levi go about a year ago, now that he was back on their radar, her boss wanted Levi brought in. It didn't mean Selene was going to help him.

"No matter what we'll be following you via satellite and tracker."

"I know," she repeated. For this op there would be a team of agents on standby but no one directly tailing her. It was too risky. Tasev was careful so even though she planned to use the NSA's micro-technology on herself, the tiny trackers could be disabled electronically. Tasev would never know she had one on herself or Levi. He'd just have to send out an electronic pulse to disable any in the vicinity and it would neutralize their trackers.

"He could hang you out to dry," Wesley said, reiterating his earlier statement in a rigid tone.

"He won't." He might try to screw her over in the end, but she didn't think he'd actually hang her out to dry. Not in the sense that he'd leave her to fend for herself on an op. She still wasn't positive that he wasn't going to let his need for revenge drive him, so she wanted to keep him as close to her as possible. Like that old saying: Keep your enemies closer. Not that she liked thinking of Levi as an enemy.

"If Tasev killed his wife, he could. You don't know how Levi will react. And we need Tasev alive, at least at first."

"No, you need Schmidt alive."

"If Tasev has more cells, we need him. He could have sent more than two teams out."

"How'd you find out about that anyway?" she asked.

"Anonymous tip."

"Bullshit."

"That's all I can say."

"Fine. You know what I want but you make the final decision. What's it gonna be?"

"Levi's in. Just get Tasev's base and we can end the bastard."

After they disconnected she turned to find Levi sitting on the edge of the bed, his dark eyes glittering with too many emotions to define. "So?" he asked, his voice hard.

"You're in for the op."

"You didn't give Wesley all the details."

"I will. He trusts me to make calls in the field."

Levi watched her with a mix of confusion and caution, as if she was some exotic animal he couldn't figure out.

"What?" she asked, feeling self-conscious under his inspection.

"I can't figure you out."

Frowning, she gathered her clothes from the bed. "How so?"

"You weren't in the military." A statement. "But you're trained. And I know some of Selene Silva's cover ID was based on truth, though you're too young to have done all of the ops. So that means they started building the ID with you in mind, even before you were allowed in the field." They couldn't have created her to be a trained assassin if she didn't know how to use a multitude of weapons and he was willing to bet she was responsible for some of the operations that created the cover ID.

"If there's not a question in there, I'm getting changed." She started for the bathroom, needing some space from Levi.

To her relief or disappointment, she wasn't sure, he didn't try to stop her. Once inside the bathroom she sagged against the closed door. As soon as she was dressed they'd have to go over the plan for tonight in serious detail and if she was posing as his lover she knew that she'd have to be comfortable around him in the way that lovers were.

She wasn't sure how she felt about that, especially since she wished she knew what it was like to be his in the bedroom.

Tasev ended the call he'd just made when it went straight to voice mail. Again. He'd called each man he'd sent out. Twice. No one was answering. On a mission everyone went dark, but everything should have been in place by now and they should have been on their way back to Miami. For eight of his men to completely fall off the radar meant only one thing.

They'd been caught.

Or betrayed. He'd been so careful, sending in small but trained teams. This had been his testing ground. Staring at his phone for only a moment longer, he shoved it into his pants pocket and strode from the room. The mansion he used as his base was expansive but the man he wanted to speak to was nearby.

Moments later he found Grisha talking to one of the

perimeter guards, laughing about some stupid sports team. That was something Tasev didn't understand—sports. Their fascination with such idiocy wasn't his concern now.

Both men looked over when they saw him, the guard straightening. Grisha's posture didn't change as he nodded in respect at Tasev.

With a jerk of his head, he had the other man scurrying away. The property was surrounded by a high wall and in addition to his static guards, he had men constantly moving around with no specific agenda other than to keep the grounds secure. Not to mention he had anti-surveillance hardware in place everywhere, making this place virtually impenetrable.

"You never told me how you got those blueprints," Tasev said. When Grisha had acquired the plans he hadn't asked how he'd gotten them. Tasev thoroughly checked out anyone he did business with but he didn't micromanage. He was too busy and anyone stupid enough to cross him ended up tortured and dead. Now, however, he wanted to know how the man had acquired such sensitive material.

"No, I didn't." There was no sarcasm in his statement, but definitely an edge to his voice.

"How did you get them?"

Grisha paused a long moment, the scar around his neck pulling as his neck muscles clenched. Likely in annoyance. Finally he shrugged. "A woman I fucked gave me access."

Different architecture firms had done the plans for each plant. Before Tasev could point that out, Grisha continued, "She works for the firm who designed the

Florida plant and had a contact with the Georgia firm. I can be very persuasive," he murmured, clearly pleased with himself.

Tasev relaxed a fraction, but didn't let his guard down. "My men haven't checked in," he said, gauging the man's reaction.

It wasn't much, but his eyebrows slightly raised. That might as well be full-on surprise for a normal person. It didn't mean Tasev trusted Grisha, but he was reacting the right way at least. "Can't you track them?" Grisha asked.

"They went dark right before the op."

He nodded once. "Of course."

Since he didn't plan to torture Grisha to find out if he'd been the one to betray him—yet—he changed topics. If Grisha was guilty, Tasev would give him enough rope to hang himself in the next twenty-four hours. "What did the German say at your sit-down?"

"The female is beautiful and intelligent and he believes she is The Wolf. She knew too many details about some of the confirmed kills. And she knows her weapons. Interestingly, he said that she left Shah's party with a man who was supposed to meet with him later that evening. Isaiah Moore."

Tasev frowned at the familiar name. The German had forwarded it to him along with a short list of people interested in doing business with Tasev, and Moore's name had been on it. He was the only one who hadn't done the preliminary meeting with the German. Instead of voicing his thoughts, he just nodded. "Thank you."

Making his way back to his office, Tasev knew exactly whom he'd call to find out if his men had been arrested. He had various people in law enforcement on his payroll—of course they didn't know his real name. He also planned to find out how his men had been caught. No one had known what they were doing except Grisha but Tasev had put a tail on him when he'd gone to see the German so he couldn't have betrayed him. All his vehicles were bugged and he hadn't made any calls or texts. Unless . . . He pulled out his phone and texted the guard he'd ordered to follow Grisha.

Less than ten minutes later Matvei arrived at his office, looking nervous as usual. It didn't matter the situation, Matvei always looked guilty of something. Which was frustrating because he was impossible to read. Luckily the man was too dumb to ever cross Tasev.

Tasev had left his door open because he didn't want to be bothered with having to get up. "Close it behind you."

Matvei nodded, his shaggy blond hair falling over his forehead. "Everything okay?"

"When you followed Grisha this morning was he ever out of your sight?"

Matvei blinked, his blue eyes revealing surprise at the question. "No. Not once."

"And he went straight to the German's?"

"Yes." He quickly launched into a recap of the route Grisha had taken and how long it took him to get to the German's. It was clear Matvei was proud of himself for tailing Grisha.

But Tasev was certain Grisha knew he'd been followed. He wasn't a mindless soldier like Matvei. "That'll be all," he murmured, dismissing the man.

The closer he came to completing his mission the

more ruthless he'd been in spying on his own men. It wasn't impossible that Grisha had betrayed him, but he would have had a very small time line in which to contact anyone. So whom would he have contacted? And why would he have gotten the blueprints in the first place?

Tasev frowned at his own paranoia. Just because it seemed as if Grisha was the only man who'd known about the op this morning didn't mean it was so. Any of the eight men he'd sent could have mentioned it to the rest of the crew. Still, Grisha had been with him for the shortest period of time so he was automatically suspect for anything. Well, Matvei had been with him for relatively the same time frame but he didn't know enough to betray Tasev anyway. His gut told him that Grisha wasn't guilty, but he had to know for certain.

And laying a trap for Grisha to fall into would be easy enough. He'd just have to give him something too big to pass up. If he said nothing Tasev would know he could be trusted.

Chapter 11

Safe house: a house in a secret location, used by spies or criminals.

Levi slipped on his custom-made Armani jacket, almost completing the civilized appearance he was going for. He and Selene had come back to the place he'd been staying a few hours ago. He hadn't been willing to stay at the NSA-owned condo, safe house or not.

When he reached for the tie he'd laid on his mattress, Selene strode into the bedroom and shook her head. "I'd lose the tie." Wearing loose gym shorts and a sports bra, she had two small boxes in one hand and a zipped-up black garment bag in the other. Momentarily distracted, his throat tightened at the sight of her sweaty and half-naked.

Ignoring her statement, he frowned at what she was holding. For the last half hour she'd been working out in the backyard area. Every time he'd looked outside she'd been doing push-ups, sprints, tabata crunches, and other forms of cardio. Less than five minutes ago he'd seen her shadowboxing in the empty pool. Watching her had been mesmerizing. She hadn't said, but it was like she had a routine before a mission.

Which wasn't out of the ordinary. Most operatives did. But that didn't explain the other stuff. "What the hell is all that?"

"Clothes for me and something for us," she said, tossing the garment bag on the bed. She handed him one of the boxes.

"Where the hell did it come from?" he shouted.

"I had it dropped off. And before you get all crazy, let's not pretend that you planned to come back here after tonight." Her testy tone dared him to contradict her.

He gritted his teeth, hating that she was right. This place was burned now that she knew about it—and clearly the NSA—and the only reason he'd come back was to wipe down anything he might have missed. He'd already packed up his meager belongings a couple of hours ago and moved them to another safe house. He was ninety percent sure Selene hadn't followed him, but even if she had, he wouldn't be staying at that place either. He always tried to think three steps ahead. "I thought you were wearing the dress," he said, indicating the black gown she'd brought from her condo and hung in the closet.

She snorted. "I changed my mind. If we're going through with your plan, we're going to paint a picture of a unified front." She unzipped the bag to reveal a pantsuit similar to his. Black, sleek, Armani, and definitely made for her long slender body. Her legs would look a mile long in the pants. From experience, he knew the NSA would have her measurements on file so it made sense they would be able to have the suit made on such short notice. It was also smart to dress similarly. It would make it clear that they were more than business associates without having to say a word to Tasev.

Though he tried to remain unaffected by her, his gaze trailed over her slightly sweaty body, landing on the outline of her nipples in her sports bra, skimming over the flat planes of her stomach and down her legs. The woman had tan, shapely runner's legs and right now all he could think about was what it would be like to have them wrapped around his waist. Or his face.

He jerked at the image of that and tore off the top of the box in his hand with more force than necessary to reveal a simple, likely platinum, watch. He recognized the brand as being insanely expensive. "A watch is an ineffective way to track us," he said, looking back up at her.

She rolled her eyes and pulled out her own watch, which was a smaller, feminine version of his. "There's no tracker on it. Watch me." With elegant fingers, she grasped the middle of the timepiece and twisted the band back and forth in what he realized was a combination of sorts. It clicked open and she grasped the ends and pulled, revealing a retractable garrote wire.

His eyebrows rose. "Impressive."

"When they scan us, it'll show up as a normal electronic device and even if they use an electronic pulse to disable it, it won't affect the weapon. The code is two clicks clockwise, five counterclockwise, then three clockwise."

As she'd instructed, he clicked until his watch revealed the weapon. Hell, yeah. He didn't mind going in unarmed because his hands were the ultimate weapon but he liked having something like this as backup. And he was glad Selene had something to protect herself with. Not that he planned to let anything happen to her, but he knew more than most how things could go sideways in the blink of an eye. After reviewing it, he retracted it and put the watch on. A perfect fit. Not that he'd expect any less from Burkhart.

"We need to leave in an hour," he said, meeting her gaze again.

"I know. It won't take me long to shower and get ready." When she started to move past him, he held out an arm.

"From the moment we leave here we're playing a role."

She frowned at him. "This isn't my first op, Isaiah." She smoothly used his alias, as she'd been doing most of the day.

He grasped one of her hands and pulled her close but she held up her other hand, pressing against his chest.

"I'm sweaty. I don't want to mess up your shirt."

That was the last thing on his mind, but something he could quickly remedy. He stripped off his jacket then started on the buttons of his shirt, keeping his gaze pinned to hers.

Her pale eyes flared as she realized what he was doing. "Just because we're posing as lovers doesn't mean—"

"I know," he bit out, not wanting to hear whatever she had to say. "But we're going to kiss and you can't blush at the sight of my bare chest."

She looked as if she wanted to say something, but paused as he slid his shirt off, her eyes tracking over every inch of his exposed skin. And damn if he didn't get hard at the hungry look in her eyes. Her cheeks were flushed, but not from nervousness. She was turned on and whether she was acting or not, she looked the part.

He sure as hell wasn't acting. When she watched him like that, everything else seemed to fade out and all he could think about was hours of raw, primal fucking. But it would be more than that between them. Even if he wanted to keep things strictly physical, that was an impossibility with Selene. She'd woken something up inside him, even if he couldn't define what it was. She made him *feel* again. It was disturbing and confusing, but he couldn't deny the truth of it. "Touch me," he demanded, feeling like an ass for ordering her around, even as he craved her hands on him.

To his surprise, she didn't shy away. Instantly she reached out and slid her hands up his chest as if she'd done it a hundred times, her fingers gentle against him. He tried to fight it, but he shuddered at the feel of her moving over his skin. She stopped at his shoulders, her fingers just barely settling over him.

Her pale eyes seemed to darken as she watched him with a mix of nervousness and need.

"You can't be nervous around me. You've seen every inch of my naked body many times," he murmured, watching in fascination as her cheeks flushed a darker shade of red. "Seen, touched, kissed, and licked all of it." What he wouldn't give for that to be the reality. His cock ached at the thought of those pouty lips taking him in her mouth.

She still looked nervous, but taking him by surprise, she moved one of her hands from his shoulder and slid it behind his neck. He loved the possessive way she held him. When she went up on her tiptoes, he met her halfway as he slanted his mouth over hers.

He tried to tell himself to be gentle, to go slow, but everything in his mind short-circuited around Selene. Considering her hands were actually on his body, it was a miracle he was even thinking at all.

He didn't know where to put his damn hands because he wanted to touch her everywhere. Sliding one up her spine, he didn't stop until he held the back of her head. Her hair was in a ponytail so he grasped it lightly and tugged.

She moaned into his mouth, her tongue flicking against his in erotic, eager strokes. Yeah, this wasn't acting. Or he hoped it wasn't.

He grasped her hip and tugged her fully to him as he rolled his hips against hers. She groaned again, letting out the most needy sound as his erection rubbed against her abdomen. He loved how tall she was, her body a perfect fit to his. When her fingers tightened on his shoulder and she leaned harder into him, his grip on her hips flexed. Her breasts were pressing against his chest and the sports bra she wore did nothing to hide the fact that her nipples were tight with arousal.

Damn it. This was just supposed to have been for the benefit of the op.

Breathing hard, he stepped back. As he did, a rush of guilt bulldozed into him. He tried to stop it, to shove it back down, but it erupted all the same.

She saw it in his face.

Eyes narrowing slightly, she didn't look hurt so much as angry. "If you're going to order me to touch

you, don't look so fucking ashamed after we kiss!" she
snapped out, then seemed to catch herself, her expression going carefully neutral.

He drew in a sharp breath. "I'm not ashamed."

"And don't lie to me either." Her breathing was as
erratic as his as she turned away from him to grab her
toiletry bag and the garment bag.

He let out a growl of frustration and grabbed her
upper arm, forcing her to look back at him. "It's not
shame. It's . . ." *Just say the damn words.* "I think *she*
would have liked you."

Selene's expression immediately softened, which
pretty much told him that yeah, Meghan would have
liked her. They were different in so many ways, but
they both had a good core, were good people. Selene
didn't say anything though.

He forced himself to continue. "I do feel guilty, but
not because of you. It's the whole damn situation." Because he felt like he was in a free fall around her and
couldn't seem to catch his breath. "There's no logical
reason for it, I know that, but it doesn't seem to matter.
I don't want to stop whatever this thing is between us
from happening." Saying the words made him feel exposed, something he wasn't used to.

Her pale blue eyes were unreadable now and he was
under the impression that she didn't believe him.

That pissed him off, even though it shouldn't. "You
think I'm fucking lying?"

She rubbed a hand over the back of her neck and
sighed. "I don't know what to think, Levi. This"—she
motioned between them—"could be an act for all I
know." For the briefest moment, she revealed a raw

vulnerability before she covered it up. But he knew what he'd seen.

It wasn't an act, but there wasn't a whole lot he could do to prove to her he wasn't a liar. "Did someone hurt you?" He shouldn't be asking right before an op but hell, he wanted to know more about her. Wanted to know everything that made this woman tick.

Clutching her toiletry bag to her chest, she gave him a jerky shrug. "Not in the way I think you mean."

"But you lost someone." *Leave it alone*, he ordered himself. Now was not the time for this.

She nodded.

"Tell me who."

For a moment he thought she would, but then she gave a brief shake of her head. "After the op I will."

"I'll hold you to it." And he would. No doubt.

Wordlessly, she headed to the bathroom. When she shut the door behind her, the most cynical side of him wondered if this was part of an elaborate plan for Wesley to bring him in. The NSA clearly knew where he was now. He was basically a sitting duck. So he was just going to have to trust Selene not to betray him.

Trust.

That word was so foreign to him even thinking it raked against all his senses uncomfortably.

Unable to sit still, he redressed, put on the watch, then did another sweep of the house out of habit. He needed to get out of the damn bedroom. He knew he'd wiped down all the surfaces he'd touched and removed everything of his but rechecking made him saner and kept his mind off Selene in the shower. Naked. With water rolling down that tight body. Covering places he wanted to kiss, lick, stroke . . .

Fuck.

He had to get his head in the game. To think. Focusing, he thought about the way she'd talked to Wesley earlier. It had been interesting. Her tone had been respectful, but there had been a sense of familiarity and almost softness in her voice. Like when one spoke to a parent. The darkest part of Levi told him to file that information away and use it against Wesley if necessary but Levi knew he'd never do it. That pissed him off.

She pissed him off. Another lie.

God, he was like some randy teenager unable to get his mind off the one woman he should want nothing to do with. Selene had the ability to screw up his mission and years of planning. For all he knew she was playing him. So why didn't he believe that?

He rolled his shoulders as he entered the bedroom, trying to ease some of the tension out of them. It was a fruitless effort. When Selene stepped from the bathroom, all the air left his lungs in a whoosh.

They might be dressed similarly, but he had nothing on her. Like a dying man, he drank in the sight of her. He'd been right about the pants, they made her legs impossibly long. The jacket had a deep V, no lapels, and an asymmetrical fastening that could have looked odd, but completed the edgy look. At first he didn't realize she had anything on underneath, but she wore a nude camisole that molded to her body like a second skin. Her hair was pulled into a tight bun at her nape, which made sense. Long hair could be used against her so she was taking away that option. And her stilettos would be another good weapon. Though nothing would be as good as the image she painted. On an intellectual level he understood that was why she was dressed the way she was.

Sex was the oldest trick in the book and using her body would make even the most trained agent distracted. Clearly.

"You look . . ." Swallowing hard, he trailed off as he met her gaze. He was surprised by the subtle hint of insecurity that flashed in her pale eyes.

Lips pulled tight, she smoothed her hands down her pants. "What?"

"Fucking hot."

She blinked once, then let out a short, loud laugh he felt all the way to his core. "That's such a guy thing to say."

He picked up the box with her watch from the mattress. "I *am* a guy."

Her full lips quirked up at the corners. "I know, I just . . . I've read your file. I expected you to be more polished." She held out her wrist for him.

The intimacy of the moment wasn't lost on him. The way they were getting ready together felt familiar and right and . . . almost normal. But he didn't do normal anymore. Hadn't thought he could do it ever again.

After he snapped the watch in place, he didn't let go of her, but rubbed his thumb gently against her pulse point, savoring the feel of her soft skin. She shivered under his touch, her gaze pinned to his. "You strip away every ounce of civility in me, Selene." She made him feel primal and raw and exposed in a way he didn't grasp when she looked at him. And he wanted her to understand that there was nothing polished about him when it came to her. "When we fuck, nothing about it will be *polished*."

She sucked in a breath at his words, her pupils dilating as she swallowed hard, the pulse point on her neck fluttering wildly. And when she didn't negate his words and tell him he was an idiot for thinking she'd allow him to possess her body, that primitive man inside did a fist pump as if to say "hell yeah."

Withdrawing her wrist from his hold, she took a step back. "We need to focus."

He nodded, knowing she was right. "Agreed. I'm sure you're already aware of this, but the meeting place won't be where the actual meet goes down."

"I know. It's standard operating procedure for these types of things."

"Have you ever done one with someone like Tasev?"

She paused, then shook her head. "I don't think there's anyone out there like Tasev. I'm usually looking at a target through a scope or assisting an op from the command center."

"But you've created assets." Her relationship with Alexander Lopez was proof of that.

She nodded and gave him a look that said she wondered why he was stating the obvious.

He cleared his throat. "For situations like this, we'll meet someone under his command, be searched, then likely hooded and taken somewhere."

She nodded again. "I know."

"Are you okay with being hooded?" He watched her carefully, thinking of the way she'd reacted when he'd tried to put one on her. So far she'd held her own, but he'd never worked with her in the field. He had to be prepared for any situation.

"It wouldn't be the first time so, yes, I'll be fine." Her words were sharp and brooked no questions.

Of course he had another dozen to ask her now, but he held his tongue. "Good. Listen . . . if shit goes south and you have a way out, take it."

She blinked at him, clearly confused. "What?"

Against his better judgment, he loosely grasped her hip, tugging her close. He didn't need an excuse to touch her and even though he knew he should keep his distance he wasn't going to deny himself the chance to hold her for another couple of seconds. "If you have to sacrifice me to get out, do it."

Now she just looked pissed. She batted his hand away and pushed him once in the chest. Not with any force. "We're teammates. We go in together, we leave together. That hasn't changed since you left."

"Saving hundreds of thousands of people and killing Tasev are the only things that matter. If that bastard ordered the killing of my wife, I want him dead and I don't care if I have to die in order for that to happen." So far he hadn't talked openly about Meghan but knew he needed to now. He needed Selene to understand. "So if you have to sacrifice me, do it. And kill Tasev. That's all I ask."

She swallowed hard and for the first time since he'd met her, her expression was damn near unreadable. Instead of responding, she simply turned from him and strode from the room.

Wesley clicked off the image of one of the interrogation rooms, hiding his frustration from his team in the command center. The men they'd brought in from the water plants were refusing to speak. They hadn't even asked for attorneys. They just flat out weren't talking.

After three hours with his normal team of interrogators, Wesley had gone in himself and still returned with nothing. So far they had a decent amount of intel on them from their fingerprints and DNA but those men were clearly more afraid of Tasev than anything anyone else could do to them. While Wesley wanted to go hard at them, he knew that wasn't the best place for his energy right now. Playing psychological warfare with criminals could be a long process and they didn't have time. They'd gotten lucky with that tip and there was no guarantee they'd get another one. They had to cut the head off the snake. And according to Dr. Schmidt, they had only days to do it.

Wesley pushed up from the computer station he'd been using and stood behind his six analysts, all at computers working together like a well-oiled machine. He'd pulled in his best for this op with his favored field guys ready and waiting for an order. "Where's the north satellite feed?" he asked, not needing to speak to anyone by name. Whoever had the answer would respond.

"Two seconds," Karen said as the live image popped up on one of the ten large screens on the main wall.

They were in a secure, soundproof room with no windows and no way to access without serious clearance. There were so many layers of guards before this floor—and everyone in this room was armed—that Wesley wasn't worried about a breach. It was part of the reason he was able to focus completely here.

He scanned the images: some satellite feeds, other CCTVs around the city, and one was a live video coming from the vehicle Selene and Levi were in. A team had dropped it off for Selene and while she knew it was there she hadn't said anything about it or looked at it. Wesley had no doubt Levi was aware of it too.

Wesley still questioned his decision to let Levi go in on this op but the man was incredibly talented. It had nothing to do with weapons training, though he had an impressive resume. Levi was a chameleon, sliding into various roles in a way Wesley had rarely seen in his long career. After Selene sent Wesley Levi's airtight alias, he'd known that she'd be working with Isaiah Moore and no one else.

Tasev was elusive—that being an understatement—and too many lives were at stake. And Wesley wanted revenge for Meghan too. Not as much as Levi, considering she'd been his wife, but Wesley had loved her too. They all had.

"We're nearing the final turnoff," Selene murmured, her voice coming through his earpiece.

Wesley watched her sitting in the passenger seat of the SUV. The small camera they'd placed in the vehicle was part of the GPS dash, giving them a view of Selene and Levi. Selene was almost completely immobile, her body rigid as she scanned her surroundings. That was normal for her on ops, which made him breathe easier.

Levi had a typical grim expression on his face as he drove, but his body language was relaxed. Yeah, he was ready for the op. The meeting place was an abandoned warehouse in the middle of an abandoned neighborhood. At the last minute the German had contacted Selene and changed the original meeting place, giving Wesley's people no time to get set up in advance. They'd expected it, but he still didn't like the situation.

"Two guards outside the warehouse. Armed," Levi said quietly.

"Narrow in on their faces," Wesley ordered.

One of his analysts did, using a satellite feed to zoom as close as they could. But the angle was bad, the men looking out toward the SUV, so they captured only the top of their heads. Only if they looked up into the sky could Wesley get a good look at them and plug their faces into facial recognition software.

"They're motioning for us to slow," Selene said.

A moment later both windows rolled down and they got a semi-decent view of the two guards. They held weapons on Selene and Levi but didn't say a word, just surveyed the interior before the one on Levi's side motioned them to move forward.

"Running their faces through our software," one of the analysts said. "It's only sixty percent accurate because of the distortion."

It would have to be good enough. Not that it really mattered. Tasev wouldn't have men important to his organization standing guard. Hell, Tasev likely wasn't even here. Levi and Selene would be taken to him. This was the part Wesley hated—sending his people behind enemy lines.

From one of the feeds he watched as the warehouse door rolled up. Selene and Levi remained quiet as they started moving. They went from the relative darkness of outside to a pitch dark inside the warehouse.

Even with the video it was impossible to see much and neither of them was saying a word.

Right as Levi said, "Shit," the video shut completely off as if someone had flipped a switch.

"Selene?" Wesley said her name quietly.

No answer.

"Their communicators and the SUV are dead," Karen said, her fingers flying across her keyboard. "I can't get a read on the GPS system, the video, or the extra tracker we placed. It's all dead."

"EMP burst," Wesley muttered, knowing what Tasev had done. The terrorist had either used an EMP gun or cannon to disable the SUV's microprocessors and everything else electronic inside it. "Everyone stay focused."

There was a steady hum of activity among his people, but Wesley had learned to tune out the voices and noises a long time ago. Less than three minutes later the warehouse door opened again and another SUV drove out.

"Karen, stay on the first vehicle." Because he had no doubt they'd use multiple vehicles to attempt to dissuade tracking. Tasev had stayed hidden for so many years for a reason. The man was beyond careful.

"Maxwell, track the second, Pierce the third, Welch stay on the—shit." Vehicles zoomed out one after the other, eventually totaling fifteen. He cursed before revising his earlier orders and reassigning who tracked what vehicle while silently praying that Levi and Selene stayed alive.

Chapter 12

Night vision device (aka NVD): an optical instrument such as goggles that allows images to be perceived in relative darkness.

Selene forced her breathing to remain even and un-affected as she grappled to slow her increasing heart rate.

Steady.

Calm.

Breathe.

In the dark interior of the warehouse with a spot-light on her and Levi, she stood with her arms and legs spread as a man with a shaved head, blue eyes, and a wicked-looking scar on his neck scanned her with a metal detecting wand. Her watch and small earrings pinged but after further inspection she was allowed to keep both. She also had to deal with a pat down. Even though the man looked intimidating his search was quick and clinical. Since she knew what could happen to her on these ops she tried to compartmentalize her emotions. It was why she was on birth control. She might be trained and confident in her ability to protect herself to an extent but she couldn't take on a small army of men by herself. Having Levi with her was the biggest relief.

Next to her, he was undergoing the same treatment, his expression almost amused as they searched him. The sight of that crooked half smile helped her relax more than anything else could have.

When two men appeared from behind two of the set-up spotlights with hoods in their hands, she prepared herself for what was to come. She'd had to do it before and it was part of the job. Being hooded could make her lose focus though and that was dangerous. A slipup of any kind could get them both killed and ruin the op, effectively cementing the deaths of countless scores of people. Something she wouldn't let happen. She grasped on to that knowledge and forced herself to breathe through the building panic inside her.

"We stay in the same vehicle," Levi said, the first words he'd spoken since they'd been escorted out of their ruined SUV. His focus was on the scarred man.

The blue-eyed man flicked a glance between them, pausing once before he nodded at the two others.

"I hope you at least washed the hoods," she said casually, looking at Levi and shaking her head. "I hate it when they don't wash them." Saying the flippant words helped ease more of her tension. That was something she'd learned at a young age—act like a badass and it was easier to be one.

Fake it 'til you make it.

Levi's lips quirked up, the last thing she saw before being plunged into darkness as the hood covered her face. Her breathing was amplified, the warmth of it heating up her face.

She heard a snap, and then the heat from the spotlights dissipated. Next a hard grip on her elbow led her about ten feet forward. Her heels clicked on the concrete so she focused on the sound, letting it steady her.

"Step up," the man holding her elbow said.

On instinct, she reached out and grasped what she quickly realized was the doorframe of a vehicle. As she stepped up, she guesstimated it was an SUV by the height of the running board. Or a truck, but an SUV would make more sense for transporting them. Tasev's men would be able to get more guards inside.

Even with the spotlights on them before, she'd been able to make out shapes that looked like vehicles but it had been difficult to gauge how many were there.

Once she was settled inside the vehicle a strong, male hand grasped hers. "I'm next to you," Levi said.

She squeezed back, using his strength to channel her own as the engine started and they were taken to their destination. Now was not the time for her to sit back and relax.

As the SUV jerked with an abrupt start she started counting, spacing how long it would take for them to make the first turn out of the warehouse parking area. Since there was no guarantee their team with the NSA could track them the entire way she planned to mentally calculate where they went using her ears. When music started up, she gritted her teeth.

It was an obnoxious electronic beat but at least it wasn't too loud and there weren't any words. The energy in the vehicle was tense. Even with a hood she could sense it.

These men—four if she had to guess, two in the front and two behind her and Levi—didn't know if they were setting up Tasev so they'd be on guard, focused, until they'd reached their destination. Everything the NSA knew about Tasev said he'd torture and kill anyone who screwed up.

Sixteen counts before they turned left. She knew Levi was doing the same thing, but she couldn't depend on him to remember everything. They wouldn't even be able to record the details of their drive until after they'd left the meeting, and who knew how long that would be.

It also didn't matter that there were eyes in the sky watching them. From this moment forward, they were operating as if they were on their own. For all purposes, they might as well be because they had no way to call in backup if shit went sideways. She wanted to be confident that everything would go off without a hitch, but ops never did. Never, ever. Something always happened, whether it was the thing you prepared for to go wrong or something else. But she refused to let fear rule her. Not with so much at stake.

Nathan Ortiz eased open the oversize glass-pane door of the abandoned house Levi Lazaro and Selene had left a half hour ago. Burkhart wanted him to do a sweep of the premises, but Nathan knew it was a waste of time. Burkhart did too, but they had to do their due diligence just in case Lazaro had left something behind.

Which Nathan found odd considering Burkhart had

told him and the rest of the team on this Tasev op that Lazaro was doing contract work for the NSA.

It was complete and total bullshit.

For some reason Burkhart was allowing Lazaro to be on the op and if Nathan had to guess, he was telling everyone Lazaro was a contract worker to cover his ass in case things blew up in their faces.

But that didn't explain why Burkhart would want Nathan checking up on Lazaro now. Or why the man wasn't at one of their safe houses. Instead it appeared that he'd been basically squatting. Sure, it was a hell of a place to squat, but it didn't make sense if Lazaro had been brought in for the op through normal channels.

Nathan hadn't seen Lazaro in a couple of years, not since his wife had been killed. That thought turned his stomach. He didn't know the details—almost no one at the agency did—but he'd heard the whispers that it had been bad. It had to have been for Levi to just disappear.

Maybe he'd been working for Burkhart all along, but Nathan didn't think so. None of this made sense, but he had his orders: Look for anything Lazaro might have left behind and take it to Burkhart alone. That was it.

Nathan's rubber-soled shoes were silent as he crossed the dusty, hardwood floor of what he guessed would be a living room if it had furniture. He didn't worry that he was leaving footprints because there was no way in hell Lazaro would be coming back here. The home was right on the water with big open windows everywhere and no damn curtains so he didn't need to wear night vision goggles.

Moving quickly and quietly, he paused by a pillar

bathed in shadows and listened intently. Houses and other buildings that were empty had a "feel" to them. After spending years in the Marine Corps and getting the best damn training out there, then being trained by the NSA, he could usually tell when a place was devoid of life.

This one was.

He still didn't let his guard down because for all he knew Lazaro had left booby traps behind. Nathan cleared each room methodically. The only room with any sign of life was one of the bedrooms. There was a mattress and dresser with no dust on it, but there were no personal items to be found anywhere.

Not a surprise. Nathan knew this was a waste of time. Once he was positive the place was clean, he tucked his weapon back in his shoulder holster and left out the front door instead of sneaking out the back. It wasn't as if the doors were even locked and there was no one around to see him leave.

Using the shadows as cover, he casually made his way down the silent street. He'd parked half a mile away. As he walked, he slid his earpiece in, put his battery and SIM card back into his phone, and turned it back on. For stuff like this, even small tasks that were part of a bigger op, they always went dark. He called Wesley and was surprised when Karen picked up the call.

"Ortiz, what's your status?" she demanded.

"Heading back to base now," he said, breaking into a jog at her uncharacteristic tense tone. Karen always kept her cool, so he knew something was wrong.

"Don't. We've got a situation. There were more vehicles than we planned on at the meet and we don't know where the team was taken."

Shit. Not good.

"You're going to be part of the eyes on the ground. I'm going to direct you to the vehicle nearest your location. Then you and Dax will tag team tracking them. I'm patching him in now."

"Got it. I'll be at my vehicle in ten seconds." Heart racing, he picked up his pace. In any op seconds could mean a matter of life and death. And he had a bad feeling that's exactly what hung in the balance for Selene and Lazaro.

Chapter 13

Tradecraft: the methods developed by intelligence operatives to conduct their operations.

Levi allowed himself to be guided along by a loose grip on his elbow as he and Selene walked down what he was certain was a stone driveway. Their hands hadn't been tied, which was standard for something like this. They weren't captives and Levi understood the need for hoods. If Tasev hadn't gone to all this trouble, Levi would have doubted they were really about to meet the man at all.

After an hour of driving, the SUV had finally stopped and they'd been escorted out, hoods still on. The soft clicking of Selene's stilettos let him know she was next to him—that and her peaches and cream scent. For the most part the men in the vehicle had been silent, clearly on guard for an attack.

Which had been good for him since he'd been keeping track of every turn and outside sound. Unfortunately he guessed that half of their drive had just been them going around in circles. Still, as soon as they were able, he was writing down everything and retracing their steps as best he could. Tasev had gone to a lot of trouble to make sure they didn't know where they were, which might mean he was staying at this location.

Levi heard a door being opened. Then someone grunted, "Stairs." After a short walk up four brick stairs that he could see beneath the bottom of his hood, they entered a room. A foyer if the gleaming wood floor he could just barely see was any indication.

With the hood on, it was hard to smell much. The interior of it was hot and moist and he couldn't wait to tear the damn thing off, but even so he just barely scented lemons. As if someone had recently mopped or cleaned. Yes, they were in someone's home. He doubted it was Tasev's permanent place of residence, if the man even had one, but this could be his Miami base.

Levi had to tamp down all emotions inside him. At one time he'd been a perfect agent, a perfect actor, able to blend in anywhere. Since his wife's death he'd turned into a rage-filled machine, ready to strike down anyone that got in his way.

Until Selene.

Now he had her to worry about as well as the safety of countless civilians. Fuck him, why did he have to even care about a bunch of people? Strangers who meant nothing to him?

Because he'd once taken an oath to defend his country against any threat, foreign or domestic. No matter what had happened, that meant something to him. He could still help the NSA and get his revenge at the same time. He could find out if Tasev was guilty, then make him wish he'd never been born. A quick death for Tasev would be too easy.

No way in hell would that happen. The man would suffer for a long time before he took his last breath. That part of Levi had changed and he knew it. He'd never relished death or suffering before. Then he'd lost everything that mattered.

But . . . he had other people to think about now. Selene was counting on him to keep his shit together and do this job.

Selene.

All he had to do was think her name and it brought him back to the here and now. Fuck everything else, he wouldn't let her down.

When his hood was suddenly yanked off, he blinked, letting his eyes adjust to the light as he took in his surroundings. Selene was next to him, her hood removed as well. Her expression was a mask, completely cool and unreadable. Good. Seeing her like this made it clear why Wesley valued her as an agent.

He'd been right; they were in a foyer. A very nice one with polished floors, real wood if he had to guess, and a couple of Monets on the wall. Probably real too. So Tasev liked a certain lifestyle. But what drew all his focus were the seven armed men. Two stood in front of him and Selene while four others were spread out. One was at the bottom of a set of stairs, he felt two men behind them even though they hadn't spoken, and two were on either side giving them about ten yards of space.

It seemed like overkill but Selene's reputation was fierce as The Wolf. She'd been right at the party when she'd told Levi that he shouldn't have had the info on The Wolf's alias, but he'd needed something for an op and his wife had given it to him off the books. Even though he knew that Selene was trained and part of her cover ID was based in truth, the only way to truly know how a person operated in the field was to work with them firsthand.

As they were scanned again with metal detecting wands—which *was* overkill—the man scanning up one of Selene's legs said something vile in Russian about what he'd like to do to her.

Levi made a growling sound low in his throat, knowing he sounded like a fucking animal and not caring. The man's gaze snapped up to him and whatever he saw there made him freeze for a moment before he resumed his scan, this time moving quickly and professionally.

Once they were done, the man with the scar on his neck stepped around from where he'd been hovering behind them. "Time to meet the boss," he said in a voice with a faint accent that might have been Russian, but maybe something else. From the way he walked it was clear the man was trained.

As they strode down multiple hallways, all littered with armed guards, Levi realized Tasev wanted them to see firsthand how much protection he had. It was a psychological thing. The show of force made sense, but Levi ignored that as he drank everything else in.

The handles and locks of the interior doors all looked good, but they weren't high-end from a security standpoint, just expensive and decorative. As they turned down a dead-end hallway he spotted only two doors. The farthest one was metal—reinforced if he had to guess. Otherwise, why have one? There was a guard standing next to it. The door was out of place among the shiny teak floors and matching polished wood trim. And there was a biometric scanner next to the door. Oh yeah, Levi was getting in there eventually.

The other door was wood and when the scarred man knocked on it, Levi could hear the solidness of it. This one was reinforced too.

A moment later a man wearing a black T-shirt and black fatigues opened the door. His gaze scanned over the scarred man in front of them, then Levi and Selene, with his gaze lingering on Selene a little too long for Levi's comfort. He kept his expression impassive though.

In Russian, the scarred man told the man in fatigues that Levi and Selene were clean of weapons and bugs. The man in fatigues nodded once, then uttered something about Selene looking like a good fuck.

It was stupid of them to speak in front of them like this, even in another language. From behind the door, a commanding male voice ordered for them to enter.

Selene and Levi trailed after the scarred man as the other one stepped back. The door shut behind them with a click.

Levi scanned the well-lit room, taking everything in with a sweep. Masculine furniture, thick heavy draperies covering huge windows, wood floors, three armed men—and Tasev sitting behind a big desk like he thought he was a fucking king.

Tasev's dark gaze was assessing as he looked at Selene and Levi. His dark-brown hair was closely cropped to his head and his eyes were intense. Nothing about his gaze was sexual though, as he watched Selene. Just assessing.

And it was definitely Tasev. Though the photos they had of him were older and grainy, Levi didn't doubt the identity of the man before them.

A rush of anger flooded his veins at the sight of Tasev. The man deserved to die for all his crimes whether or not he'd ordered Meghan killed, but Levi ordered all those thoughts back into the darkest part of his mind. He needed his game face on now.

"So you are The Wolf," Tasev said quietly, his gaze pinned to Selene's.

She stood there in a semi-relaxed state and nodded.

"Should I call you Selene or The Wolf?" His voice was softer than Levi had expected.

"Selene."

"It is likely not even your real name though, yes?"

Selene just shrugged, the action subtly shifting the deep V of her jacket and drawing attention to her body. It was a subtle movement and the oldest trick in the book, but Tasev's gaze flicked down to her cleavage for a fraction of a moment. Seconds counted in this business and it was clear she'd use anything in her arsenal to come out on top. In was then that Levi realized why Wesley had chosen her for this job. She was very good.

"A name doesn't matter anyway," Tasev continued. "But your skills do. I would like a demonstration to prove you are who you say—"

Before he'd finished, Selene struck out at the nearest man—the one who said she looked like a good fuck— with her foot, kicking him in the inner thigh with that sharp stiletto. He cried out in a mix of surprise and pain. Before he'd fallen to his knees, she kicked him in the face and slammed him down on the ground. Levi forced himself to stay immobile as the scarred man and two others withdrew their weapons. All his protective instincts roared to the surface in a rush of rage.

Tasev remained where he was and Levi knew the men wouldn't do anything unless he gave an order. It was the only thing that kept him sane. Though he knew he looked calm on the outside, inside, his heart was erratically beating as he had to restrain himself from attacking every man pointing a weapon at Selene.

She wrenched the man's arm behind his back as he writhed in pain. She wasted no time removing a pistol from his back waistband and sliding it away from him. Looking up at Tasev, her eyebrows rose. "Good enough or would you like more?"

"Put your weapons down," Tasev ordered in that soft tone.

His men immediately followed orders, sheathing their pistols with practiced efficiency. Only then did Levi's heart rate begin to return to normal. Sort of.

Tasev didn't bother looking at his men, just flicked out his hand in a sharp gesture. "Grisha, you stay. You two, leave and dispose of that weak piece of garbage," he said, clearly referring to the man on the ground.

Selene rose in a fluid, graceful movement, letting the other men take the injured one away as he made protests and apologies. Levi tuned him out, not caring that he'd likely be killed in the next couple of minutes. Anyone working for Tasev deserved to die.

As the door shut behind the other men, Tasev looked between Selene and Levi, his focus sharpening on Levi. "You are her guard and you let her fight her own battles?"

"I'm not her guard." Levi had no doubt that Tasev knew he'd been at Shah's party. Considering how thorough he'd been tonight, Levi didn't think Tasev would leave anything to chance. He knew who Levi was—his alias—and was testing him.

"I'm his," Selene added.

Tasev's gaze narrowed. "We haven't been introduced, Mr. Moore."

Yep, the German had told Tasev about him. Levi nodded once. "You may call me Isaiah. Selene and I work together. I apologize for the subterfuge in having Selene set up the meeting. I wasn't certain if you were who you said you were or if this was a setup." Because Tasev had been supposedly dead for five years.

"I understand the need to be careful." He motioned for them to sit in the two seats in front of his desk.

The man named Grisha didn't move from his post to Levi's left. He stayed just far enough out of reach that if he drew his weapon it would be impossible for Levi to take it from him without a few long strides. Smart.

Levi and Selene sat almost in unison.

"Are you truly The Wolf?" Tasev asked.

Selene nodded as Levi said, "Yes. She did some work for me a couple of years ago before I brought her on with me full-time."

Tasev's gaze flicked down to their matching watches, but he just nodded as he looked back at Levi. "So Selene is not offering her special services to me?"

"She can if you and I decide to do business together."

Tasev was silent for a long moment, watching Levi. It might have been a tactic to make Levi and Selene nervous but he didn't think so. Tasev was thinking about something, possibly weighing his options. Levi could practically see the wheels turning in the man's head. "Your résumé is impressive," he finally said.

Levi simply nodded since Tasev hadn't asked a question. He never filled silences.

"Why did you leave Shah's party the other night without meeting with Gregor?" Levi found it interesting that Tasev called the German by his first name.

It might mean nothing but he still filed away the information. He wasn't sure why Tasev was asking such an obvious question but maybe he wanted to get a read on Levi when he was telling the truth. It would make it easier for Tasev to gauge when Levi was lying. But Levi had been trained not to give anything away through his own body language or even micro-expressions. Those were a lot more difficult to control and in some cases impossible to completely hide. Luckily most people didn't pick up on them. "There was no point in staying once Selene had the meeting in place."

He nodded, then looked at Selene. "You arrived at Shah's with Alexander Lopez."

She nodded.

"How long have you known him?"

"Long enough." There was a small bite to her words, making Levi hide a smile. She was playing her role perfectly. A high-priced assassin with no employer—and it was clear Levi wasn't actually her boss, but more of a partner—would not deal with authority well or suffer stupid questioning.

Tasev's lip pulled up slightly as he looked back at Levi. "You've worked with some of my associates and still managed to remain clean in the eyes of the law."

Isaiah Moore had indeed done that. Of course, all Isaiah's supposed associates were now dead.

"So, why do you want to do business with me?" Tasev continued.

"Money. We can be a benefit to each other. I know that Paul Hill is in prison and—"

"He's dead."

Levi didn't bother hiding his reaction, wanting Tasev to see what he looked like when he was genuinely surprised. His eyebrows rose the slightest fraction. "Since when?"

"A couple of hours ago."

Levi didn't ask if Tasev had done it because he didn't care and even if he did, it would seem odd for him to question the man. "With Hill out of the way there will be others looking to take over his many businesses. After some inquiries into Hill your name came up so I'm guessing you were in business with him. I don't know if you're taking over for him but if you are, I do a lot of international shipping." He didn't need to say more than that.

If Tasev was interested they would eventually go over the tedious details of shipping illegal cargo and how Levi would keep everything appearing legal.

"Tell me about your pharmaceutical company," Tasev said, getting right to the heart of the matter.

Even though a sharp sense of relief slammed into Levi at the man's words, he feigned surprised in the same way he'd done moments before. "It's one of my legal operations."

"Do you have a fully functioning lab at Moore Pharmaceuticals?"

If anyone actually looked into it they'd find an abandoned building, though Wesley was in the process of giving it a quick makeover complete with fake personnel. There would be cars in the parking lot with employees heading to and from work. It would be set up as if everything was on the up-and-up. Something like that was a piece of cake for one of Wesley's teams. Levi already had an answering service in place for it, just as he did with all of his "legal" companies. "Yes."

"Would you be able to mass-produce something in a limited time frame?"

This was more than Levi had hoped for. But Tasev had clearly taken the bait from Levi's résumé. He punched down the sense of hope inside him that soon he'd be able to destroy the man who had taken everything from him. "That's vague, but if the price is right anything is possible. What they do at the lab is out of my area of expertise, but my team is highly capable. Without speaking to my lead scientist, I'm certain they'll need to know what needs to be mass-produced before giving a definitive time line. And, this is assuming that whatever the drug is, is already created. Which also means my scientists will want access to the creator."

Tasev grunted, the sound neither affirmative nor negative. Leaning forward, he placed both arms on his desk, the flash of excitement in his eyes surprising. "What would you say if I told you that a deadly toxin would be released on American soil, killing hundreds of thousands, maybe more, and we could legally make billions mass-producing the antitoxin?"

Levi smiled, tapping into his full predatory nature

and letting Tasev see what he wanted him to. "I think it's likely we can come to an agreement." Tasev might not realize it yet, but he'd already subconsciously made the decision to work with Isaiah and The Wolf. The way he'd said "we" was a giveaway, as was that flash of excitement in his eyes.

Tasev smiled back, though it was more of a baring of teeth. No matter what happened, Levi wanted this guy dead. He spoke of killing so many innocent people as if it was nothing. "I'll want to see your lab soon but if everything goes as smoothly as I think it will, we'll talk about reviving Hill's former enterprise."

"We can take my personal jet whenever you'd like," Levi said. There was no jet but if he needed to make it happen he'd get his hands on one either through the NSA or from one of his assets.

Tasev nodded once, then half tilted his head in his guard's direction but didn't quite look at him. "Grisha, leave us."

After the scarred man shut the door behind him, Tasev leaned back in his chair and looked at Selene. "Tell me about Alexander Lopez."

For the first time since Levi and Tasev had started talking Selene slightly shifted in her chair, flicking a gaze at Levi—as if asking for permission. Once he nodded she looked back at Tasev. "I don't talk about my contacts or my clients. Ever. If you don't like it, we don't do business together."

It was slight but Tasev relaxed at her blunt words. He stood and nodded at the door. "That's good. Now I have someone I want you to meet."

They left the room with Tasev leading them, completely unguarded. Levi tamped back the energy humming through him. Tasev felt safe in this place and showing them his back was sending a silent message that he thought himself untouchable. Maybe he was.

For now.

But his days were numbered.

Chapter 14

Kidnap: taking someone away illegally by force.

Claus sat across from his daughter where she'd laid out food on the metal lab table. He'd requested red wine for dinner tonight. An expensive vintage he was pleased to see Aliyah enjoyed. Tasev had always given him anything he requested as far as supplies or food. The man might be a monster but he wanted to keep Claus happy.

Until he fulfilled his purpose.

And Claus wanted Aliyah as comfortable as she could be considering she was a captive and terrified for her life. "So tell me why you broke up with your last boyfriend." Since he'd already discovered the coding for the antitoxin he'd been working a little less. Not enough to draw attention but he was soaking up all the time possible with his daughter and getting to know her as much as he could.

Because he feared it would be the only chance he got. He had two days left to give the antitoxin to Tasev and he hadn't heard anything from Meghan. Not that she could actually contact him but Claus had assumed she'd have sent someone to help him and his daughter by now.

Aliyah shrugged in response to his question and Claus forced himself to keep his expression relaxed when all he could do was worry. "It's silly but I didn't feel that *thing*, I guess."

"That thing?"

"You know, that intense attraction that separates him from anyone else. He was good-looking and intelligent and on paper perfect for me but . . . no lasting spark." She speared a piece of salmon and shrugged again in a way he'd come to realize was a habit for her.

"I understand about sparks." He'd had it with her mother but it had been fleeting.

As if she read his mind, Aliyah asked, "Did you and my mom . . . What was it like when you two met?" Her voice was soft and unsure. It was the first time she'd broached the subject. Until now they'd talked about her job and her life growing up. He wanted to know everything.

He put his fork down and started to answer when the main door above them opened, making a sucking sound as it slid to the side. Claus gave Aliyah his knife and nodded toward the area where she slept. "Wait there," he murmured.

She clutched it tightly to her side, her face pinching tight with fear as she slid off the swivel chair and strode toward the bed positioned under the stairs and gangplank. Tasev could realistically do whatever he wanted, but Claus tried to stay separated from his daughter when one of Tasev's men came to see them. It would be easier for him to threaten to take his own life and for her to defend herself with one of the weapons they'd been creating.

Claus looked up, watching as Tasev himself strode in and his heart rate ratcheted up. It was late evening, which was much too late for Tasev to be here. He normally visited in the mornings, wanting to know Claus's progress. But perhaps he was getting antsy.

A cold thread of fear raced down Claus's spine, but he tried to appear unaffected. His gaze instantly moved to the two individuals behind Tasev: a man and a woman.

For a moment he forgot to breathe. It was Levi Lazaro. He didn't know much about the man at all, just that he was Meghan's husband. Claus and Meghan had been friends and had loved discussing art and literature but he'd never spent any time with her husband. Though he had seen his picture and knew who he was. Claus wasn't sure what Levi did for the NSA but they must have received his message after all.

Levi looked at Claus but his expression didn't change. He didn't recognize the blond woman but perhaps she worked with Levi. If he was here though, he wouldn't be working under his real name. Looking off to the side, as he always did, Claus avoided eye contact as Tasev and the other two descended the stairs. Claus fought against the burgeoning hope inside him. Could they really be saved tonight? Could this nightmare be over so quickly?

"This is an impressive setup," Levi said, looking around, acting as if he had no idea who Claus was.

Tasev grunted something and the blonde looked at his dry-erase board. Really looked at it, as if she was reading it. Claus thought that was odd, but maybe she was a scientist.

"Doctor," Tasev said, nodding at him.

Claus remained near the table where his fork was. It wasn't the best weapon but he could use it if necessary.

"Mr. Moore, this is the doctor who is going to change history. He's transformed a type of botulism into a superior strain and is currently working on the antitoxin."

That was technically true about the botulism but Tasev's terminology was so simplistic. As if taking a foodborne type of botulism and turning it into something out of science fiction was so easy. Claus, however, didn't correct him.

"In the next two days I'll be hitting major American cities so if you don't come up with the antitoxin, even more people will die than originally planned," Tasev said, his gaze directly on Claus, likely trying to play on his conscience.

"He only has one assistant?" Levi asked, drawing Tasev's attention away from Claus and to where Aliyah was crouched on her bed, watching the newcomers warily.

"She's not his assistant. She's my insurance that he does everything I ask. Family is a powerful motivator."

Out of the corner of his eye Claus could see the blond woman attempting to look at the back of his double-sided dry-erase board but when Tasev turned, she smoothly moved back and suddenly appeared bored as she glanced around the lab.

"He kidnapped me!" Aliyah shouted, her angry voice slightly echoing around the room. "And whoever you are, you're both monsters for working with him."

"Aliyah!" Claus said, wanting to silence her. Tasev

was smart enough to know he needed Claus but the man was occasionally unpredictable.

She huddled against the mattress, wrapping her arms around her knees. Thankfully Tasev just ignored her and turned back to Levi. "You have seen my lab. I will want to see yours." There was a familiar edge to Tasev's voice as he spoke to Levi—or Mr. Moore.

Levi nodded casually, ignoring Claus and Aliyah. "As soon as you're ready. I don't know if you plan on keeping him around"—he nodded at Claus—"but my scientists will most definitely want to talk to the creator so don't kill him just yet."

Though Levi didn't look at him or give any type of signal, the man had to be here for them. And he was trying to keep them alive.

Tasev laughed, the sound cutting and sharp. "I think we're going to work well together. Come, let's share a drink to a new partnership."

As they left, the woman glanced over her shoulder and met Claus's gaze. For a moment her expression softened before she turned from him, her back ramrod straight as she headed up the stairs.

"They're going to kill us anyway," Aliyah said as she stood, trembling. Even though she was terrified the anger in her eyes was raw and clear.

"Let's finish eating," he said, hoping to draw her back to the table.

She looked as if she wanted to argue but nodded and made her way back, knife in hand.

"Tasev can be unstable," he murmured, all he would say about the man. "Don't give him a reason to take it out on you."

"I hate just waiting to die. Because that's what we're essentially doing." She took a big swig of her wine, downing the entire glass, the fire in her eyes flaring even brighter. He loved her fighting nature. She'd been traumatized and thrown into a terrible situation but she'd been keeping it together incredibly well.

It made him proud as a father.

Even though he hated the idea of giving her false hope, he took the risk. Silently, he pushed his food around his plate, and spelled out "help is coming" with his rice pilaf before he scattered the grains and took a bite.

She blinked rapidly, as if fighting tears, then took the bottle of wine and refilled both their glasses. "Don't think I've forgotten our conversation. I want to know more about you and my mother."

It was the last thing Claus wanted to talk about, but for Aliyah he'd do anything. At least she seemed more settled because now in addition to the fire he saw hope.

He just prayed that Levi and the woman had truly come to help them.

Chapter 15

Burn phone: prepaid disposable phone.

Selene blinked in surprise as her hood was whipped off. After sharing a drink with Tasev, she and Levi had been escorted from the property in the same fashion they'd been taken. The second time being hooded was easier, partially because the meeting had gone so well and all she could focus on now was taking Tasev down.

"You're sure this is where you want to go?" the scarred man asked as he pulled up to one of the drop-off terminals at Miami International Airport.

Levi had told the man where to take them and though the man named Grisha had given them a surprised look, he hadn't questioned them until now. Levi just grunted and opened the door. They'd still had four guards in the SUV with them but the atmosphere had been more relaxed compared to the drive to Tasev's place.

Selene wasn't stupid enough to think that more men hadn't followed. Tasev was sure to attempt to track them. Which was why they'd come to the airport. Unfortunately this airport didn't have storage lockers so one of her teammates had stashed a bag of clothes and burner phones for them in one of the public bathrooms.

Selene moved out after Levi, not bothering to glance back at the SUV as they made their way to the sliding glass doors. It was late enough that it wasn't rush hour, but this airport always had a steady stream of activity. They planned to use that to their full advantage.

A cool rush of the air conditioner rolled over them as they entered near a Delta check-in area. Knowing exactly where they were, Selene started to calculate how long it would take them to make it to the designated bathroom, which was roughly four terminal entrances away. Not too bad.

Levi took her hand in his, threading his fingers through hers, and tugged her in another direction. "This way," he murmured.

"Our stuff is the other way." Something he had to know. She'd seen him poring over the layout to the airport earlier. Just like her, he didn't like to leave anything to chance.

"We're not using it." He scanned their surroundings as they casually strode around a group of tourists with matching yellow shirts.

"Why not?" Everything they needed would be in their stash bag; clothes, phones, and even keys to a car Wesley had left for them in one of the parking lots.

Levi didn't respond, just continued walking. They passed a Starbucks, Pizza Hut, and a sushi bar before he guided them into a big store with books and touristy crap. "Grab generic-colored T-shirts for us, flat shoes for you, and a travel or tote bag," he said before heading to a section of travel books, prepaid calling cards, and throwaway phones.

She knew what he was doing and didn't blame him. He didn't want clothes or phones from the NSA because she had no doubt Wesley had tagged some of the belongings in the stash bag. But that didn't explain what he planned to use for transportation.

Selene didn't question him though because there was no point. Hurrying to a rack of clothes, she grabbed a sage green T-shirt with a picture of Florida on it since it was the least ugly out of the pathetic selection. At least the men's clothing section was somewhat better. She found a plain black T-shirt with a small logo of Florida on the pocket for him. The shoe selection was the worst of all but she settled on a pair of dark blue Ked-style sneakers—for fifty freaking dollars—because they were the only ones dark enough to semi-blend in with her pants. She didn't need anything that would make her stand out worse than the shirt and if they had to run from anyone, doing it in her stilettos wasn't the best plan. She also grabbed a wire-bound notepad with Mickey Mouse on the front. Levi might think it was weird but she planned to use this as soon as she could. With her eidetic memory she could recall pretty much anything, but all those math symbols from Dr. Schmidt's dry-erase board could get jumbled if she didn't get them down on paper soon. Sure she'd have everything transferred but it might be in the wrong order. Since she was pretty sure that was the antitoxin he'd been working on, she needed to get this to Wesley as soon as possible.

She met Levi at the checkout counter with a blue-and-white-striped tote bag. He had two plain black ball caps and four burner phones. Wordlessly he bought everything with cash.

Pausing at the exit of the store, he reached out and cupped her cheek, gently stroking his thumb over her skin. A shiver rolled through her even though the timing was stupid. "The one named Grisha is at ten o'clock, outside the Armani store sitting on a bench."

"I see another one at two o'clock by a sunglasses kiosk." And there would be more they didn't see.

Levi nodded, as if this was expected—because it was. It would actually be pathetic if Tasev didn't try to have them tailed. "I'm going to head west, you head east. Pick a populated bathroom and change," he said as he slipped one of the phones in her tote bag. "Ditch what you can, then wait five minutes before exiting. Try to leave with a crowd of people. Then head to the third level of the south garage."

She'd memorized the layout of the MIA so she knew how long it would take her to get there if there were no snags. And she expected to be followed. They'd have to lose their tails in the heart of Miami somewhere. Selene started to nod but was suddenly struck with the realization that Levi could ditch her.

Hell, he had no reason to stay with her if he'd memorized the drive to Tasev's place. If he had, he could easily get back there himself and take out Tasev. Before she could voice anything, Levi grabbed her hand in his and headed west, taking her with him. "New plan."

"Why? What's happened?" A shot of adrenaline surged through her. Had he seen more of Tasev's men?

"I can see you think I'm going to cut and run so we're going to find a ride together." He sounded annoyed but his grip on her hand simply tightened.

"I didn't—"

"Yes, you did. Don't fucking lie to me," he snapped, cutting her a sharp look.

She kept her mouth closed because he was right. Instead of stopping in one of the bathrooms they got on a shuttle and headed to the north parking garage. The south garage would be a better place to escape from because the exit would quickly take them to a main highway where they could blend into traffic.

At the north garage main floor, Levi nodded toward one of the stairwell doors instead of the elevators. Once inside, he stripped off his jacket.

She looked around for cameras but didn't see any. Not that it seemed to matter to Levi because he was already moving into action.

"Change," he ordered, moving with a beautiful liquid grace as he pulled the plain T-shirt on over that deliciously muscular body.

Forcing herself into action she quickly changed into the T-shirt and sneakers and shoved her other clothing in the tote bag. She took the ball cap from Levi and pulled her tightly wound bun through it.

"We'll head to the third level and find a vehicle to steal. They've probably got a tail waiting for us at the exit but we'll just lose them on the streets," he said, grabbing the bag from her and moving for the stairs.

"Works for me."

Silently they raced up the flights of stairs, both pausing at the third-floor door before Levi eased it open to scan for anyone. Once he nodded that it was all clear they hurried out into the garage. Still no sign of a tail.

Levi pointed that he was headed left and she should go right. That panicky feeling welled up inside her as she worried he'd ditch her, but she ruthlessly shoved it back. If he wanted to leave, he would and there was little she could do about it unless she planned on shooting him. Not that she had a weapon handy—and she'd never actually shoot him.

He seemed to sense her train of thought because he cursed before crushing his mouth over hers in a hungry, intense, and far too short kiss before he raced away, moving like a lethal panther.

She barely had time to catch her breath after that kiss. Even though she could taste and feel him lingering on her lips, she ignored it and briskly walked toward the nearest row of vehicles. The rows in the parking garage stretched farther than she could see so she figured starting close was smart.

After passing up a dozen newer-model cars she found an old Pontiac that had to be from the eighties. Since she didn't have anything useful to pop the locks, she leaned back against the nearest car for support and lifted a leg, ready to kick out the passenger window. It would be noisy but that couldn't be helped. As she started to haul back and attempt to fracture the glass enough that she could break it out in pieces, an engine rumbled loudly nearby.

Ducking down to hide, she heard her name being called. Popping back up, she saw Levi behind the wheel of a souped-up black Mustang. Either a '67 or '68.

A sharp bolt of relief rolled through her that he hadn't left her. Rolling her eyes at the type of vehicle, she raced from her hiding spot and slid into the passenger seat. "Seriously? A muscle car?"

He laughed low, the wicked sound making her nipples tighten against her will. She was in so much trouble where this man was concerned. "We'll trade it out as soon as we lose them, but for now this is the best option because it's fast, durable, and there are no airbags."

"Only car old enough to steal?"

His lips quirked up at the corners. "Yeah. Fucking hate those newer models."

The newer the vehicle, the harder it tended to be to take unless you had the right equipment. And it wasn't like she ran around with a car thief kit twenty-four/seven. Though maybe she should start.

As they wound down the garage, heading for the main level, Levi shot her a sideways look. "You seriously thought I'd ditch you?"

She shrugged and glanced around, looking for a possible tail even though she knew the likelihood of that was slim. Tasev's men would be waiting to follow them as soon as they exited the garage. It made the most sense. "It's not that crazy."

He was silent but she could feel the anger pulsing off him every second that passed, as if it was a live thing and she knew this conversation wasn't over. Just on hold. Ignoring him, she pulled the notepad from the tote bag and breathed a sigh of relief when she found a pen in the glove compartment.

"Can you watch for the tails alone or do you need more eyes?" she asked as she flipped it open to the first page. Heart racing, she started writing down everything she remembered. Some of the symbols made no sense to her, but she knew they would to someone.

"Yeah . . . holy shit, you remember all that." It was more of a statement than a question as he flicked a look at the pad.

"I basically have an eidetic memory," she muttered, trying to tune him out even though that was pretty much impossible. By just being in the same room, the man was a huge distraction.

He let out a low whistle but didn't say anything as she worked. After he paid the parking attendant and they exited, Levi straightened next to her, his entire body becoming rigid and controlled as he maneuvered onto the airport road that would take them to the highway.

"How many are there?" she asked, her pen still flying over the pad.

"Three."

Damn, Tasev wasn't messing around. She trusted Levi enough to get them out of there so she focused on her task. Levi was using some serious evasive driving skills, making random turns and gunning it at yellow lights. She didn't bother trying to pay attention to where he was taking them or memorize their path. She couldn't let anything distract her from her own task.

Fifteen minutes later she finished all she'd seen in that lab—which unfortunately wasn't everything since there had been more writing on the back of the board— and fished out one of the new throwaway phones.

It took a few minutes to activate it but once she did she took multiple pictures and sent them all to one of Wesley's private cell numbers with a message telling him what it was and that she'd check in soon. She wouldn't call him until she had a secure line. As soon as all the pictures went through, she deleted them from the phone. She'd save the notebook for Wesley too but she wanted him to have the information as soon as possible.

She grasped the side of the door when Levi suddenly took a sharp turn. "We're down to one," he said. "Grab all our stuff."

Shoving the notebook into the waistband of her pants, she unstrapped her seat belt and held the tote bag in her lap. Bright neon lights and the wild flashes of color from the Miami nightlife were a blur as they cruised down Ocean Boulevard. She wasn't sure what Levi's plan was but she trusted him whatever it was.

So far he'd been straightforward and competent. And he'd changed his original plan when he'd realized she thought he'd leave her. Selene didn't know how to feel about that. It could be another calculated way to gain her trust, but she didn't know what the point would be. Of course there was a chance she was missing something . . . that he had another angle she didn't know about.

As he took another turn down a quiet side street with no parking allowed, she was surprised when he jerked to a halt and parked. "Come on," he snapped as he pulled his door open and jumped out.

She was right with him. He tossed the keys into a storm drain as she fell in step. They weren't running, but when headlights flashed behind them they picked up their pace into a jog. Thankfully there was no one on the street. "What's the plan?" It wasn't as if they were in a race for their lives. Tasev wouldn't have let them go if he'd wanted them dead so she knew the men following them would give up eventually.

"Metrorail's right around the corner. I don't feel like driving around all night humoring these fuckers," he muttered.

"I don't have any small bills with me." As far as she knew the Metrorail took only ones or fives. "We can use the Metromover instead." It was free to everyone.

"I've got an EASY pass for both of us."

Though she was surprised, Selene didn't say anything. Sure enough, when they reached the end of the street a Metrorail stop was across the intersection. Thank God.

There was no guarantee that one of Tasev's men wouldn't somehow follow them on the Metrorail but it was doubtful. And she had no doubt she and Levi could lose them anyway. It was just tedious and wasted valuable time.

Once they were on the transit system, she and Levi found two empty seats in the car. Instead of sitting immediately they both stood, scanning all passengers for anyone who looked out of place. As the doors closed they sat, with Levi wrapping his arm around her shoulders. The action took her by surprise, but she leaned into him, soaking up the feel of his strength.

"I can't believe you have EASY passes."

"I'm always prepared," he murmured against the top of her head. "And I can't believe you thought I'd fucking ditch you." He spoke low so no one around them could hear.

The car wasn't that crowded anyway and they had three seats in between them and anyone else.

She tried to pull back so she could look at him, but he held her tight, his body rigid with an unspoken tension. Oh yeah, he was pissed. Sighing, she laid her head on his shoulder. "Can you blame me?"

He didn't respond, only speaking a few moments

later when a pregnant Hispanic woman with a toddler in tow approached them and asked if the seats next to them were taken.

"So, Spanish and Russian," she murmured. "What other languages do you speak?" She could tell that he'd understood that asshole back at Tasev's. It was stupid of the men to have spoken in Russian not knowing if they understood it but maybe it had been a test. Who knew?

"Don't act like you don't know," he said quietly.

She cringed at the edge to his voice as she was reminded that she had an advantage by knowing more about him than he did about her. It would definitely annoy him. "I know what your file says but that doesn't mean it has everything pertinent."

"You first."

"Russian, Czech, Spanish, Italian, German, a little Norwegian—which means I can also speak passable Danish and Swedish." With her memory she simply had an affinity for languages. Plus, so many of them had the same roots it was easier to pick up say, Italian, once she'd learned Spanish.

"Show-off," he muttered, a trace of humor in his voice. "So you speak Spanish too?"

"Yeah. Where'd you learn yours from?" His file hadn't said if it had been school.

"My grandparents on both sides emigrated from Spain and my parents made sure I learned the language."

"European Spanish?"

"Castilian."

"Ah. Is that how you picked up Arabic so quickly? Your file said you were a quick study."

He chuckled softly. "Yeah . . . That thing you did with the equations, did you pay attention to our route when we were driving?" She noticed he was careful not to mention that they'd been hooded or to say anything else to draw attention to them.

"Yes. When we stop again I'm going to write it all down and compare it with a map of the city, see if I can cross-reference our pacing."

"Good. I kept track too so we should be able to narrow down the location."

She stiffened slightly. So he didn't know where Tasev's place was. He still needed her. It was why he hadn't ditched her.

Leaning close again, his breath was hot against her ear. "You and I are going to have to talk about your trust issues."

Selene didn't respond because there was nothing to say. Besides, she didn't want to talk with Levi. And wasn't that the problem. She wanted to do things that didn't involve any talking. Well, maybe it did if you counted dirty talk.

No. Focus.

Sighing, she closed her eyes and replayed everything in her head that she remembered from the drive to Tasev's place. Sometimes the practice helped her to drag up something saved in her memory bank that she might have missed otherwise. She might have an eidetic memory but her memory certainly wasn't perfect. And Levi played hell on her concentration at the best of times.

Chapter 16

Unmanned aerial vehicle (UAV): aka drone, an aircraft without a human pilot physically aboard. Controlled by computers or a pilot at another location.

Levi stood next to an oak tree as Selene talked to Wesley on one of the burner phones he'd bought at the airport. This was one he'd be ditching soon enough. They were at a park about five blocks from one of his safe houses. In a safe part of Coral Gables at this time of night, it was quiet and secluded. Perfect for their privacy needs.

From her half of the conversation he'd gathered that the equations she'd sent to Wesley were legit. According to the team of scientists the NSA was using, Schmidt was on the right track with the antitoxin to the toxin.

The toxin he'd created. Not that Levi would throw stones. It was clear the man had done it to protect his daughter, but what else had he done to save the girl and his own skin? All Levi knew was that Meghan had been going to see Schmidt before she died. She was dead and Schmidt was alive and working for Tasev.

Levi wanted to know if the man had been involved

in her death. For all Levi knew, the doctor had lied to the NSA. Maybe he'd gone into business with Tasev, then realized how dangerous the terrorist was and now needed a way out.

From what he knew of the man Levi didn't think so, but he didn't care either way. He just knew that if Schmidt had been involved in Meghan's murder, he was dead too.

With a sigh of annoyance, Selene ended the call and handed the phone to him as she stood up from the metal bench. He took out the battery and shoved the pieces into his pocket. He'd been listening to her conversation with Wesley and she hadn't given any indication that she was leading Wesley to them.

"You know they could probably figure out where we're going if they wanted to track us," she said.

He shrugged. Maybe, maybe not. They wouldn't be using satellite or drone resources right now if he had to bet. Levi doubted he was worth *that* much to Wesley, especially when he had bigger problems to deal with. And there was no other way the NSA could track them. They were in a suburban area with no CCTVs. Of course, they could use another angle and try to figure out where his safe house was based on unoccupied homes in the area. But he hadn't picked an empty home this time.

An old asset was allowing him to use his own home while the man was out of town on business. If the NSA managed to link Levi to his asset, then he could see them finding him and Selene, but that was a long shot.

"I want a few hours of sleep without worrying that Wesley will bust me."

Selene rolled her eyes. "Let's get out of here. I want to record everything I remember from the drive. Does this place have Internet?"

"Yep."

"Good. Then what are we waiting for?" She still held on to the blue-and-white tote bag, clutching it to her side as she watched him warily.

He knew he should wait until they were at the safe house for this conversation but if he did, he'd end up kissing her and then they'd end up naked. Which he hoped happened, but first he wanted to hash some stuff out. "I want to discuss the fact that you assumed I'd leave you."

"I did . . . until I realized you haven't figured out where Tasev's home is either."

He gritted his teeth, angry at her, even though he couldn't blame her reasoning. The truth was, if she was anyone but Selene, he'd seriously consider ditching her. But he couldn't hang her out to dry. Even if he could let a countless number of people die—which he couldn't—he'd never leave her to deal with the fallout because he'd left her. She'd vouched for him to Wesley and while Wesley still made the final decision about ops, she'd stood behind him instead. For all he knew it could seriously damage her career or call into question her competence. He couldn't be sure what the fallout would be, but there would be consequences. "Believe what you want, but I promise that I won't fuck you over. We're a team until this thing is through and we both get what we want."

Her pale gaze locked on him for a long moment before she nodded. "I won't screw you over either."

"Because you think you owe me?" She'd still never explained what she'd said to him at Shah's party, though Levi could guess it was because of Meghan helping her.

Selene shrugged. "At first yes, and, okay, yes, that's still why but I think you got a raw deal when everything happened. I'd never say this to Wesley but I don't think the agency handled things the way they should have. I think he was stunned by your wife's death and even though he's been looking for her killers for two years, I don't think he should have kept you off the investigation—even if it was protocol. And I know he tried to keep you out of the loop. If someone pulled that crap with me, I'd have gone off the reservation too and taken things into my own hands. Meghan deserves justice. It doesn't matter that almost no one knows what happened to her, her killers got away with it, and if they know she was an agent, they think they got away with fucking over our government in the process. Which means others will know too. All terrorists need to be aware that there will be consequences to their actions, that we will hunt them down to the ends of the earth if they come after our people."

He blinked in surprise at the passion in her voice as she finished. "That's quite a speech."

"It's how I feel," she snapped, her tone defensive.

Even though talking about his dead wife with the woman he wanted more than his next breath should have been weird, it wasn't. It was freeing. He liked that Selene knew exactly who he was, what Meghan had meant to him. Acting a part and lying all the time to maintain his cover was damn exhausting. "I believe you."

"Well, I guess I'm going to have to believe you too." She played with the hem of her tacky tourist shirt as she eyed him, still a little wary.

"So reassuring." His voice was dry.

She shrugged and changed the subject. "I want to get out of here. We need to start on the mapping."

Knowing she was right, he nodded. Everything else could take a backseat until they figured out where the hell Tasev was located.

Wesley stood next to Karen's desk with his arms crossed over his chest. Urgency hummed through him and he didn't fight the sensation. He knew that Selene would figure out where Tasev was located soon. He'd heard it in her voice when he'd asked her.

She hadn't said so directly though and it was because she was with Levi. And Wesley was done letting her go completely dark with him. Not when they were so close to discovering Tasev. He needed eyes on Selene. Now. She was one of his best agents and more than that, he worried about her in a way he didn't other agents. Not because she wasn't capable—he'd never have put her in the field if she wasn't so damn good—but because he loved her like a daughter. He'd never had a family other than the Navy and now the people he worked with and Selene meant more to him than anyone. He'd never forget the first time he'd met her; she'd been scared and still defiant as hell. And she'd had all sorts of demands of what she wanted if she agreed to work for him. It had been mostly bluster though, her attitude. Something he understood about her now. After losing her family she'd been alone and had put up walls against everyone in an effort to protect herself.

"The phone went dead but I pinged their location," Karen murmured as she continued typing commands into her computer. Her words pulled Wesley out of his head. "Patching Carafano in now . . . Carafano, you're on with me and Burkhart."

"Hey Stafford," Eric Carafano said, his voice light and teasing. "Miss me?"

She snorted. "What's your location?"

"The drone's closing in on the coordinates you gave me. Just one . . . minute. All right, we've got three subjects visible. Your screen up yet?"

"No," Karen said, frustration in her voice as she continued working her magic on the computer.

It didn't matter how much technology they had, sometimes delays were inevitable. Wesley didn't react because there was nothing he could do as they waited for the same screen to pop up on their end. Carafano was manning the Miami drone all the way from Maryland.

"That's all right, I've got a clear visual of the neighborhood. Not much movement this time of night. I see two subjects moving together east and one subject with what appears to be the heat signature of a very small animal. Which one am I following?"

"The two subjects," Wesley said.

"On it."

"Our screen is up," Karen said almost simultaneously.

Wesley looked up from Karen's computer to the bigger screen on the wall behind it.

Carafano continued tracking the two heat signatures leaving the park where Karen had last pinged Selene's cell phone signal. Now all they had to do was wait for them to stop somewhere. And Wesley knew they'd have to. It was late and they'd need rest. Levi might be trained and highly motivated, but he was still human and needed to recharge.

Karen was silent as she pulled up another screen with a map of the Miami neighborhood where the drone was tracking. The couple passed a few more heat signatures as they made steady progress down various streets. Eventually they stopped at one house and from the angle of the neighborhood map, it appeared as if they entered through the back door instead of the front.

"Stay on them another twenty minutes," Wesley said to Carafano. He wanted to make sure it was them and that they stayed put.

Before he could ask Karen for the address she said, "E-mailing you the address and coordinates now."

"Good. Run a check on the owner of the house and any connection to subject one." Wesley didn't say Levi's name out loud since Carafano was still on the comm. He hadn't been read in on the op because it wasn't necessary. Wesley just needed him to be his eyes in the sky right now. For all he knew the house was abandoned, but something told him Levi wouldn't use the same MO two times in a row. He'd want to mix things up.

"On it now," she said, moving into action.

"Get me if you need me," he said to her. Then, "Thanks, Carafano. Appreciate the assistance."

"Anytime."

Wesley clicked off the secure channel and headed for his office. First he called Ortiz and ordered him to head to base. Then he dialed Jack. It was late but the man should be up. Wesley just hoped he was willing to take a last-minute mission.

Wesley didn't even know if he'd need Jack, but he believed in being prepared. And if it became necessary to detain Levi there was no one he trusted more than Jack.

Chapter 17

Blown: discovery of an agent's true identity or a clandestine activity's true purpose.

Selene looked at the map on Levi's laptop, then the foldout map he'd found at his asset's house. Levi hadn't actually said they were staying at an asset's house but he'd had the security code and didn't seem concerned about anyone returning home. He also wasn't concerned with keeping the lights off so no one would know they were inside.

A man definitely owned the house, considering the heavy masculine furniture and the ridiculous oversize flat-screen television on one of the living room walls. That and the surround sound were dead giveaways. She guessed it could belong to a friend of Levi's but she doubted it. He hadn't had many associates listed in his files and none of them were in Miami so it stood to reason that whoever owned this house owed Levi or Isaiah Moore—or one of his other aliases—a favor.

"What do you remember next?" Levi asked as he traced a pencil along one of the streets.

"I . . ." She closed her eyes, trying to recall how many

seconds had passed from the last turn. "Maybe ten seconds of driving, then we stopped, but not for long. After that we took a left-hand turn."

When she opened her eyes, she found him nodding as he eyed the map critically. "It should be this street then. I can't tell from either of the maps, but I'm guessing it was a stop sign." They'd narrowed down Tasev's house to a specific area southwest of downtown Miami. Tasev's place had to be in Coral Gables. Where exactly, she wasn't certain.

But she had her suspicions. Unfortunately for Levi, she wasn't going to tell him. Guilt swelled inside her but she couldn't reveal the location yet. She didn't want to screw him over and if she had to kill Tasev off the books a couple of weeks from now after the op was over, she would. She just . . . couldn't tell him her suspicions on the location yet. For all she knew he'd leave in the middle of the night and mess up their entire op in his quest for revenge. She trusted him but she also knew that she wasn't exactly objective right now. And the truth was, right now wasn't about her. She had to do what was best for the op, for the hundreds of thousands of innocent people out there. If that meant holding back information, she had to do it.

"What next?" he asked, zooming in on the online map.

She shook her head. "I don't know. I started to panic a couple of times because of the hood." Which was actually true. But she did remember what direction they'd gone in next and she was almost a hundred percent positive that Tasev was staying in the same damn neighborhood as Shah: Tahiti Beach.

It would make sense, considering how exclusive and

cut off the area was. And she remembered them slowing down for a guard gate, so the neighborhood Tasev was in was gated. There were a lot of gated communities in Miami, but not many in the area they'd narrowed it down to.

Levi watched her for a long moment, his dark eyes unreadable. She couldn't tell if he believed her or not so she remained expressionless. Finally, he scrubbed a hand over his face and turned back to the computer. She resisted the urge to let out a relieved breath. Now was not the time to relax.

"We need some fucking sleep," he said, more to himself than her.

They'd been going over what they remembered for almost an hour and comparing it to their maps. Some things were impossible to say with certainty so they'd had to guesstimate driving times.

"We *need* to rescue Dr. Schmidt and his daughter." Selene hated the fear she'd seen on that woman's face.

"If he had anything to do with Meghan's death, he's dead too." Levi's expression was almost defiant as he watched her. As if he expected or wanted her to argue with him.

Selene just rolled her eyes and collapsed back against the leather couch, throwing an arm over her face as she leaned her head back. "Think you can hold off killing him until we get the antitoxin?" she muttered. She was mentally exhausted and didn't have the energy to get into anything with him. It was always like this after an undercover situation. She'd get a dump of adrenaline, then not exactly crash, but slow way down. Even with how tired she was she still couldn't turn off her attraction to him. It still simmered right under the surface, that awareness of him driving her insane.

"Where do you want to sleep?" he asked. She felt the couch depress as Levi sat next to her.

She dropped her arm and tilted her head toward him. "You don't want to keep going?"

He shook his head, something in his gaze making her stomach flip. She ignored it . . . for the moment.

"I need to send what we've got to Wesley. They might be able to narrow it down faster than us."

"We've still got two days according to Schmidt's message, right?"

"Yeah." But that didn't mean anything. Tasev could split town or decide to send out another team to poison another water source and they might not get a tip this time. Anything could go wrong and they needed the NSA on this.

Levi didn't respond, just watched her like he was picturing her naked, his train of thought clearly different from hers. It was jarring and erotic at the same time. She didn't *want* to want Levi like she did, but there was no fighting it.

But she knew what she had to do. She had to tell Wesley her suspicions about where Tasev's base of operations was.

Levi would see this as a betrayal, she knew that. It wasn't actually one but she had a feeling he wouldn't care.

No matter her feelings for him or how raw a deal he'd gotten, she still had to put innocent people first. Damn it, she had to send the information to Wesley. She also knew that as soon as she went behind Levi's back, things would be over between them. He wasn't the forgiving type even if her actions were justified. He wouldn't care.

No matter how much her gut told her Levi didn't want innocent civilians hurt any more than she did, he was still a wild card. Grief made people unpredictable. She couldn't take the risk that he would let his rage get in the way. Because if she trusted him and she was wrong . . . no way that was going to sit on her soul. She'd been wrong about people before, specifically a man she'd been involved with, so she knew it was easy to be blinded to what was right in front of you. She simply didn't have the right to risk that many people's lives.

She opened her mouth to convince him that they needed to contact Wesley. A last-ditch effort before she did it anyway. Before she could speak Levi moved faster than she'd imagined possible, covering her mouth with his in a dominant, possessive display that stole her breath.

She'd been aware of him all damn night but this was a shock to her senses.

His slid his big hand around to the back of her neck, cupping her nape gently. His hold made her feel too many things.

The most selfish part of Selene didn't care that she was breaking all sorts of rules by doing this. She wanted Levi in a way she'd never wanted anyone.

She ordered herself to shove him off, to put an end to this but as his tongue flicked against hers, she realized she had no self-control. He'd completely stripped it from her.

When she found herself clutching his shoulders she

knew she'd lost her damn mind. But not entirely. She snapped her head back, her breathing erratic as she stared into his dark eyes. "Levi—"

"I want to hear you shouting my name as I thrust into you," he whispered darkly. "I want to taste your release on my tongue as you ride my face."

She felt her face flame at his words. She'd never thought a man talking dirty to her could be a turn-on, but there was something so primal about the way his voice shook and the way he looked, as if he wanted to devour her.

You can't.

She slid a hand down to his chest and lightly pushed. "Levi—" she started again but he cut her off when he grabbed her by the hips and tugged her so that she had to straddle his lap. Her knees sank into the couch, pushing her farther over his erection. She couldn't fight the moan that escaped at the feel of that thickness between her legs.

"Here or one of the beds?" he murmured against her mouth.

"Bed." It was all she could manage to squeeze out even though she knew she should have said no. But she knew herself well enough that she'd regret it forever if she didn't take this time with Levi. Because she'd never get another chance after tonight. For once she was going to be selfish, to take what she wanted. The intense attraction to him had surprised her probably as much as it had seemed to shock him and she just couldn't walk away from this kind of chemistry.

The word had barely left her lips before he stood with her in his arms, his long muscular legs eating up the distance down the hallway to the nearest bedroom. The guestroom she'd seen earlier. It was bare except for a queen-size bed with a blue comforter set. And a bed was all they needed. She didn't give a shit about the decorations.

Taking her by surprise, he set her down on the edge of the bed and slowly reached out and cupped her cheek. He was being so gentle it stunned her. She'd expected him to more or less pounce so this took her off guard. "What are you doing?" she whispered, not surprised when her voice shook. She was barely keeping it together. Her entire body hummed with a raw awareness that she knew only he could satisfy and it seemed as if he wanted to take his time.

Keeping his gaze on hers, he let his hand fall and reached for the button of her black pants. Wordlessly, he undid them before helping her shimmy out of them. The whole time he kept his eyes glued to hers, the heat in that dark gaze growing with each second.

She could feel herself falling under his spell, helpless to stop it as he reached for her touristy Florida T-shirt. She was already damp between her legs and they hadn't even done anything. Her nipples tightened as she thought of him seeing all of her. He might have seen a flash of skin in the bathroom of that first safe house but that was different. She didn't plan to throw soap at his head this time.

Acting braver than she felt, Selene lifted her arms and let him tug the shirt and her skin-tone camisole top off. Once she was completely bared to his dark gaze she couldn't even think about covering up. She loved the way he was staring at her, as if she was the most desirable woman on the planet. It was thrilling and made her feel powerful in a way she'd never imagined.

When he knelt in between her legs, she grew even wetter. She should probably tell him she hadn't done the actual deed before, but what if he stopped? She'd fooled around with guys in the past and had almost made the decision to sleep with her first and only real boyfriend, but when she'd discovered what a piece of garbage he was, things had ended and . . . right about now she wished she had a little more experience.

"Where'd you just go?" Levi murmured as he slid a hand up one of her bare thighs.

His palm was hot against her skin and she wondered what it would feel like to have him cupping her most intimate area. It seemed unfair that she was practically naked except for her thong and he was still dressed. Especially since she wanted to see and touch everything she'd been fantasizing about.

"Nowhere," she whispered, reaching out for his T-shirt. Yeah, that had to go.

"Don't lie to me. Not here." As he spoke, he slid his hand the rest of the way up her thigh and teased the edge of the barely there black lace, dipping underneath until his finger teased the top of her mound. He wasn't even close to her clit, but her inner walls clenched in need just the same.

"I was thinking . . . that this isn't casual for me." Shit, why had she said *that*? A man like Levi didn't want to hear that.

"You think it is for me?" he asked as he withdrew his hand.

Just when she was about to mourn the loss of his

touch, he cupped her mound over her thong. She held on to his shoulders to steady herself, feeling more exposed than she ever had, but at the same time completely free.

Levi might hate her once everything was said and done but for now she knew she could trust him with her body. She'd been fantasizing about this since he'd approached her at the party.

Slowly, he rubbed the heel of his palm over her clit. "You gonna answer?" he demanded in a harsh whisper.

"I don't know." It was the truth. She didn't know what *this* was for him. Even so, she trusted him right here and right now.

"I haven't been with anyone since my wife. I haven't wanted to—until you. This isn't fucking casual." His dark eyes glittered with so much emotion it made it hard to breathe.

She tried to rein the words back in, to keep from telling him what he deserved to know—what she didn't want to say. But she knew she had to. It wasn't even that big of a deal, but he had a right to know. "I haven't been with anyone. Ever."

He blinked as he stopped rubbing his palm against her clit. At least he didn't completely remove his hand. "What?"

She shrugged, suddenly feeling exposed in a way she hadn't seconds ago. "It's not like I've been saving myself for marriage or anything. And it's not like I'm completely inexperienced. I've done . . . stuff. I was recruited young and I haven't had a conventional upbringing I guess." That being the understatement of the freaking century.

He slowly started moving his palm again, the friction wonderful. "How old were you?" he asked, sliding her thong completely to the side so that it was flesh to flesh.

His callused finger teased the entrance of her slit but he didn't penetrate or make a move to tease her clit any harder. Combined with his intense gaze on her face it was hard to concentrate on his question. Just the feel of him caressing her like this was so different from her own touch.

Her fingers dug into his shoulders as she found her voice. "Sixteen."

He frowned at her answer and she understood why. It was incredibly young but her job had saved her life in more ways than one and she'd be forever grateful. "How old are you now?"

She was glad he hadn't stopped what he was doing but she couldn't believe he wanted to talk. Obviously he didn't care that she was a virgin so why talk? Unless . . . iciness slid through her veins as another thought occurred. What if this was about information gathering?

Levi's hand dropped, his gaze darkening as he placed both hands on her bare thighs. "What?" he bit out, as if he'd read her mind.

"Why do you want to know how old I am?" She hated that she was so mistrustful but after the way she'd grown up and considering her job, it would be weird if she *wasn't* this way. Her mistrust was also part of the reason she hadn't slept with anyone before. Even with her ex, she'd never truly trusted him, not with her body. Something she could see now with perfect hindsight. But with Levi, she knew who he was. Or she thought she did. And no matter what, she trusted him in this.

For a moment he looked angry. Then he sighed and leaned forward, brushing his lips over hers. "I want to know everything about you but not for any ulterior motive. The only answer I need to know is if you're on birth control."

She nodded. All female agents went on birth control before an op and she'd been on so many over the years she'd just never gone off.

"I'm clean," he rasped out, his voice shaking. Even his hands trembled against her. It made her feel better that she wasn't the only one shaken by what was happening between them.

"So you still want to . . . ?"

He let out a sharp sound that might have been a laugh before he pushed up from his kneeling position and slanted his mouth over hers, his tongue teasing and demanding and making everything inside her wake up and take notice.

Okay then, that answered her question.

In a completely dominant display he covered her body with his, grabbing her by the hips. As she clutched on to him he moved them farther up the bed so that she was stretched out beneath him. The feel of his taut, muscular body above hers made her shudder. She arched into him, her nipples brushing against that rock-hard chest and she cursed that his T-shirt was still in the way.

When he pulled back from her, she was afraid he was stopping, but then he began feathering little kisses along her jaw as one hand moved from her hip to her breast. He didn't stroke her nipple like she wanted though; he just held her breast carefully while he nibbled down to her ear. His teeth pressed down on her earlobe and she swore she felt the action all the way to her clit. That shouldn't have even been all that erotic, but it was Levi's mouth on her body. It didn't matter that it was just her ear. Unable to stop herself she let out a moan.

Unsure what he planned, she felt as if she was walking on a tightrope, just waiting to fall. It was clear he knew what he was doing and for that she was thankful.

"If I do anything you don't want just tell me to stop, okay?" he murmured against her neck as he finally rubbed a thumb over her hard nipple.

Her inner walls clenched at the erotic caress. "I want more than this," she blurted, then cringed.

His head popped up so that he was looking directly down at her. "More?" He pinched her nipple between his thumb and forefinger.

She nodded and somehow found her voice. "You're going too slow," she whispered.

A wicked smile spread across his face that she felt all the way to her toes. It softened his normally harsh expression, making him look years younger. That look should be illegal. "I just didn't want to scare you if I went too fast," he murmured. When he spoke there was a raw vulnerability in his voice. He was normally hard to read but he was being serious.

He was worried she'd back out? Hell no.

"I'm twenty-three," she whispered, answering what he'd asked earlier, wanting him to know more about her, wanting him to know something real. "My parents and sister died when I was fourteen and because of certain skills I have, I managed to do just fine on my own for about a year and a half. Then I got on someone's radar. Someone bad. That's when Wesley saved me." There was a whole lot more to that story but now wasn't the time and she didn't want to strip herself completely bare. At least not emotionally. But Levi deserved to know more about her. It made what they were about to do feel . . . right.

He watched her for a long moment, his gaze intense and searching. Taking her by surprise, his lips curved up again in that wicked way that made her body tremble with need. "Shit, twenty-three."

The way he said her age made her smile. She knew how old he was from his file. "Ten years isn't that big of a difference." She'd never been a kid anyway. She'd never had the chance. Her smile fell when he dipped his head and sucked her nipple into his mouth. "Oh . . ." She didn't know what to say; couldn't have found any words anyway as he sucked the tight bud into his mouth.

She felt the tug all the way to her pulsing clit, as if the two were connected by a wire. When he made a groaning sound against her breast, the vibration hummed through her, getting her even more worked up.

She'd touched herself before and fooled around with a couple of guys in addition to her ex-boyfriend, but nothing had ever felt this good. She knew it was because this was Levi's mouth and hands on her.

He cupped her other breast while he continued his torturous assault with his tongue. Flicking and teasing her nipple, he lashed the hard bud in a rhythm so erotic she could barely catch her breath. He used a slower rhythm with his thumb and forefinger on her other nipple. The difference in tempo was making her pant out his name.

"Levi, more." Damn him, he was going to tease her as long as he could. The black silky scrap of material covering her mound was so soaked it was a little embarrassing.

But at least he was rock hard between her legs. The clothing between them did nothing to hide his need for her. Knowing he wanted her as much as she wanted him sent a sharp thrill through her.

She rolled her hips, enjoying the feel of his erection sliding over her covered mound. She wanted him inside her. Finally he shuddered, showing a thin crack in that hard veneer.

So she rolled them again. He surged up, his cock rubbing against her insistently. She slid her fingers into his dark hair, needing more contact with him.

To her disappointment he tore his mouth from her breast. When he started a hot path of kisses down her belly, she immediately tensed.

Levi froze at her navel and looked up, his dark eyes cautious. "You okay?"

She nodded, her throat tight. She was more than ready for sex but oral sex felt more personal and intimate. And she didn't care how much the media made it out to be no big deal, it was to her.

"Don't lie or hold back," he whispered before dropping a kiss on her stomach. He didn't go any farther though, just traced a design over her bare skin with his tongue, making her shudder. "If you're worried about me going down on you, you should know I've been fantasizing about burying my face between your legs since you let me touch you on Shah's dock. I wanted to fall to my knees then, even knowing who you worked for, and make you scream my name in pleasure."

His words made her face flame but he wasn't done.

"I've been imagining what your pussy will look like spread for me, how pink your lips will be and—"

"Levi." She didn't know what else she intended to say, only that she needed him to stop talking before she melted into a puddle right there.

That grin was back as he once again dipped his head against her stomach. This time there was no stopping him. He grasped the edge of her panties and tugged down, practically ripping them off her.

When she was completely bare to him, her legs spread for him to see all of her, she couldn't believe she'd ever been nervous. The hungry, possessive look in his dark eyes stole her breath. He truly wanted her for her. This wasn't about the job or anything else, just pure hunger and wanting to please her.

He paused there for a long moment just staring at her, his gaze raking over her entire body from head to toe as if he wanted to memorize every inch of her. When those eyes narrowed back on the juncture between her thighs her inner walls tightened.

She slightly lifted her hips, meeting his mouth as he covered her most intimate area. She thought she'd been ready but at the feel of his tongue swiping up the length of her slit, she groaned out his name. "Levi."

The sound of his name on her lips seemed to spur him on. He grasped her inner thighs with enough pressure that she couldn't move her legs, holding her in place. The sensation of being restrained by him was oddly erotic. She slid her fingers back into his hair, loving the feel of holding his head while he pleasured her.

He teased her mercilessly, his talented tongue stroking her up and down, tasting all of her before he focused on her clit. He teased her with just the right rhythm to make her body tremble and her inner walls convulse with the desperate need to be filled. Then he pulled back from her sensitive bundle of nerves and resumed his teasing.

"More," she demanded, unable to stop the word from tearing from her throat.

He practically growled against her slick opening and maybe that was what he'd needed from her. Still holding one thigh, he released the other and gently teased her lips apart as he focused on her clit with his tongue.

As he continued stroking her, she jerked against his mouth, unable to show any sort of control.

Slowly he started sliding a finger inside her, groaning as he pushed deeper. She clenched around him, savoring every second. A small part of her had expected discomfort but there was none. Of course, his finger was different from his cock. Still, he felt amazing as he stretched her with one, then two fingers, moving in and out of her.

It was too much and not enough. Her nipples tingled in awareness and her inner walls clenched tighter and tighter around him as she rushed toward climax. She might have pleasured herself before but this already felt different.

More intense.

When Levi made an almost growling sound against her clit, she lost it. Something inside her was set free as he increased his strokes. The orgasm that had been building inside her crested before pushing her into a freefall of sensation as all her nerve endings lit up in pleasure.

Uncaring about how she looked, she didn't hold back, rolling her hips against his face as her orgasm seemed to go on forever, pulsing out to all her nerves as she came down from her high. Her eyes closed and her head fell back against the sheets as she let the pleasure take over.

When he completely withdrew his fingers, her eyes snapped open. Levi crawled up over her body and slowly peeled off his shirt, revealing inch after delicious inch of the most perfect male form she'd ever seen. She'd seen him before but now she could look her fill and drink in those taut, muscular lines. She might be satisfied but she wanted so much more; she wanted all of him.

She went to unbutton his pants but he moved back out of her reach and quickly shucked them himself. That was when she discovered he went commando. Another burst of heat flooded her at the sight of his thick erection. She couldn't wait to feel him inside her. Moving like a sleek panther, he was back on the bed in seconds, moving between her thighs, his hard length insistently nudging at her opening as he leaned down to kiss her.

She could taste herself on his lips and was surprised by how erotic it was. Reaching around his big body, she dug her fingers into his back as he pushed deeper inside her. Being stretched and filled by him was the most wonderful sensation. Pulling back from his wicked mouth she watched him as he thrust completely inside her, fully burying himself.

There was a slight give as she molded around his thickness but no pain like she'd expected. Just a fleeting discomfort. Oh, she was sure she'd be sore later but this was wonderful. And she knew it was because this was Levi.

Thankfully he didn't ask how she was doing, just watched her face intently as he pulled back out.

The way he stared at her was so intimate that she was tempted to look away. But she wanted to see his expression as he came.

Her inner walls started clenching around him in the same way they'd done around his fingers and she realized she might climax again. It seemed impossible but her entire body was over-sensitized and primed.

His neck muscles pulled tight as his thrusts grew faster and more unsteady. Taking her by surprise, he reached between their bodies and began rubbing her clit again. She let out a gasp and arched up. His mouth descended on one of her breasts again and she couldn't have stopped the tidal wave of sensation if she'd wanted to. Which she didn't.

Another orgasm crashed into her, flooding all her senses as Levi groaned against her sensitive flesh.

Grabbing her hip with one hand, his thrusts grew faster as he buried his face against her neck. She held on tight, wrapping her arms hard around him as he lost himself inside her in long, hot strokes.

She wasn't sure how much time passed as they lay there. She stroked her hand up and down his spine as he nuzzled her neck in the sweetest way. It seemed so out of character for Levi but she loved this side to him. Loved that he allowed himself to be vulnerable at least in bed. Maybe it was just her imagination but she didn't think so. This, right here with him, turned her heart over.

Eventually he pulled back, his eyes glinting with an emotion she couldn't define.

"Is it always like that?" she rasped out, physically and emotionally spent.

He shook his head, a ghost of a smile tugging at his lips. "Next time it'll be longer." That wasn't what she meant so she pinched his side and earned a grin from him. "No, it's not always that intense. Give me a sec," he said as he withdrew from her.

Frowning, she watched as he hurried to the adjoining bathroom. The way his ass muscles flexed made every feminine part of her flare to life again, even though she should be completely sated.

When he came back with a washcloth she realized what he was doing and her heart melted. He stretched out on the bed next to her. Wordlessly he cleaned between her legs in gentle strokes, the action almost more intimate than everything else they'd shared.

"How do you feel?" he murmured.

"Amazing." The answer was immediate and honest.

With a half smile he kissed her forehead, nose, then mouth. It was sweet and almost-but-not-quite chaste. "I should have done the gentlemanly thing and said I couldn't take your virginity," he murmured though there was no conviction in his voice.

She snorted indelicately. "Well, thank God you're not a gentleman. And you didn't *take* anything, dummy."

His eyebrows rose. "Dummy?"

"Yeah. Don't say dumb stuff after wonderful sex. I

can't believe that's what I've been missing out on."
Though something told her that had more to do with
her and Levi's combustible chemistry than anything
else.

His grin widened as he brushed his lips against hers
again. "It'll be even better the next time."

She wasn't sure there'd be a next time but for now,
she could pretend because she desperately wanted to
believe that there would be. Even if she knew better.
Stretching out next to him, she curled against him, savoring his strength and warmth.

He rubbed a hand down her back. "So . . . I know
what you said earlier and you don't have to answer,
but how is it you were still a virgin? Honestly? Have
you looked in the fucking mirror," he murmured, his
words light.

A small laugh escaped. "It's not one thing or a single
reason. I . . ." Keeping her head on his chest, she traced
her finger over one pec. "Sex involves trust. At least for
me."

His body went impossibly still. "So you trust me?"

She couldn't answer that without lying so she went
for mostly honest. "I trust you with my body." Because
the truth was, she didn't think he'd betray her in the
sense that it was intentional. But she also knew that his
internal anger might be triggered and he could make
poor decisions—which could inadvertently hurt a
bunch of innocent people. She rushed on before he
could respond. "When I was first recruited I was young
and had no interest in sex. I was also . . . in counseling
for a while, thanks to Wesley."

"Really?"

Nodding, she pushed away from him slightly and propped her head up in her palm, her elbow on the bed, but kept her body curled against his. "Yeah, not because of sex stuff or anything, just because I freaking needed someone to talk to. By the time I was old enough to even think about the opposite sex, Wesley watched me like a hawk. He was a little ridiculous." He'd been the definition of the overprotective father figure. Something she was actually grateful for. Her own parents had been wonderful and though no one could ever replace them, Wesley didn't need to. He was family to her now.

Levi's mouth curved up. "Good."

She blinked at his possessive tone, then smiled. "Anyway, I did manage to fool around a little with a couple of guys going through training but no one ever really . . . rang my bell, I guess."

"No one?"

She lifted a shoulder. "Well, not until I was about twenty. I started dating this guy. Actually dating. It was really nice; made me feel normal I think on some level. He was a few years older, smart, had military experience and we were going through a lot of the same intense programs together. He was really good."

When she saw Levi frowning, she tweaked one of his nipples. "Get that look off your face. He was a super douche, just let me get to that part."

A ghost of a smile tugged at his lips as he slid a hand up over her bare hip to settle higher on her waist. "Am I going to want to kill super douche?"

She snorted. "He's not worth it—trust me. You know how hindsight can be a bitch?" When he nodded she continued. "I won't bore you with the details but it bothered him how good I was. It just never occurred to me to, well, not be who I am. To give you an example, at the range I was almost always the top shooter. And I tested better than almost everyone. That's mainly because of my eidetic memory but I also tend to think outside the box, try to look at every angle."

"And he couldn't take it?"

She shook her head. "Nope. And the thing was, he had a lot of strengths, was way better than me and anyone in our group setting up tactical offense situations. But, long story short he tried to sabotage one of my simulated ops to make me look bad. I didn't know it at the time but Wesley did. Or he suspected anyway. The second time he tried something shitty, Wesley kicked him out of the program."

Levi's eyebrows rose. "Whatever happened to him?"

She shrugged. "He works for the FBI I think. Don't know and really don't care. After that 'lovely' experience, I didn't bother with relationships. I was too busy anyway. So there you have it."

Half smiling, he cupped the back of her head and brought her mouth down to his. When he brushed his lips over hers, she felt her entire body heat up again. She knew this time between them wasn't going to last long so she was taking full advantage of the sexy, strong man next to her.

Chapter 18

FUBAR: military slang for "fucked up beyond all repair."

Selene stared at the phone in her hand. The burner phone she'd used to call Wesley earlier. Levi had left it just lying in the tote bag, a clear sign that he completely trusted her. Which just made her feel even crappier.

She needed to call Wesley now, to let him know where she thought Tasev's place might be. The sooner she told him, the sooner he could get a team into action. Hell, she just needed her own laptop and she should be able to narrow it down using her custom-made programs. They had to save Schmidt. There was no other option but for her to do this and she refused to let innocent people die because she couldn't get it together.

Levi was in the shower and even though the thought of joining him was more than appealing she'd begged off, telling him she was hungry.

Just do it, she ordered herself. She hated that it felt like a betrayal to him but her duty had to come before her feelings for Levi. They needed to save Schmidt and get that damn antitoxin.

"What are you doing?" Levi's voice made her jump a fraction and turn from where she stood at the kitchen counter. His jaw was tight, his expression hard.

Holding the phone and battery in one hand, it was pretty damn obvious. "I have to call him," she said, not needing to specify who.

Levi just stood there, completely naked but his hair wasn't wet. Crap, he hadn't even gotten in the shower yet. She could hear the water running so maybe he'd forgotten something—or maybe he'd just been checking on her because he didn't trust her.

"Towel," he growled, as if reading her mind. "So what was that in the bedroom? You wait until I'm distracted so you can call Burkhart? Why not just wait until I was asleep?" His words were harsh, demanding, and he sounded almost hurt.

Which destroyed her. "It wasn't like that and you know it." It hurt that he could even think that.

That dark gaze burned right through her. "I know that minutes after we fucked you're out here ready to sell me out." His voice shook with barely controlled rage, each word dripping with anger. His chest rose and fell rapidly, his fists clenched into tight balls at his side.

"I'm not selling you out! What the hell do you expect me to do, Levi? I can't hold off any longer." Too many lives were hanging in the balance. How the hell could she get up every morning and look in the mirror if she knew she'd let people die?

"So you know where Tasev's house is?"

She shrugged. "Not exactly but I have a good idea."

"Were you going to be here when they took me in?

Or were you going to run so you wouldn't have to watch?" he snarled.

Hurt stabbed through her as she shook her head. "Don't do that. You know I'm not betraying you. That's not what this is about." But it hurt like hell that's what he assumed she was doing.

His jaw tightened as he watched her for a long moment. She wanted him to say something, anything, but he finally turned and strode from the room. A moment later the door to the bathroom slammed with such force she jumped.

She wanted to go after him and plead her case but knew it was pointless. She'd known this would happen eventually; she just hadn't expected it to hurt so damn much. Her chest ached, as if she'd just lost something priceless and knew she'd never get it back. Throat tight, she hurried to the bedroom and tugged on her pants. She was wearing the T-shirt Levi had discarded and even though it was stupid, she kept it on. She liked the way he smelled and this was the last damn time she'd see him so she wanted to hold on to that bit of him as long as she could. After slipping on her sneakers she left everything else but took the phone.

It was all she needed anyway. Outside in the driveway she put the battery back in the phone and made the call. She knew Levi would be leaving in the next sixty seconds and she wasn't going to stick around for an all-out confrontation. Deep down she wondered if he even cared enough about her to have one.

Wesley picked up on the first ring. "We just got another tip. Tasev's gonna hit five cities tomorrow morning."

A burst of adrenaline shot through her like a cannonball. In that moment she was thankful she'd decided to contact Wesley. Everything else took a backseat to saving so many lives. She just hoped Wesley could send someone to pick her up pronto. If not, she was stealing a car. "I think I can locate his base. I just need my laptop—and some clothes." She raced down the sidewalk, heading back toward the park she and Levi had come from earlier. It would be a good point of pickup even though she had a feeling Wesley already knew where they were. And if he didn't, she didn't want to give him the exact location for Levi. Didn't matter that Levi was probably already on foot, booking it to God only knew where.

"Ortiz is on his way to get you. He's got everything you'll need. Where's Levi?"

"Not with me."

"He hurt you?" he demanded.

She snorted. It was almost unfathomable that Levi could hurt any woman, something Wesley knew. "No. How far out is Ortiz?"

"Hold on . . . Tracking your phone now and you should see him in just a sec. Dark SUV."

As she turned left down another quiet residential street the lights from an SUV parked by a curb flashed on and off once. "I see him. What are you going to do about Levi?" she asked, knowing Wesley wouldn't just leave him alone. Her boss might have been willing to let him go a year ago but Levi was back in Wesley's orbit again. "You clearly knew where I was. Has Ortiz been waiting here long or did he just arrive? How'd you find us?" She hurled questions at Wesley, needing answers even though she'd already guessed the last one. He'd likely triangulated the cell before she ended the call to him in the park, then tracked them with a drone.

"Ortiz just got there and he was coming to get you. And how do you think I found you? Drone."

"You still didn't answer my question about Levi."

"I've got someone on it. Don't worry." His tone warned her not to push it but she didn't care.

"Don't hurt him." There was a threatening edge to her words she hadn't meant to let slip out. Wesley didn't miss a thing.

There was a long moment of silence on the other end. "Hurting Levi is the last thing I want to do."

It wasn't the assurance she'd been looking for, but the truth was, if Wesley sent someone after Levi he wouldn't be there anyway. Hell, he'd probably already left that house seconds after her. Maybe he'd figured out where Tasev was or maybe he'd try to follow her. Still . . . "Wesley, I'm serious."

He let out a frustrated sigh. "He won't be hurt. I swear."

That was all she could ask for. "Thank you." She slid into the front seat of the SUV and nodded once at Ortiz, who immediately pulled away from the curb. Her computer was sitting on the center console. Someone must have grabbed it from the safe house. "Give me a couple of minutes to narrow down the location and I'll call you back."

Wesley didn't respond, just disconnected, which was pretty typical when they were in an op like this.

She flipped open her razor-thin laptop and turned it

on. "You bring me clothes?" she asked Ortiz, already turning around in the seat to look.

"Clothes, shoes, a vest. It's nice to see you too, by the way." There was a teasing note in Ortiz's voice.

Despite her dark mood she half smiled as she grabbed the long black T-shirt and black rubber-soled shoes that reminded her of diving shoes. Instead of trying to change in the front she jumped in the back and used the space to start stripping. Now wasn't the time to worry about modesty and Ortiz was a professional. The classically handsome man might look like he should be on a movie set, but he was rough around the edges like everyone else who worked for Wesley. Last thing he'd be distracted by right now was a half-naked woman in the backseat.

"Where to?" he asked as she started changing. He'd brought her what they all considered operational clothes. Which meant Wesley had already planned for her to go in on this op. *Good.* There was no way she was sitting on the sidelines. She'd noticed that Ortiz was also dressed in black from head to toe and strapped down with weapons.

"Tahiti Beach neighborhood. I'm pretty sure Tasev is there," she said as she slid back into the front seat and pulled her laptop into her lap.

Ortiz had grown up in Miami so she wasn't surprised that he didn't bother inputting the area into the SUV's GPS.

"What kind of weapons did you bring for me?" she asked as she started opening the programs she'd need.

"A SIG and your KA-BAR. Got an MP5 if you need. They're all in the back."

"Thanks." She didn't bother with small talk as she worked and Ortiz didn't try to make conversation either. Not that she'd expected him to. They'd worked together before and he was effective. She wondered if he knew anything about Wesley's plans concerning Levi but resisted the urge to ask. She wasn't sure what her boss had told everyone about Levi's involvement and figured it was better to remain quiet on the subject.

They weren't very far from the exclusive neighborhood, which was good. As they neared the turnoff, she looked up as a thought occurred to her. "How are we getting in?" There had been a guard at the gate for Shah's party. Something she should have thought of earlier. Which said a lot about where her head was. She mentally shook herself. She had to keep her head on straight or risk getting killed.

"Don't worry about it."

She wanted to ask, but didn't. Instead she focused on the map on her screen. Mentally calculating the distance from the guard gate to how far she and Levi had traveled once entering the neighborhood she was able to narrow it down to one of two houses. As they pulled up to the gate, Selene started to shut her computer screen but stopped when she saw Dax step out from the small guard building.

The former Delta Operative just grinned at them and waved them through.

"How'd Wesley get him in place so fast?" She hadn't even told him about Tahiti Beach neighborhood.

"He's been alternating operators out since Shah's party. Wanted to keep an eye on who comes and goes. Nothing to do with Tasev. This is just Dax's shift."

"Clearly no one's seen Tasev."

Ortiz shook his head. "Or any of his known associates."

"He could be traveling via boat," she said, thinking of the layout of the neighborhood and wondering if this was even the location at all. Her gut told her it was.

"Or not leaving his place at all," Ortiz muttered.

"Yeah. Head here." She pointed to the house on the screen, letting him see the layout.

Ortiz nodded and kept to his slow speed. It was close to two in the morning and most of these homes had walls or hedges for privacy so she wasn't worried about anyone seeing them.

As they neared the house, she tapped her earpiece and called Wesley.

He answered on the first ring. "Yeah."

"I need someone to run an address for me." Something she could easily do herself, but she didn't want to waste the time when they had a team of people. She wanted to know who owned the home. It definitely wouldn't be in Tasev's name, but if it was owned by a shell corporation or something shady, it would be a good sign that they were on the right track.

After she gave him the location and he rattled it off to someone else he came back on the line. "You think Tasev is in Shah's neighborhood?"

"Yeah . . . Hold on and don't hang up." As Ortiz had been driving, she'd been scanning the neighborhood's wireless Internet and security systems. It was all pretty standard, with some on the high end of security, but the house she suspected as Tasev's had layers and layers of encryption. She could easily break into the others and the fact that the firewalls on this residence were so dense told her a whole lot about the owner. "I think this is it."

"Should I park here?" Ortiz asked.

"No, go down a couple of houses. I should still have a wide enough range." Because the system wasn't set up for long-range infiltration, she'd have to be within a specific scope to work her magic.

Ortiz grunted something that could pass for a response as he continued driving.

"We've got the house up on satellite. And, shit, there are a dozen bodies moving around on the grounds," Wesley said.

"Guards." Ortiz murmured what they were all thinking.

"What kind of security system does the place have?" Wesley asked before giving orders to someone in the background to gear up.

"I'm not sure, but it's not run-of-the-mill crap. Is Karen there?"

"Yeah."

"Can you have her patch in to my computer?" Selene asked as she chipped away at the encryption. The security at the house was set up on a wireless system, which made her job a hell of a lot easier.

"She's shadowing you now. We see what you see."

"Good, just give me one sec." Her fingers flew across the keyboard as she sliced through a vulnerability in the security, giving her access to the actual security system.

As a multitude of video screens showing various angles of the exterior and interior of the home popped up she grinned to herself. She recognized the main foyer and the hallway that led to where the doctor was being kept hostage. Immediately she fired up another program and began recording everything. If they were going to break in she'd have to put the camera system on a loop so whoever was watching wouldn't see them breaking in. It wouldn't work for long, but it would do for a last-minute job. "This is it, Wesley."

"You're positive?"

"Not that he's in there now, but yeah, this is the place Levi and I were in." Saying Levi's name sent a pang of regret through her.

"Stay on the line." He muted it and she knew he'd be giving orders to his team.

"Karen, when you ran the address did you get the blueprints?"

"Yeah. Sending now."

"Thanks." The security system was intense, and showed the layout of where each security marker was on a very rough blueprint. It must have been what the security guys used to monitor the house wherever there wasn't a camera.

Selene compared what she had to what Karen sent her, quickly reviewing the blueprints side by side. They matched. She allowed herself a small breath of relief. Her plan was definitely doable. "I can't disable the whole thing at once. I mean, I could, but if anyone in there is half trained, they'll be able to boot it back up within a couple of minutes and it will put them on alert. I can, however . . ." She trailed off as Tasev stepped out of his office.

"Shit," Ortiz muttered beside her. "That's really him."

Tasev paused in the hallway, then turned toward the

metal door where an armed man stood guard. He said something to the man, who nodded, then walked away and fell in step behind Tasev.

"We need someone in there now," she said as Wesley came back on the line.

"I've got an assault team on the way. Can't believe Tasev is there," he muttered more to himself than them. "Ortiz, you're going to take point on—"

"Wesley," Selene interrupted. "We need to go in *now*. The only reason I'm in the system undetected is because it's doing an automatic backup. In roughly ten minutes they'll know an intruder's piggybacked onto their system. If you want to do a hard infiltration it won't matter and I'll disconnect now, but . . ." She trailed off, not needing to finish. If they could get in covertly there'd be a much smaller chance of the doctor getting killed or blood being spilled. Once they got the doctor and/or the antitoxin, their team could go in hard. Getting that antitoxin was all that mattered.

"Can you guide Ortiz?" he asked, not shooting her down immediately.

"Yes, but I should go with him. I've been inside. Karen can guide both of us. She's locked in to my computer." Something Wesley very well knew.

"What happens if you lose connection to the system?" he asked.

She inwardly cursed. She was hooked in wirelessly and if something went wrong—as it always did in an op—she'd have to be the one to reconnect. Not to mention she was better with security systems than Karen. It would be a tricky game of disconnecting certain doors or windows for Ortiz's infiltration. "I'll stay."

"Ortiz, if you get caught, just stay alive long enough for the team to get there," Wesley said, his tone serious.

"I can do that, but I don't plan on getting caught. Where am I going in?" he asked Selene.

"As long as Karen helps you avoid the patrols, I can get you in here." She turned the screen toward him and pointed out the best point of entry. "I was only inside once, but according to the blueprints this extra kitchen has two doors, one on the side of the house and one that leads to the back. It's the closest point of entry to where you need to go."

"Extra kitchen?"

"The place is thirty thousand square feet. Now, I can disable a door but you'll have less than twenty seconds to pick the lock and get in. It needs to appear like a blip in their system. Right now I'm recording a loop for each camera and as soon as you're ready to infiltrate, I'll take over their system and run a shadow program. You're going to need to go from here"—she used her finger to trace a path to where Tasev was keeping Schmidt—"to here. Once you reach the door it'll get tricky. He's got a biometric scanner—dual retinal and handprint—and there's no time to bypass it, but I can crash it so you can get in using a code on the keypad." Selene had recognized the brand and in case of a malfunction there was a backup keypad installed along with the scanners.

Ortiz just nodded, his expression neutral, and she knew he was in straight battle mode. He might look like a pretty boy but he was trained and lethal. There weren't many people Wesley would send in alone on a last-minute op like this. Even though she hated that

Ortiz wouldn't have any physical backup, she knew if anyone could free the doctor and his daughter, he was one of the few.

"Before you get the doctor out there's more writing on the back of his dry-erase board I didn't get to see while we were in the lab. I'm not sure if they've got a jammer in the room or not but if you can take pictures and send them to Wesley before you get out, do it." Because if he didn't get out alive or couldn't get Schmidt out alive, they still needed the doctor's work.

Ortiz nodded again and after he and Wesley spoke for another few seconds, he slipped from the vehicle. Selene slid into the middle seat and reached back for where the weapons were. She had an anti-reflective screen on her computer so any outsiders wouldn't be able to see the glow but she liked to be prepared for any scenario. If she was attacked, she'd be ready.

Focusing on the screen, she saved the recordings from the cameras and listened as Karen guided Ortiz onto the property. Soon it would be Selene's turn to make sure Ortiz got inside undetected and stayed alive. She'd done last-minute ops before but nothing like this. They'd done no prep-work and that scared the hell out of her. She knew it was why they all trained so hard, but it didn't alleviate her fear that not only was Ortiz's life in her hands, but the doctor's and his daughter's as well. She couldn't screw this up.

Vibrating with anger, Levi started to get in the shower but twisted the knob off, his hand clenching around it as he just stood there.

He wanted to be angry at Selene, but he wasn't so

much angry at *her* as he was the whole fucking situation. She'd never been part of his calculations for this mission and she was screwing everything up.

Right now he didn't want to shower because he didn't want the smell of her off him. He knew how messed up that was, but he didn't care. "Fuck," he muttered to himself before he turned and headed back to the bedroom. He couldn't leave things like this with her. And he wasn't sticking around for one of Wesley's teams to pick him up. Though deep down, Levi knew Selene wouldn't sell him out like that. If he truly thought she would, he'd have already escaped out a window and disappeared into the night.

They needed to talk.

And damn it, she was right. He might not get to torture the shit out of Tasev like he wanted, but if he could bring the man down and stop his operation, that would be even better revenge—because it would have been what Meghan wanted.

As he stepped into the bedroom, he froze.

Jack Stone leaned against the doorframe of the open door, his arms crossed over his chest, casual as fuck as he stood there watching him. As if the man had every right to be there.

"If you wanted a peek at my dick I would have sent pictures," Levi growled, stalking to the bed, where he grabbed his discarded pants. "What the hell are you doing here?" He glanced over Jack's shoulder, wondering where Selene was, needing to see her like he needed his next breath. He knew what he felt for her was real and already heading into territory that started with a capital *L*. He wasn't there yet, but he was falling fast.

Or hell, maybe he was already there and didn't want to admit it.

Jack just snorted and let his arms drop. It was subtle, but his stance was defensive, as if he was prepared to brawl.

Levi wasn't afraid of anyone, including Jack, but he respected the man's abilities. If there was anyone he had to go up against in hand-to-hand combat, Jack would be his last choice because he wasn't sure who would win. Not to mention, he loved Jack like a brother. It didn't matter that they hadn't talked in almost a year and that Jack most likely hated who Levi had become, Levi still cared about his old friend.

And he hated that he did. Jack reminded him of his former life, of what he'd lost. Of who he wished he still was.

"Selene send you in here?" he asked as he looked for his T-shirt, then remembered she'd been wearing it.

"Selene's gone."

Levi's head snapped up. Those two words pierced through his chest, making it hard to breathe. He'd been in the bathroom for only two minutes. He'd thought she'd make the call to Wesley or . . . fuck, he didn't know what he'd been thinking. He clearly hadn't been thinking, that was the problem. "Why?"

Jack shrugged, the casual action pissing Levi off when his heart was racing out of control. She couldn't have left. If he'd thought that she'd run he would have . . . hell, he'd have tied her to the bed. Good thing he'd placed a tracker on all the burner phones. He hadn't been willing to risk that she might leave him. And not because of his mission. He didn't want to lose her. He wanted . . . everything from her. Something real. A commitment. He knew it was impossible for them to have a real future but he didn't care. He'd take whatever he could get from her and he didn't care how weak that made him. After everything he'd lost he should have known better.

"Why are you here?" He thought about going for one of his weapons, but didn't bother. He'd never use a pistol or blade on Jack. Probably why that bastard Wesley had sent Jack in the first place. Levi's hands clenched into tight fists.

"Wesley wanted to make sure you don't do anything stupid."

Too fucking late. "I thought you retired. You back in the game?"

He shrugged again, probably because he knew it pissed Levi off.

Levi couldn't rein in his temper any longer. "Give me a fucking answer, Jack. You think you can bring me in? Really want to risk sending your corpse back to that pretty wife of yours?"

Jack's pale eyes glinted dangerously as he took a step forward.

He held a hand up and took one step back as a sign. He'd never kill Jack to avoid being taken in. And damn it, Wesley knew it. "Fuck, I'm sorry. I'm . . . I shouldn't have said that. I'd never . . ." Levi scrubbed a hand over his face.

Jack's jaw tightened as he eyed Levi with a distrust that hadn't been there moments before and it was his own damn fault. "Don't mention her again." The former operative's voice was low, deadly. Jack rarely shouted or raised his voice. And he didn't bother with threats—he just did what he needed to do.

Levi recognized that he was treading a very thin line with the legendary operative. "So what's the deal? Why are you here?" If Wesley had wanted him dead or to bring him in he would have sent an assault team, not Levi's former best friend.

"Like I said, to stop you from doing anything stupid. Wesley's got a team going after Tasev and he doesn't want you getting in the way."

Levi took an angry step forward but paused as reality set in. "Is Selene on that team?"

Jack nodded and once again that knife pierced his chest. He knew she was more than capable, but he didn't want her going after Tasev with anyone but him. Hell, Levi didn't want her involved at all. She brought out all his protective instincts in a way that rattled him to his core. It didn't matter how skilled she was. There was no way in hell he was letting her go after Tasev without him.

Because no one would protect her like he would. He'd already lost one woman he loved to that monster. He wouldn't lose another.

Chapter 19

CS gas: a chemical used to temporarily incapacitate by dispersing via an aerosol method. Often used by law enforcement for riot control in the form of grenades or aerosol cans, the tear gas irritates the eyes and/or respiratory system, causing tearing, sneezing, coughing, and vomiting.

"Five, eight, four, six, zero," Selene said into her earpiece, watching Ortiz on the monitor. "You've got less than ten seconds."

Weapon in his left hand, Ortiz punched the numbers into the keypad with his right, moving with a lethal efficiency that highlighted his training. He'd infiltrated the house like a machine, doing exactly what she and Karen instructed. He'd had to kill two guards and stash the bodies as best he could. So far no one had noticed their disappearance but Selene knew that wouldn't last long. She didn't have audio over the video feeds but she could hear the soft click of the door opening through her earpiece as Ortiz opened the door and stepped through.

From this point on they wouldn't communicate, but she could hear him moving, the sound of his shoes stepping over the metal gangplank to the stairs. She didn't have eyes in the room and she'd bet her retirement account the lab was bugged.

When a soft clicking sound came over her earpiece and she could no longer hear Ortiz, she frowned. "Karen, you hear that?"

"Yeah. I think we lost Ortiz. There's gotta be a jammer in there."

Since he couldn't respond they wouldn't know for sure but she couldn't hear any movement anymore. She had to operate as if he was okay though. He hadn't alerted them to anything when he'd entered the room and if something had been off, he'd have known immediately.

On her screen a guard rounded the corner and eyed the hallway, then headed in another direction. It was as if he was looking for someone. Probably one of the missing guards. Selene's heart rate kicked up but she kept her breathing steady. Ortiz knew how much time he had to get in and get out. She glanced at her watch. Sixty seconds to go.

If he couldn't get Schmidt and the daughter out of the house, there were a lot of places to hide before the backup team arrived. She knew Ortiz would make the right decision. If it was her, she'd stash them in the wine cellar or just hole up in the lab, but that was his call and he had operational latitude.

Though she tried not to stare at her watch, it was hard knowing that her teammate was in there and she couldn't give him immediate backup. She scanned the recorded videos she'd made, then pulled up the real-time feed only she could see. Tasev was still in sight, talking on his phone outside next to the waterfall that sloped into the massive pool. As he spoke, the man who'd been in the hallway strode up to him and interrupted him.

That couldn't be good.

Thirty seconds to go and Ortiz needed to be out of there. "How far out are the teams?" she asked.

"Twenty-five minutes," Wesley said, even though he wasn't with Karen. He'd opted to ride with the teams coming to raid the place. That was one of the things she loved about him. Even if he wouldn't be going in on the op, he was on the ground as much as possible, a solid support to his people.

Too long. "We might have a problem. You see the guy talking to Tasev?"

"Yeah, we see it," Wesley muttered. "Hold off," he ordered, meaning don't say anything while Ortiz was in the lab.

He had twenty seconds now. Enough time to get the prisoners out and on the way to safety. Her heart raced out of control, the adrenaline pumping through her unstoppable. Tasev put his phone down and turned to talk to the man, his body language tense.

Come on, Ortiz, she silently ordered him.

She jumped as a loud thump slammed into the front passenger-side window. Grabbing her weapon she ducked down as another thump hit the bullet-resistant glass.

Shit, shit, shit.

A tidal wave of adrenaline shot through her. "I'm under attack. Likely a fifty cal. The glass is spidering out. Another hit or two and they're in." She grabbed her laptop from the floorboards and started typing furiously, doing the one last thing she could to destroy Tasev's upper hand. "I'm uploading a virus to his security. You're going to lose visibility but so will he." She didn't dare move from the floorboards to see how many assailants were waiting. She wasn't making herself a target even if the windows were bullet-resistant. Too bad true bulletproof windows didn't actually exist.

Wesley and Karen both cursed. Then Karen said, "I don't see anyone on satellite. Wait . . ."

Thump.

Whoever was shooting had to have a suppressor on the fifty-cal. She could hear the discharge now but it was muted.

Thump.

The glass wasn't going to hold much longer.

"Someone's moving out of the hedges, rifle in hand," Karen said, her voice tense. "He's hitting the window with the gun."

Slam, slam, slam.

The SUV shook with the impact of the tango starting to punch through the laminate and glass.

Selene leaned back, crouching down behind the driver's seat and angling her SIG toward the passenger window. Gloved fingers appeared through the growing hole. She wanted to start firing but exercised calm and waited in the shadows behind the driver's seat. She couldn't be sure if anyone could see her yet and she wasn't giving away her location.

When the glass started to bend back and a full hand came through, she fired.

Someone cursed savagely in Russian, making her

inwardly smile. Next she shot her laptop twice, blowing it to pieces.

"You hit him but there are two more men arriving now." Karen's voice was tight. "Hang in there, Selene."

She didn't have a choice. Staying low, she kept her weapon aimed at the window but then a small canister was shoved through the hole. "Tear gas," she growled as she shoved up and dove into the very back.

The distance wouldn't protect her. Nothing would but a gas mask and unfortunately she didn't have one.

Her eyes, nose, and throat started burning with tears, mucus running down her face as she hunkered down, still clutching her weapon. She'd been through this before during training but it didn't matter. She wasn't immune to it and it burned like a bitch. Nausea bubbled up, but she fought it. She grasped her weapon tight, ready to fire blindly. If she was going down she was taking as many of them with her as she could.

"Hang in there!" Wesley shouted.

She tuned everything out as she tried to swipe away her tears and focus through the haze of gas. A man wearing a mask suddenly appeared over the back of the seat, reaching out for her with one hand. He'd probably unlocked the SUV but she couldn't see or hear shit at this point.

Everything was blurry but she fired through the back of the seat since she couldn't force herself to get up. Her muscles were clenched too tight in pain. She heard screaming and cursing and tried to fire again but the nausea she'd been fighting took over.

Her stomach heaved and she started puking as something hard struck the side of her face. She lifted her arm to protect herself as she flew back into the two rear doors. One of them opened and she fell out onto the pavement, unable to stop choking.

Disoriented, she tried to push up when pain suddenly exploded in the back of her head and blackness took over.

Ortiz tapped his earpiece as he descended the stairs, his MP5 drawn. Below the stairs he saw a woman huddled on a mattress, her eyes wide. A man he recognized as Claus Schmidt stood by a dry-erase board, his eyes bleary as if he'd just woken up. In his hand he held a cutlery knife.

Ortiz held a finger to his mouth as he quickly scanned the rest of the space. It was large, but there weren't many places to hide except behind two long, rectangular tables. Silently he moved around them before focusing on Schmidt, who now stood protectively in front of his daughter.

Ortiz pointed to his eyes, then around the room, hoping the doctor understood. The man shook his head but pointed to his ears.

So the room was bugged like Selene had thought.

He nodded once and headed for the dry-erase board. Just like Selene had said there was writing on both sides. He took pictures of everything since he wasn't sure what she'd transcribed. He tried to send it to Burkhart, but the phone wouldn't work.

Hurriedly he looked around and saw a pad of paper on one of the tables. He grabbed the pencil next to it and scribbled the word "antitoxin" on it with a question mark. The girl flinched as he strode toward them but the doctor remained calm as Ortiz handed the pad to him.

Schmidt pointed to his head, then to his daughter, himself, then upstairs. Finally he pointed to the word "antitoxin."

He wanted their freedom in exchange for the antitoxin. Yeah, Ortiz didn't blame him. The doctor knew that they'd move heaven and earth to get him out alive with that bargaining chip.

Ortiz nodded and pointed at the girl to move. She stood on shaky legs and moved behind her father. At least she wasn't crying. He couldn't deal with a histrionic principal.

Using hand signals he motioned for them to stay behind him as they crept to the stairs. On silent feet they all ascended the first set of stairs, his weapon on the door.

When the soft click of the door opening sounded, he gritted his teeth. Sweeping out one arm behind him, he urged them to the side so they'd be more protected by his body. The second a man wearing all black fatigues stepped through, he fired a double tap, striking the man in the neck and chest. His suppressor absorbed most of the sound so if someone wasn't directly outside it was unlikely anyone had heard.

As the man fell off the balcony, blood spurting everywhere as he slammed against the tile floor at an odd angle, the girl screamed in horror. Even though the shots had been muted, her cry would have alerted whoever was listening.

Running footsteps came from outside the door.

Well, hell. Shit was about to get a whole lot dicier

now. "Move back," he ordered them, breaking silence. "We've got to take cover."

Because he planned to hunker down and wait for the assault team. If it was just him he'd fight his way out, but he couldn't risk either of the principals getting killed.

Chapter 20

Auditory exclusion: a form of temporary loss of hearing occurring under high stress. In combat, a temporary filtering of irrelevant noise including gunfire.

Levi grabbed a button-down shirt from the closet while Jack still stood in the doorway. He weighed his next words as he finished getting dressed. Before he could say anything though, one of his burner phones rang from the tote bag.

"Is that a new style, a man purse?" Jack murmured as Levi headed for where it sat next to the side of the bed, unexpected humor in his voice.

Despite the situation, a small smile tugged at his lips and for a brief moment he remembered how easy things used to be between him and Jack. "Don't hate when you know you want one. And it's a man *bag*, not a purse." He shot Jack a glance and was glad to see his former friend half smiling too. Levi snagged the ringing phone, all humor fleeing when he saw the number. It was Tasev.

The terrorist had one number for Levi, to a burner phone he kept charged at another location. Anyone who called him on that phone would be forwarded to whatever phone Levi had routed the number to. In this case, he'd routed all calls to this current burner. When he ditched it, he'd reroute it to his next one.

Why the hell was Tasev calling so soon after their meet? Levi pressed the green button to answer the call. "Yeah."

"You want to tell me why I found your assassin whore hacking into my security system?" Tasev's voice was razor-wire sharp.

His words made the bottom of Levi's world drop out. That monster had Selene. His throat tightened and he knew his expression must have showed his horror because Jack straightened, taking a couple of steps into the room. Levi tuned him out though. "What the hell are you talking about?"

"I found your Wolf breaking into my home with another man. Looks as if they want to break out my doctor."

"Don't fucking lie to me," Levi snapped, forcing himself to play his role of criminal asshole. "What game are you playing?"

There was a short moment of silence. "I'm not playing a game, Mr. Moore. Now explain yourself or I'll kill your bitch."

"I have nothing to explain. I'm not sure that I even believe you. What could she possibly gain by breaking in? We want to do business with you. Long-term business that will be profitable for all of us. She's seen the numbers." Full-blown panic hummed through Levi but somehow his voice remained steady. As if he was more annoyed than anything. Not terrified, even though for the first time in years, he was experiencing true, crushing terror.

"She's told one of my men that she's here out of revenge and that you knew nothing about it. That she's been using you all along too. Maybe the little assassin is telling the truth."

"Using me?" he growled. "Fuck that. Where is she?" he demanded, heart in his throat.

"Are you willing to meet with me? Alone and unarmed?" Tasev asked, a test.

One Levi couldn't fail. "Yes. I have nothing to hide and if she's been lying to me I want answers. This doesn't make sense."

"Fine. Come alone to my home, no weapons."

"I need the damn address first," he snapped.

Tasev chuckled, the sound like fingers on a chalkboard. "You are either very smart or very stupid. I'll have someone pick you up."

Levi rattled off the address of a park very near where he suspected Tasev was for the pickup before ending the call. "They have Selene," Levi said as he turned to Jack, who was slipping his cell phone into his pants pocket.

"I know. Wesley just told me. They're twenty minutes out."

He'd done some calculating and had figured out Tasev was in one of three neighborhoods. With the pickup from one of Tasev's guys he should still get there sooner. The thought of losing Selene gutted him. "I can't let her die. I *fucking* can't." And that was all he could squeeze out. He wasn't sure if he loved her but it felt a hell of a lot like it. And he was going to tear Tasev apart with his bare hands.

Jack's pale eyes widened, maybe at Levi's tone or what he saw in his expression. Then in standard Jack-fashion, he made a split-second decision and nodded. "Let's go. I'll stay invisible at the park but be your backup in case Tasev just tries to kill you outright."

Arms cuffed behind her back, Selene stared straight ahead at the wall of the freezer. Tasev had a freaking walk-in freezer. Probably liked to hang dead bodies in here and look at his handiwork. Sick freak.

Chills snaked through her, making her teeth chatter, but she clenched them together trying to calm the effects on her body. It was useless though. She needed to start moving and get her blood circulating faster.

The freezer was empty except for some shelves, the chair she was sitting in, and another chair. Tasev had had one of his guys drag her in here. He'd demanded to know why she was here and who the man in the lab was and what his intentions with the doctor were. Which told her that they hadn't managed to get to Ortiz yet.

She said a silent prayer they never got to him. She knew by now that backup was about twenty minutes out so he just needed to hold on. And she had no doubt Ortiz could stay alive and keep the doctor alive. Saving all those lives was all that mattered.

Her only regret was that she hadn't told Levi she loved him. She didn't care how short of a time they'd known each other. When you knew, you simply knew, and she didn't see the point in analyzing it. She loved him.

And now she was going to die.

She wondered how much he'd care. The thought that he wouldn't hurt worse than anything.

She just hoped he killed that bastard Tasev. She'd lied to Tasev, telling him she was after the doctor out of revenge for what Tasev had done to her friend Meghan. Which had some truth in it. Tasev had killed a woman Selene had known and she had details to back up her story. It was the only thing that might keep her alive long enough for the teams to arrive. She doubted it, but she wasn't going down without a fight.

She tensed as the freezer door opened. She expected to see Tasev come back in. He'd been gone for less than sixty seconds.

Instead two men strode in. She recognized both as guards. One had blond hair, dark eyes, and a bandaged hand. Crap. It had to be the man she'd shot. The other was the one she knew as Grisha, shaved head, scarred neck, and all-around scary-looking bastard.

The one with the bandaged hand came to stand directly in front of her, holding a blade. Her KA-BAR. She refused to meet his gaze, looking at his torso instead. It didn't matter that backup was on the way. Anything could happen in minutes and a mere sixty seconds could feel like an eternity of hell while being tortured.

The man ran the dull, back edge of the blade down the side of her face. "So pretty. For now."

She didn't respond, which was certain to annoy him. Terror forked through her at what could happen to her, but she didn't focus on her fear. Victims did that. She was a fighter.

He grabbed the other chair, the scraping against the floor in the enclosed area jarring to her senses. A shiver raked through her, more to do with the cold than anything else. The adrenaline rush from earlier and the gas attack in the SUV had left her overly weak. At least she could still think straight.

The man turned the chair around and straddled it about a foot away from her. Their first mistake was in not binding her legs. Though she wasn't exactly surprised. Tasev was an egomaniac and she was "just a woman." He would think he had her beat no matter what because of the sheer opposition. Too bad for him he was wrong.

"Your boyfriend is on the way," the man said. "We've got a bet going who's going to hurt you more, him or Tasev. My money's on Tasev." He let out a wicked laugh.

Oh God, what a moron. She was glad he was talking though. The longer he talked, the better chance she had to survive. She had to be down to seventeen minutes now. She'd been knocked out for less than a minute, because she'd come to as she was being dragged through the foyer. Mascara and her tears still streaked her face. But hell, she was alive so that was something.

"Lucky for me Tasev lets us have his leftovers and you are one tasty morsel." There was a slight accent to his voice so she focused on that, not his vile words. It was how she compartmentalized. And seriously, who said words like "tasty morsel" anyway? She clenched her jaw and kept looking straight ahead at a point over the man's shoulder.

Grisha had moved closer. Maybe he wanted to hurt her too. She twisted her wrists against the back of the chair and bent her thumb all the way back. There was just enough wiggle room to get it out. But she couldn't be obvious about it.

"Almost as tasty as your redheaded friend."

Against her will her gaze snapped to his. Instantly she cursed her reaction, but it was too late.

Grinning evilly, the guard tapped the edge of her blade against her knee. "That got a reaction. You really are here because of that whore. Tasev wasn't sure if you were lying or not."

Selene clenched her teeth, willing herself not to say anything. Her position was awkward, but she slipped her thumb under the cuff. It scraped against the back of the chair but he didn't seem to notice. Unfortunately Grisha took a step forward. Crap, did he suspect? She shifted her wrists and let her thumb fall back into place. Her heart pumped overtime but he just moved in behind the other guard. Now she had to start over.

"I had a lot of fun with her. We all did."

"I'm going to kill you," she growled, the guttural words tearing from her throat. This man had actually been part of hurting Meghan? Of doing unspeakable things to her? Of breaking Levi's heart? If it was the last thing she did, Selene was going to kill this bastard and feel no remorse. "What kind of monster rapes a pregnant woman?"

His eyes narrowed on Selene's face. Moving faster than she anticipated he backhanded her with his non-bandaged hand.

Pain exploded in her cheek and the iron taste of blood filled her mouth. But she wouldn't be stopped. "I'll tell you what kind, a fucking degenerate. Big strong man hurts a weak, pregnant woman. You want a fucking medal for that? Go fuck yourself," she spat. She twisted her wrist again, working faster this time.

Her thumb slipped free and she clutched on to the cuff to keep her hands in place and to keep it from jangling against the back of the chair.

Instead of responding, he just laughed at her. When his gaze flicked down toward her chest, she took advantage of his distraction. She struck out with her boot, kicking at the leg of the chair, tipping him off balance.

He cried out in surprise and she moved fast, slamming her cupped hands down on his ears in one violent attack. The ear slap was one of the most basic self-defense moves and it worked every time if done right.

The guard shouted and jerked back from her, falling onto his side. She stood, ready to attack Grisha but he moved for the other man, blade raised over the man's chest. The guard kicked at Grisha's ankle, knocking him off balance.

Without pausing Selene grabbed the nearest chair and bashed it across the guard's chest. She heard a cracking and knew she'd broken his ribs. Good. He deserved to suffer for what he'd done.

Before she could move again, Grisha moved lightning fast, grabbing the guard and rolling him onto his face. He wrenched the guy's arms up hard, making him cry out in pain as he secured his wrists behind his back with cuffs.

"What the hell?" the man snarled, struggling under Grisha's hold.

Yeah, Selene was thinking the same thing. Keeping the guard pinned, Grisha pulled a blade from a sheath on his belt.

"You raped a pregnant woman?" he growled, disgust in his voice.

Selene glanced at her fallen KA-BAR, wanting to dive for it, but not wanting to gain Grisha's attention. She had no idea what his endgame was.

He saved the decision for her and kicked her blade over to her. Grisha didn't look up as he said, "You can kill him if you want. It doesn't matter to me. We need to get out of here."

Okay this guy clearly wasn't what he seemed. She snagged her blade and took a step toward the pinned man.

"The baby's not dead! I saved it!" the guard shouted.

Selene froze. Grisha paused, his gaze meeting hers as if the other man's words had surprised him too.

Ice flooded her veins in one searing blast as the guard's words fully registered. She knew that violence and trauma could force a woman into early labor. But he couldn't mean . . . "Her baby lived?"

"I'll tell you everything! Just don't kill me." Suddenly he sounded pathetic and whiny, the change making her want to order him to grow a pair.

Mindful of Grisha since she still didn't trust the guy, she walked around the front of the fallen guard's body and pressed her boot to his face. "You'll tell me everything or I'll cut off your nuts and make you eat them. Would you like that?" she growled, sounding savage even to herself.

"I'll help you start." Grisha started to turn the guy over but the man started whimpering.

"Tell me everything. Now," Selene demanded, digging her boot into his cheek.

"She . . . she went into labor. No one expected it but . . ." He trailed off, squirming against their hold.

"What did you do with it?" Selene hated calling the baby an "it," but she didn't know the gender. When he didn't answer right away, she nodded at Grisha, hoping the man understood what she wanted.

Grisha flipped him over and sliced through the guy's belt and pants with ease. Before he could scream, Selene covered his mouth with her foot.

"Wait, wait," he said, his voice muffled.

She withdrew her foot. "Last chance." Selene hated playing hardball like this, especially when she wasn't sure Levi's child could have survived. But if there was even a chance she had to do everything in her power to find the child.

He stared up at her, his face looking distorted because of his upside-down position. "She bled out after having the baby. One of the new guys was supposed to get rid of it but dropped it off at the hospital." He muttered something in Russian that sounded like "weak fool."

Selene forced her voice to remain steady. "So you didn't save the baby?"

His eyes narrowed. "Not me personally but I didn't tell Tasev what that fool did so, yes, I did save it."

She found it hard to believe that someone in Tasev's organization showed even that much mercy as to save a baby but even monsters had limits. "So Tasev knows nothing about this?"

He shook his head. "The man who saved the baby died not long after. Killed in a gun battle. No one but me knows."

"You don't even know if the baby survived," she spat, needing him to give her more information and fast. They were running out of time.

He started nodding furiously. "She *did*. One of the women I fuck regularly has a cousin who works at the hospital and the kid lived."

That was all she needed to know. And they were out of time. She had to save the doctor and get out of here before Tasev showed up. Selene looked at Grisha and nodded.

He understood completely because he cut the man's throat before the guy could even squeak out a protest.

She stepped back as the man started gurgling. Ignoring the river of blood she took a step back, still not trusting Grisha completely.

"We need to get out of here now," he said as he stood, casually wiping his blade on his pants.

"Okay." She had no clue who this guy was, but she wasn't going to question him. At least not at the moment. The only reason she was agreeing was because she needed to help Ortiz save Schmidt and his daughter and time was running out.

"Matvei, foyer, now," Tasev snapped into his radio. That stupid bitch had disabled his security system so he was working blind. Didn't matter, soon enough she'd tell him everything he wanted to know. At least he had men sitting on the lab. He wouldn't risk an attack now. Not until he knew more from the woman. He needed to know what her endgame was and if her partner in the lab was the only backup she had. For all he knew the man in the lab would kill Schmidt and ruin his plans.

Unfortunately he had another problem to take care of and he couldn't find the bastard. He was ninety percent sure that Grisha was a mole. He'd given him intel on an incoming shipment of illegal cargo. The information had been false, but now a couple of his shipping containers were being watched by someone in the government. He wasn't certain who, but it was definitely law enforcement. He didn't want to believe Grisha was a mole but after what had happened with the water plants, he knew it wasn't a coincidence that after Grisha had become aware of both situations—even if one was untrue—law enforcement had become involved. Tasev didn't know or care what agency the man worked for. He just wanted to eliminate the problem and move on to more important things.

Because that bitch had screwed up his visibility he couldn't locate Grisha. Luckily he'd put Matvei on him earlier.

Twenty seconds later the blond man hurried onto the polished wood floor of the foyer, his shaggy hair falling across his forehead as it always did. "What do you need, boss?"

"Where's Grisha?"

"I don't know. Saw him by the pool an hour ago but he's not on shift tonight. I don't think."

Tasev gritted his teeth. "Find him for me. It's important. If he won't come with you, kill him."

Matvei's eyes widened but he nodded and hurried away. He turned back to the two men waiting near the front door for the arrival of Isaiah Moore. "The lockdown?" he asked the one on the left.

"The property is secure. No one will get in or out and I'm sending a man to the front gate. He will take over for the guard and report back any new entrants into the neighborhood. He's getting dressed in the uniform now."

The death of a nameless guard meant nothing, especially since Tasev planned to be gone by sunrise. He didn't care if the woman he'd captured worked for the government or was truly a world-class assassin. His base had been compromised and he wasn't certain how much Grisha had passed on about him so he would have to relocate. "Good work."

His radio buzzed. "Mr. Moore is here."

"Bring him up." He looked over his shoulder, hoping Matvei arrived with Grisha in the next fifteen seconds. He planned to put a bullet between the traitor's eyes and he wanted Mr. Moore to see him do it.

The fact that the man had agreed to see Tasev after his employee had tried to breach Tasev's home told him that it was unlikely Moore was involved in all this. But only time would tell.

The true test would be when Tasev starting torturing her. If Moore stood back while it happened, he would be allowed to live and they would hopefully start a lucrative business relationship.

Chapter 21

Infiltration (military): movement into enemy territory
by individuals or small groups, using the weakest or
unguarded points of entry. Avoiding contact with the
enemy is preferred but not always possible.

"Wait," Selene said to Grisha, if that was even his
real name. She bent down to the dead man and
took his Makarov pistol. SIGs were her preferred weapon
of choice but this would do. As she started to check the
magazine the door made a soft snicking sound.

Tensing, she raised her weapon and crept off to the
right side. Grisha did the same, moving to the left, his
weapon aimed at the door.

When it opened, her heart rate kicked up a notch as
she readied to shoot Tasev or any number of his guards.
A blond man popped his head in. To her surprise he
grinned when he saw the body before he looked at Grisha, who was already lowering his weapon.

"He's with me," Grisha said to Selene.

"Damn it, I wanted to kill Valery. Hated that guy.
Come on. Tasev knows you're a mole. We need to get
you out of here."

Grisha nodded, still holding his weapon. "We're both leaving. You can't stay here any longer. It's getting too hot and something tells me this place is about to get stormed."

She nodded, looking at her watch. She could lie to the guy but didn't see the point. He'd already helped her and he knew a raid was coming. No need to deny it. "Thirteen, fourteen minutes max." God, how could only six or seven minutes have passed? It felt like an eternity. She worried about Ortiz but knew he could take care of himself.

"Thank God," the blond said. "I'm tired of playing the dumbass soldier with no brain. Next time that's your role."

"But you play it so well," Grisha murmured, all hints of his Russian accent gone and a hint of a smile tugging at his lips, making him seem human.

"I need to get to the doctor now," Selene said, her voice urgent. She didn't have time to sit around and bullshit.

Grisha tilted his head at the door. "Let's go. The lab isn't far from here."

"You first." She might be letting these guys help her escape but she didn't trust strangers at her back. For all she knew these men were part of some hostile takeover. She doubted it, but went with her training.

Grisha didn't pause or argue, just moved in front of her and motioned for her to follow. At least Tasev's thugs hadn't taken her shoes. She knew he would have eventually gotten to that, probably when he'd decided to start cutting off her toes, but she was thankful to have them now. She could run faster and if they ran into broken glass or anything, she wouldn't be slowed down. And she had to find Levi's daughter. Before she told him there was a possibility the child was alive, she had to know for sure.

Because if she gave him false hope . . . No way in hell could she be the cause of more pain for him. Her throat tightened and she banished all thoughts of Levi.

Her earpiece was gone and she was basically working blind. She needed her wits. Hell, she just needed to stay alive long enough to tell Wesley about Levi's daughter. Because if she wasn't around to find her, Selene knew Wesley would.

Levi kept his expression neutral as he strode up the short set of brick stairs to Tasev's palatial place, the man who'd driven him at his back. He was pretty certain Jack had followed them, but he hadn't been able to see anything since he'd been hooded at the pickup point.

Jack hadn't liked the situation but there was no choice. Levi had to go into the viper's nest alone. When Levi first arrived at the address he'd seen a guard cleaning up shards of laminate and glass outside the property. Inside the wall he'd seen a busted up SUV he hoped Selene hadn't been in. But deep down he knew she had.

If Tasev had hurt her, there was no force on earth that would stop Levi from killing him. He didn't care what happened to him, he just had to save her. Unfortunately he knew he was walking a dangerous edge with Tasev. The man knew his place was compromised so he'd be hyperalert and likely paranoid. He wouldn't trust Isaiah Moore at all.

One of the guards opened the front door and ushered him in to the same foyer he'd been in not long ago with Selene, with the wood floors and Monets.

Tasev stood at the bottom of the stairs, two guards flanking him from behind on the very bottom step and two next to him. Levi knew he was playing psychological games but it was pointless. Right now the bastard held all the cards because he had Selene. He was in charge until Levi could save her. He knew the backup team was on the way. Maybe fifteen minutes out now.

A fucking lifetime when you needed to keep the person you loved alive.

He knew he loved her. It was way more than lust. A different stratosphere from that. He'd give up his revenge for her if it would keep her alive. He'd even let Tasev go if it kept Selene alive. He just *needed* her to live. Because the thought of a world without her in it . . . He swallowed hard.

Time to put on his game face and act like a pissed-off business partner. It was the only thing that might keep him from getting his head blown off by one of Tasev's guards. "Where the fuck is she?" he demanded as he strode across the foyer.

One of the guards next to him took a step in Levi's direction, but Tasev stopped him with a flick of his wrist and came forward, his shoes silent as he crossed the distance between them. "You came." He seemed surprised.

"I don't believe that she betrayed me."

Tasev's mouth lifted into a feral smile. "Women are conniving, my friend. How long have you been sleeping with her? Since the beginning of your business arrangement?"

Levi gritted his teeth and shook his head. "That has been a recent development."

"Whose idea was it to do business with me?" he continued, his expression calculating.

Playing his part, Levi let out a savage curse, pretending to suddenly realize Selene had set him up.

Tasev made a tutting sound. "She probably let you think it was your idea, too. Come, let's see her. I have one of my guards entertaining her now. She shouldn't be too worse for wear. Yet." He turned toward the guards and told them to stay put.

So arrogant to go with Levi alone. Maybe he thought the guards with Selene would be enough protection. Unfortunately for him, nothing could save Tasev now. Not if he'd hurt Selene in any way.

Levi's blood turned to ice but he didn't respond, just fell in step with Tasev. He shoved out all the horrific images playing in his head and forced his feet to move. He knew Wesley's team was coming soon, so all he had to do was save Selene and keep them both alive until backup arrived. And kill Tasev if the opportunity presented itself. But it wasn't his priority.

Keeping track of their movements, he was surprised when they entered an industrial-sized kitchen. Everything looked new, as if it was never used.

"I only use the freezer," Tasev said as if reading his mind. He pointed to a large metal door.

Levi simply nodded, not trusting his voice. Fear wasn't an emotion he was accustomed to, but raw fear raged through him at what he might see when that door opened.

Tasev strode to the door and opened it. "You first."

As Levi stepped inside his panic subsided when he saw a dead man lying on the ground and a pair of handcuffs next to him. Selene had gotten away. The relief that overtook him was staggering. He turned to find Tasev stepping in behind him, his expression savage.

The bastard was pulling out his radio. Twisting, Levi lifted his arm, ready to slam his forearm into the man's throat and break his trachea.

Tasev reacted too fast, dodging to the side as his radio clattered to the floor. Moving lithely, he kicked out at Levi's inner knee, but Levi jumped back and to the side.

Levi let out an enraged snarl. He knew this was going to be a fight to the death. One he had no intention of losing because Selene needed him. Acting on instinct, he grabbed the nearest chair and swung hard.

Tasev was nimble though, clearly as trained as any of his men. Maybe more so. Probably why he'd stayed alive so long. The leg clipped Tasev's shoulder. He grunted, the sound echoing as Levi swung back, throwing the chair at him.

Tasev tried to duck but the back of the chair crashed into his face before hitting the shelves behind him. Tasev's hands jerked to his face as he stumbled.

Levi rushed at him, slamming his fist into Tasev's face. The man struck back just as hard, hitting Levi in the ribs.

He heard the impact more than he felt it, the adrenaline surging through him so potent he felt as if he could lift a car. Rolling with the punch, he struck again, pummeling Tasev's face and ribs with an animalistic savageness.

Weakening, Tasev reached for the weapon Levi knew

he had tucked into his shoulder holster. He hadn't had a chance to reach for it until now and even attempting was beyond stupid. It gave Levi the opening he needed. The fumbling movement was the last mistake Tasev would ever make.

Levi smashed his elbow upward, twisting his whole body into the blow as he struck Tasev's temple.

Crying out, Tasev stumbled, falling to his knees. Levi rammed his knee into Tasev's face, relishing the sound of bone breaking as he fell back. Gurgling on his own blood, Tasev attempted a pathetic grab for his weapon again.

Levi tore it from his holster and slid it across the floor. He wasn't shooting this bastard. That was too good for him. The most primal part of Levi needed this monster to die by his hand. When Tasev rolled over in one last attempt to crawl away, Levi jumped on him and wrapped his arm around his neck from behind.

Rolling back on the floor, Levi tightened his arm around Tasev's neck as he cinched his legs around his waist. The fucker wasn't going anywhere but to hell where he belonged.

Taking him by surprise, Tasev's hand flashed up and struck a blade down into his thigh.

The pain barely registered, Levi's adrenaline overtaking everything. He squeezed even harder with his arm, stealing the life from the man who had taken everything from him. "You killed my wife," Levi rasped out, wanting Tasev to know exactly why he was dying. "My unborn child."

Writhing against him, Tasev tried to find purchase on the cold floor, anything to fight his own death.

Nothing could save him now.

Levi stopped crushing Tasev's trachea and broke his neck, giving him instantaneous death. It was still too good for him, but Levi needed to get to Selene. Needed to make sure she was okay.

Levi relaxed his grip. Tasev's body thudded against the freezing cold floor. Shaking, he pushed to his feet.

He'd failed one woman. He couldn't fail another. Fate couldn't be that cruel to take her from him now.

Chapter 22

Going dark: when an operative cuts all communication for a certain period of time.

Selene and Grisha had their backs against the wall around the corner from the lab. Matvei, or whatever his name was, was standing guard so they wouldn't be ambushed from behind. He'd been listening on the radio and so far no one seemed to know that she'd escaped or that Grisha wasn't who everyone thought he was. She still wanted to know who these guys were working for but for now, they were on her side.

Grisha held up four fingers to Selene, then pointed to the hall. Then he pointed to himself, and made a motion that he'd go in high and she'd go in low. Grisha had given her a suppressor for the Makarov. Even though it was a little weird that he was carrying around an extra suppressor, she was taking it. Besides, she had a garrote wire on her watch so maybe the suppressor wasn't so odd after all.

They couldn't afford to alert anyone else to their presence. It had taken them almost five minutes to get to this hallway so now they were down to nine minutes before the teams infiltrated. She wanted the doctor and his daughter out of that lab and hidden before that happened. For all they knew Tasev had some fail-safe in place where he gassed the doctor if he tried to escape, killing him so he wouldn't be able to tell anyone about the toxin or antitoxin. She wouldn't put it past the monster.

Grisha counted down with his fingers.

Three.

Two.

Go.

Moving with a graceful silence that highlighted his obvious training, Grisha slid into the hallway, weapon aimed as she moved in low, her weapon forward.

The four men turned, surprise on their faces as they reached for their weapons. Shoulda had them in hand already.

Aiming, she pulled the trigger, once, twice, and kept going until her targets were down. She knew she'd hit the two men on the left side of the hallway in the head and center mass. Grisha had clearly done the same to his two guys.

"Come on," she murmured, hurrying forward toward the lab door.

The virus she'd uploaded to the security system had screwed up all their safety measures. The house wasn't even secured now. No wonder Tasev had four guards in front of the door. She looked at Grisha. "Stay back," she ordered before easing the door open. She didn't move in though, knowing Ortiz would be waiting for an attack and would shoot whoever walked in.

"Ortiz, it's me. How are the packages?"

"Alive," he called out. "You okay?"

If she said the word "fine," it was code that she was under duress. "We're good to go."

"Thank God. Coming up."

Weapon in hand, Selene turned to Grisha, who hadn't moved. "I'm with two of Tasev's guys. Former guys. Whatever. They're helping us." If they had more time—and if she thought he'd tell her—she'd ask Grisha, which definitely wasn't his real name, who the hell he worked for. It had to be another government agency.

Grisha grunted. "Yeah and me and my buddy need to leave. We'll cover you to the wine cellar. It's the best place to hunker down until your backup arrives."

She nodded. That had been her plan too. "Works for me."

Matvei appeared around the corner, his expression tight as he hurried toward them. "Tasev's dead. Just heard it on the radio. His body was found with Valery's. It must have been your partner," he said to Selene. "Everyone is leaving. They're grabbing their shit and getting out of here."

Tasev was dead? It had to be Levi. Tasev had told her that he'd be calling him, but . . . Her heart leaped at the thought. "The man with me before. Have you seen him?"

Matvei shook his head. "No, but Tasev was waiting on Moore when he sent me off to look for Grisha."

Relief flooded her. "If you see him, don't engage. He's with me."

Ortiz stepped out of the lab door, MP5 drawn as he looked between them. The doctor was behind him, his arm around his daughter's shoulder. The girl looked terrified but at least the two hostages were in good health and keeping it together. "Let's get the hell out of here . . . Oh shit, I'm back online." He put one hand up to his ear. "Wesley, yeah, I'm with her and the packages now."

She held a finger to her lips and pointed at Ortiz to follow.

Behind her she heard Ortiz murmur, "Going dark."

Heart in her throat as she worried for Levi's safety, she stepped around the bodies of the dead guards, avoiding the spreading blood as they hurried down the hallway. Moving past Grisha, she fell in step with Matvei. If Levi was truly here she wanted him to see her first and know these guys weren't tangos. She didn't want him attacking without warning.

As they neared the end of the hallway, Levi stepped into view at the far end, weapon drawn. His pistol was pointed straight at Matvei, who stopped walking, his own pistol pointed at Levi's chest.

That dark stare swung to hers and held, burning with an intensity that made the hair on her arms stand up.

"They're helping us," she said quietly.

Thankfully Matvei lowered his weapon.

In true Levi fashion he kept his up, holding it trained on the man's head. "Did they hurt you?" he asked, his gaze never wavering from Matvei.

The concern in his dark eyes was almost too much. "No one hurt me. They helped me kill the guards. We need to get Schmidt and his daughter out of here. We don't know what Tasev has put into motion and we need that antitoxin."

Levi nodded and stepped to the side, letting everyone pass as she remained where she was, his intense gaze falling on her. Somehow she tore her gaze from his and held out an arm to stop Grisha.

He raised his eyebrows, but kept his weapon loose in his other hand. "The man you killed, what's the name of the woman he saw regularly?" she asked. "The one he mentioned."

If he was surprised by her question, he didn't show it. "Galina. Lives in Wynwood. She's a professional."

A professional meaning prostitute. Or more likely a well-paid escort. Galina was a unique enough name that Selene hoped she could find her quickly. If not, she had another plan for what she needed to do. She nodded her thanks and he continued past her.

"Ortiz, I'm right behind you," she said without looking at him, keeping her gaze on Levi. "I know where the wine cellar is." She had to talk to Levi first.

Ortiz paused next to her, as if he wanted to argue, but he nodded and herded the doctor and his daughter around the corner.

"Tasev is dead," Levi said, barely a foot from her. "I had no choice but to kill him."

She wanted to throw her arms around him and kiss him senseless but now definitely wasn't the time. "You're alive. That's what matters. And so is Schmidt. But you need to leave. Wesley is maybe seven minutes out. Get the hell out of here." She didn't care if she caught hell from her boss for letting Levi go. He meant too much to her to see him brought in. She didn't think Wesley wanted him arrested anyway but still, she wasn't taking any chances.

"It's more like six, and I'm not leaving you." His expression was fierce and determined.

It melted her heart. "Levi, I don't know what his plan is for you. You've got to go now," she snapped.

He took a step forward so that they were inches from each other. The faint scent of his aftershave and their recent sex wrapped around her. "I lost one woman I loved. I'm not losing another."

The meaning of his words hit her square in the chest. He'd come for her when Tasev called him so maybe she shouldn't be surprised, but she'd thought . . . hell, she'd thought he was still in love with his dead wife. Throat tight, she unsheathed her KA-BAR and handed it to him. And suddenly she couldn't hold back what she'd refused to think about since they'd started working together. "Remember that mission you did in Cartagena seven years ago? Jimenez's compound?"

He stared at the blade—his old knife—but didn't take it as he quickly put the pieces together and jerked his gaze to hers. "That was *you*?" Shock reverberated through his voice.

"Yes." She fought the memories flooding back, how she'd felt so safe with him even back then. She'd been a scared kid and because of him she'd known everything in her life would be normal again. Or her version of normal. "I owe you more than I can ever repay, Levi. You saved me from hell. Please trust me and leave. I swear to God I'll contact you as soon as I can. I just . . . I need to do something first and I need you to trust me. *Please.*" She didn't care that she was begging. She needed him gone because first she had to find out if his daughter was alive. She'd never been much for prayer but she sent up one now for all she was worth. If any-one deserved a second chance at a family and peace it was Levi. "I love you, Levi. *Trust me.* I . . . My last name is Wolfe, with an *e* at the end." Telling him her true identity was the only way she could think to show him how much he meant to her, even more than telling him that she loved him. Agents like her didn't reveal who they were. Ever. She was giving him all her trust.

His jaw clenched tightly and she knew he wanted to argue. But they didn't have time. Taking her off guard he grabbed her by the back of the neck and crushed his mouth to hers in a quick, bruising kiss. "You'd better stay alive," he snarled before stepping back and peer-ing around the corner. "I'll follow you to the cellar."

She wanted to argue but knew it was pointless. Nod-ding, she hurried with him. They silently made their way through hallways. Matvei had been right, every-one must have been scrambling to leave because no one was in their way.

As they reached the cellar door, Ortiz stood there, MP5 in hand, looking anxious. "The doc and his daugh-ter are in. The other two left. Said we should be safe in here." He tapped his earpiece. "Wesley knows where we are."

Selene nodded, then pointed at Levi. "Did you . . ."

Ortiz shook his head.

Wesley had to know Levi was here, or she assumed he did, but she didn't want Levi getting swept up in any bureaucratic bullshit if the wrong person saw Levi here or if Wesley decided to haul him in. Relief bled through Selene and she looked at Levi as Ortiz headed down the stairs.

"Can you get out undetected?" she asked quietly.

Levi snorted, as if her question was ludicrous. He grabbed her hip with his weapon-free hand. She felt his possessive hold all the way to her core and hated that she had to let him go for now. "I don't want to leave you."

"You're not leaving me, unless you don't plan to see me again?" She hated the vulnerable note in her voice. It made her sound weak but at this point she couldn't hide it. She needed to see Levi again no matter what. And not for selfless reasons but because she couldn't stand the thought of him not being in her life.

"There's nowhere you can hide that I won't find you," he murmured darkly before turning and heading down a hallway she knew would take him to a garage.

The sharp sense of loss she felt as she watched him disappear was more potent than she could have imagined. Weapon out, she hurried into the cellar and locked the door behind her before descending the stairs. A lock wouldn't stop anyone, but it would alert her and Ortiz to anyone's presence.

At the bottom of the stone stairs she quickly scanned the area. Racks of wine bottles covered the three walls, but there was an alcove behind the stairs. On silent feet, she hurried inside and found Ortiz standing guard next to an open door. The door had a rack of wine bottles covering it, making it blend into the surroundings.

"They're in here." He stood back, letting her enter to join the others.

Only when he shut the door behind them did Selene allow herself a small breath of relief.

"Where's Wesley?" Selene asked.

"They're storming the place now. He went offline for the infiltration but he knows where we are."

"Why didn't you tell him about Levi being here?" she demanded.

Ortiz shrugged. "He asked if I'd seen him so he knows Levi was here but . . . fuck it, Levi saved my ass more than once when we were in the Corps together."

Selene nodded once in approval before turning to face Schmidt and his daughter. The young woman who was likely the same age or maybe older than Selene stood next to a rack of red wines, her arms wrapped tightly around herself.

"Do either of you need a medic?"

They both shook their heads and Schmidt asked, "Why did Levi leave?"

"It's not important. Do you or do you not have the cure to the toxin you created?" She tried to keep the anger out of her voice but it was difficult. The man had created something that could kill countless people and it had no known cure.

"I do. I'll finish writing out the formula now." He pulled a pad of paper from the back of his pants he must have grabbed from the lab. "Is Levi in some kind of trouble? I . . . I sent my message to Meghan hoping—"

"Meghan Lazaro is dead," Selene said softly. "Tortured and killed by Tasev two years ago." She told him bluntly, wanting to see his reaction. Because if this was all a charade, if he'd somehow known, she'd kill him herself.

His face paled and a shudder racked his wiry frame. He clutched on to the edge of a built-in table in the middle of the small room. "She's *dead*?"

"Yes."

"I . . . I contacted her two years ago when Tasev approached me. He didn't tell me who he was then, though I wouldn't have known his name anyway, but his questions were suspect. He'd read some theoretical papers I wrote and was far too interested in toxins and what they could do. I should have contacted someone sooner, but I was coming to DC for a conference and knew I could talk to Meghan then. We talked all the time anyway but . . . I wanted to tell her in person, see if she thought it was worth worrying about. She was supposed to meet me the day I was taken. I never imagined . . . Oh, God, he was probably tracking all my movements. Maybe even my phone calls. I told her enough over the phone that I might have . . . might have made it clear she worked for the US government." His voice cracked as he trailed off and his daughter wrapped an arm around his shoulders. "I'm so sorry. I never knew anything happened to her."

Selene wasn't convinced, but it would make sense for why Tasev had taken Meghan. If he even suspected Meghan knew something about him and his plans, he would have gone to any length to eliminate the threat. Clearly. "Why did it take you so long to contact her again?"

"I never had a chance until recently. I've been a virtual hostage for two years. I've"—he shot his daughter a glance before focusing on Selene again—"I've done things I'm not proud of."

"Like using live test subjects?" From Wesley's last big job that involved terrorists blowing up hundreds of people at a gala, she knew that a man named Paul Hill had been in business with Tasev and had been giving him healthy girls to dose with his toxin.

Averting his gaze, Schmidt nodded. His daughter paled beside him, but didn't say anything.

"So why now?" Selene pressed.

His gaze snapped back up. "They kidnapped my daughter so I used the opportunity. Until a few days ago I haven't had access to electronics in two years. I took a risk."

Selene just nodded at the pad in his hand. "Can you finish the formula? We have most of what was on your boards."

"I'll do it now." He pulled a pencil from his white coat and started scribbling furiously.

Selene glanced over at Ortiz, who was standing near the door, weapon ready. "You heard from Wesley or Karen yet?"

He shook his head. "No, but I'm sure it's a cluster-fuck up there."

She wasn't surprised they couldn't hear anything. This house was well insulated and huge. Nodding, she glanced around the room. "Wonder what's going to happen to all this wine."

"I bet Wesley lets us keep a bottle."

She snorted, so many emotions racing through her at once that laughing felt foreign. Tasev was dead, the doctor was safe, and Levi was in the wind. For now. She wasn't letting him go though. No way in hell.

Chapter 23

Uncle: headquarters of any espionage service.

Levi steered his rental car up to the guarded gate of the parking lot outside the nondescript gray building in Pine Mountain, Georgia. He'd been here only once before, many years ago, but he knew it was Burkhart's preferred base of operations. And he wasn't sure why.

The man had offices in Maryland, DC, Miami, and other cities that civilians didn't even know the NSA operated out of. But Pine Mountain was his favorite place.

Since Levi hadn't been able to get in touch with Selene, he was going straight to Burkhart. Even if it meant he got arrested or dragged back into Agency work that would eventually kill his soul. He had to see Selene again.

She'd told him she'd contact him in a week and it had been eight days. He couldn't take it anymore.

And he knew Burkhart was here. He'd seen him drive in an hour ago. He'd staked out the place twenty-four hours ago and while their security was excellent, the layout was the same as the Maryland office—and he'd been watching through a scope a half mile away. There was a possibility they knew he was coming, but he doubted it.

As he stopped at the guarded gate and rolled down his window, he nodded at the guard sitting behind the bullet-resistant window. The bottom half of the door was steel-reinforced. A civilian who accidentally stumbled on this place wouldn't know that, but Levi knew how their offices were set up.

"Are you lost, sir?" the man wearing plain black fatigues asked. Though he couldn't see a weapon, he knew the man was armed.

"No, I'm here to see Wesley Burkhart."

"I'm afraid you have the wrong—"

"Tell him it's Levi Lazaro."

The man paused and gave him a hard look before picking up a phone. Levi looked straight ahead, waiting for Wesley to let him in, send him away, or put armed men on him.

A moment later the gate lifted and the guard said, "Park in the third row from the front." Just like that he was in. Of course getting into the building was a whole other thing. And seeing Selene was something else entirely. She wouldn't be here of course, but Wesley would know where she was.

He glanced around the quiet parking lot as he slowly drove, sticking to the fifteen mile per hour speed limit. Just as the guard instructed he parked in the only empty spot in the third row. When he got out he kept his hands visible just in case someone got trigger-happy. He'd come unarmed because to do otherwise would send a bad message.

Glancing around, he noticed two men in black fatigues about five cars down on each side of him just standing there. They weren't moving toward him or acting hostile, just watching.

He headed for the front of the building, weaving his way through cars and the men did the same, keeping their distance. Ignoring them, he headed straight for the front door. Once he was inside he was met by two armed men, both wearing gray uniforms. Depressing color.

Both men had buzzed haircuts and were fit. The one on the left nodded at him. "You're going to go through a security scan, then a strip search. Once you're upstairs you'll go through another security scan."

Levi gritted his teeth but nodded. He wasn't exactly surprised but a strip search, really? Twenty minutes later he and an armed escort stepped out of an elevator and headed down a hallway. After they took a left, the guard stopped at the first door on the right. There weren't any more offices in this hallway and the door was unmarked.

The guard nodded once at him, then left. Guess that meant he should knock. Before he'd raised his hand, Wesley barked out, "Come in."

Bracing for the worst, he opened the door to find Wesley sitting behind his desk next to a stack of paperwork.

He eyed Levi cautiously. "You here to kill me?"

Levi rolled his eyes, knowing that was Burkhart's way of breaking the tension, and let the door shut behind him. "I should after that fucking strip search."

Burkhart shrugged, his mouth pulling up at the corners. The man hadn't changed much in two years. Dark hair, graying at the temples, piercing green eyes, and he was in good shape not just for a man in his fifties but a man any age. "Why are you here?"

"Where's Selene?" he demanded. He sat in one of the maroon chairs on the other side of Burkhart's desk.

To Levi's annoyance, Burkhart didn't seem surprised by the question. He just watched him like he wanted to see into his soul. "Why do you want to see her?"

His jaw clenched as he started to answer. When he saw a picture of Wesley and Selene with their arms around each other on one of Wesley's bookshelves, he frowned. She was younger in the picture, maybe eighteen. She wasn't exactly smiling for the camera, but she looked proud. It was difficult to tell where the picture had been taken because it was outdoors. Everything about the photo was generic. "Damn, you really did recruit her young."

Wesley shifted in his seat, his expression turning hard.

"I wasn't insulting you. She told me she'd been recruited young. I guess I just wasn't sure."

"You haven't answered my question."

"Why do you think I want to see her?" He wasn't telling Wesley anything.

"Because you love her."

Levi blinked but nodded stiffly. "Yeah. I do."

"So?"

"What the fuck do you mean, so? She told me she'd contact me in a week." And he'd been watching the clock, counting down, agonizing like a teenage girl waiting for a phone call.

"It's only been a week."

"It's been *eight* days," he growled. "Did you detain her or some shit for letting me go?"

Wesley shook his head, the protective vibes rolling off him fierce. "No. So, you love her. What does that mean for you, Levi? What are you going to offer her? A broken man still mourning his dead wife? Selene shouldn't come second best to a memory."

The questions grated over Levi's skin like shards of glass. "How's that any of your business? And Selene would never be second best," he snarled, pissed Wesley could even say that.

"She's like a daughter to me. I want to know and you'll damn well tell me or you won't see her." There was a flicker of something in Burkhart's eyes but the man was so unreadable it was impossible to tell. Hell, he'd taught Levi everything he knew.

"I will always miss Meghan," he rasped out, his throat tightening for a moment. "Always. But I love Selene." He wasn't sure what the hell he had to offer her, but he'd figure it out. He'd give her anything she wanted, do anything she wanted. The woman had saved him when he hadn't even realized he'd needed saving. "You planning on charging me with anything?"

Surprising him, his former boss snorted. "No. I know why you did what you did. And *most* of the gray stuff you engaged in wasn't on domestic soil. Besides, I don't have any proof of anything."

The tension in Levi's shoulders fled and he relaxed against the seat. If he wasn't getting arrested he could think about starting a life with Selene. A real one. That hope sat heavy on his chest though. For so long he hadn't thought of anything past revenge. These new possibilities were terrifying. "So what happened with Schmidt? Did he know about Meghan?"

Wesley shook his head, his expression grim. "No, he reached out to her for help and when she went to see him, she must have been picked up by Tasev's men. I've got some of his men in custody, though most were killed the night we raided his place, and only one has been around long enough to have known about how Tasev acquired Schmidt. He didn't keep many employees much longer than a year. Tasev was monitoring Schmidt's calls and e-mails. When he reached out to her, it set off Tasev's alarm bells. He took her because he wanted to know who she worked for, her connection to Schmidt, and if anyone she worked with knew who he, meaning Tasev, was."

Levi needed to know exactly what had happened. "You believe the doctor?"

"That he had nothing to do with her death? Yeah. I do. Plus he passed the polygraph we gave him. Doesn't mean that bastard is innocent though," Wesley muttered.

"What about Tasev's men? Any of them around when she was murdered?"

Wesley's face turned impassive. "What if I say yes? Are you going to let it go and let the justice system do its job or are you going to give up Selene and go after them?"

"The justice system is broken and we both know it, but . . . I won't go after anyone." He wouldn't do anything that could take him away from Selene. He just hoped she still wanted him; that she meant the words she'd said to him. He'd lived on them every day since.

Wesley nodded once. "Right answer. And no, none of the men with him now were part of what was done to her. They're all dead according to one of Tasev's former crew. He was with Tasev for almost three years and has been very cooperative. He also passed the lie detector test. He knew about what happened to her, but he wasn't there for any of it."

Levi had more questions, but more than anything, he just wanted to know where Selene was. "You going to tell me where she is?"

Wesley sighed and picked up the phone on his desk. After dialing a number—that Levi memorized—Wesley sat back and waited for whoever it was to pick up.

Levi hoped it was Selene, but couldn't tell if that's who he was calling.

"Hey," Wesley said, his voice softening.

A pause.

"Levi's sitting in my office."

A longer pause.

"He wants to see you now."

An even longer pause. This time Levi didn't think she was even speaking on the other end.

Finally, "Okay."

Once Wesley hung up, Levi shifted to the edge of his seat. Taking him by surprise again, Wesley stood. "Come on. Let's go see her."

Almost numb with hope, he followed his boss out and they took a private elevator to an underground parking garage and got into a luxury four-door sedan Levi had no doubt was armored. Wesley was silent as they left the compound but the energy humming from him was almost palpable.

"What is it?" Levi asked quietly after about twenty minutes of driving. "I can hear the gears in your head."

Wesley pushed out a ragged sigh, the action out of character for the man. "Your life is about to change and I'm—" He broke off and cleared his throat. "You were a good agent and I'm truly sorry for what happened to Meghan but you're getting a second chance at life. I know you won't come back, especially after today, but if you ever change your mind you'll always have a place waiting."

His words stunned Levi, but he didn't know how to respond so he leaned back against the leather seat and looked out the window. If he'd done anything truly heinous while he'd been off the reservation he was certain Wesley would have made him pay, but there was no way Wesley or anyone had proof of much of anything Levi had done in the last couple of years. And Levi had a feeling that prosecuting someone who'd once been deep Black Ops wasn't something the NSA would ever want to open themselves up to.

They were silent as Wesley drove them out of town to a rural area with a lot of forest and flat spreads of land.

When Wesley turned down a road with a sign marked private property off to the side, Levi glanced at him but it was clear he knew where he was going. The single-lane road was paved with fenced-in property that contained horses on either side. Maybe Wesley was taking him to a safe house. As they neared the end of the fenced property, the trees on either side thickened for about a hundred yards before thinning again. The paved road turned into a long gravel driveway and a two-story log and stone cabin-style home came into view.

"What is this place?"

"Selene's home."

His heart rate kicked up. Levi looked at him in surprise, but Wesley didn't glance back. It answered the question why Wesley preferred to work out of Pine Mountain. Wesley kept driving down the gravel driveway until he parked in front of a two-car garage. "They're waiting for you."

Wait. "They?"

Wesley didn't answer. Just looked out the driver's side window. For a moment it looked like he had tears in his eyes but Levi knew that was just plain wrong. Without questioning him further, he jumped from the vehicle, thrumming with an out of control need to see Selene. To hold her in his arms, to tell her he loved her and that he wanted to spend the rest of his life showing her how much. He didn't care who was at the house with her. Maybe another agent or something.

Before he'd made it up the stone steps to the wraparound porch, Wesley was already pulling out of the drive. Good. Levi didn't plan to leave Selene any time soon. Or ever. And he didn't want an audience for what he had planned.

When he reached the front door, it swung open immediately. Selene stood there wearing jeans, a blue sweater, and no shoes. She looked nervous.

Welcome to the club.

He stopped where he was, scared as hell to see her again. Especially when she hadn't called him like she'd said she would. "Hey."

She smiled. "Hey. You're here."

He nodded and she shook her head at herself. For a moment he panicked. What if she hadn't meant what she said? Things between them had been fast and intense and hell, maybe now that she'd had time to think about it she realized he had nothing to offer her. "Can I come in?"

She swallowed hard and nodded, stepping out and closing the door behind her. "Yeah. In a minute. I, uh . . . I don't even know how to tell you this."

Her words barely registered. Unable to stand not touching her any longer, he crossed the distance between them and pulled her into his arms. Holding her long, lithe body against him was the best sensation in the world. He squeezed her tight, feeling like his chest might explode when she wrapped her arms around him. "Leaving you was the hardest thing I've ever done. I meant every word I said, Selene. I love you. I don't know what I have to offer you now. Hell, I don't even have a place to call home or a job or anything to give you but I love you and I want to spend the rest of my life with you."

Her pale blue eyes filled with tears. "I love you too. More than I ever thought possible. But right now . . . I'd like you to meet someone." Her voice broke on the last word and tears started tracking down her cheeks.

Who the hell was here that would make her so upset? "Don't cry, baby," he murmured, wiping his thumbs across her soft skin, hating to see her in pain.

"These are happy tears," she whispered, pulling back from him. "Come on."

Levi didn't want to see anyone else but Selene, but

he let her take his hand and lead him through her foyer, past a dining room and living room and into a spacious kitchen where a little girl with bright red curls sat in a booster chair eating grapes from a Minnie Mouse plate. She looked up at him, then at Selene, then back at him. She smiled, revealing twin dimples in her little cheeks before she popped half a grape in her mouth.

Levi stared as a painful suspicion took hold. It was too much to hope, but . . . she looked exactly like Meghan. A complete replica of her when she'd been little. Red hair, twin dimples, green eyes. The bottom of his world fell out. His throat tightened and he tried to look at Selene, but he couldn't tear his gaze away from the toddler. He wanted to pull the little girl into his arms.

"Juice!" she suddenly demanded, taking her sippy cup and pounding it on the table.

Laughing, Selene went to take her sippy cup. A tremor racked through him and he blinked back hot tears. Levi managed to find his voice. "Is she . . ."

"She's yours and Meghan's. She's two and her name is Faith," Selene said, moving to the refrigerator while he stood there staring through swimming eyes. "I'll tell you everything when she goes down for her nap, but for now, meet your daughter, Levi." Selene's voice broke then too and he didn't even bother trying to stop the tears.

His throat was thick as he forced his feet to move. He sat across from Faith, not wanting to scare her as he catalogued each tiny feature. Her hair and eyes were Meghan but the nose and mouth were all him. God help him, he couldn't stop staring. She was a miracle.

One he wasn't sure he deserved but he was grateful he'd always have a piece of Meghan. He didn't know shit about kids and he was a big guy. What if he scared her?

Selene placed the sippy cup in front of his daughter again, then pointed at the seat next to Faith. "You can sit next to her. She's very well adjusted and not scared of most people."

Still unable to talk, he slid into the chair, drinking in the sight of his daughter.

Daughter.

It seemed impossible yet here she was sitting right in front of him. When the table started shaking he realized his knee was bouncing up and down, hitting it. He forced himself to stop and cleared his throat. He should say something. Anything.

"Nose," Faith said, pointing to his nose.

He nodded and mimicked her like a parrot. "Nose."

"My nose," she said, touching her own.

"Your nose."

She pointed to her eye next and said, "Eye." He started to repeat it when she crossed her arms over her chest and said, "love," then pointed at him and ended with "you."

He looked away, his throat clogged with tears as he started shaking. Fuck, he couldn't control the tremors racking his body. Selene's arms came around him from behind, holding on to him tight. "Her foster mom taught her that," she whispered. "But I'm pretty sure she's going to love you more than anything in this world."

A sob escaped and this time he didn't fight it. Selene

murmured soothing sounds as she held him close, rocking him against her chest. "Thank you," he finally whispered, able to get something out. He couldn't imagine all the trouble Selene had gone through to even find Faith, to give him the most precious gift in the world. And she'd clearly been taking care of her.

Luckily Faith didn't seem fazed by his outburst, she just kept chattering away, making mostly nonsensical words as she ate grapes and drank her juice.

Levi couldn't believe any of this was real, but he knew it was. He didn't know if he deserved a second chance but he was sure as hell taking it with both hands. He was going to make a life with his daughter and make sure Faith knew only love and happiness. He just hoped Selene wanted to be part of that life.

Chapter 24

Security clearance: status granted to individuals allowing them access to classified information and/or re-
stricted areas.

Wesley picked up the phone in his office and dialed
a familiar number. He hadn't heard from Levi or
Selene since he'd dropped Levi off and he didn't think
he would for a while. Later he'd have Levi's rental car
delivered to him, but that wasn't important now.

At first Wesley had been surprised at the thought of
Selene and Levi falling for each other, especially since
Selene was so different from Meghan. But maybe he
shouldn't be. They both had a steel core and had been
through some tough shit and come out okay. Thank
God Levi eventually had. Wesley hadn't been so sure
the man would ever get out of that dark abyss.

"Yeah," Max Southers said, his voice distracted.

"You at work?" Wesley asked.

"Yeah. Getting out of here soon though."

"Want me to call your office or is this secure?"

"We're fine."

He didn't plan to say anything classified but he

didn't want this conversation to be overheard. "Just about wrapped up all that shit with Tasev."

Max snorted. "Glad that bastard's dead. Saw the news and heard through the grapevine you brought down what could have been a vicious attack."

"Yeah." Toxins in general were nasty business. "Sorry I haven't called you since everything went down. I know you had a contact in his organization and I want to make sure he got out before our raid." It was likely two undercover agents according to what Selene had put in her official report, but Wesley wanted to feel out his friend before continuing.

"Hypothetically, if I had a contact, or contacts, they're alive and said to say thank you to a certain blond operative if I ever got the chance."

Wesley smiled. "Hypothetically she extends her thanks too."

"When are you going to be in DC again?"

Wesley glanced at his calendar. "Next week." He had a bitch of a schedule next week, flying to three different locations.

"Come over for dinner if you're free. Mary would love to see you."

"Think she'd cook that lasagna for me?"

Max chuckled. "Yeah."

"I'll set it up with you later." As soon as they disconnected, Wesley stood and grabbed his laptop. He could work from home tonight.

Sitting on Selene's couch while his beer sat on the side table next to him, Levi felt as if he was going to wake up at any second and discover this was all a dream, that he hadn't just met his daughter for the first time today.

It was too surreal.

For the past few hours they'd done nothing but play with her, read her books—though she tried to teethe on them more than anything—and take her out to see Selene's horses. She was way too young to ride, but Faith liked to pet them. She also had a pet bunny that Selene had apparently gotten for her a couple of days ago.

He had so many damn questions and he wanted to know why it had taken Selene so long to contact him but he understood why she'd wanted to wait to discuss everything until Faith was sleeping. She'd skipped her nap, too excited by the newcomer—him.

She'd let him hold her and hadn't seemed scared of him at all. Holding her in his arms was the best feeling in the world. Meghan would have loved her more than anything and he was never going to let any harm come to her. When Faith had done the "I love you" thing again, he'd almost had another breakdown.

Now he wanted answers and to hold Selene in his arms. But in a much different way. Today she hadn't touched him much except for when he'd first arrived and he couldn't tell if she was letting him get adjusted to Faith or what, but he wanted to touch her, even just to hold her hand. He wanted her to understand what she meant to him, that he wasn't letting her go again.

Selene came out from the guest room where Faith was sleeping, a monitor in her hand. "I've got the security system armed but now you can see her anytime you want," she said, holding out the monitor to him as she collapsed on the couch next to him.

Hell no. He hauled her into his lap.

Blue eyes wide with surprise, she settled against him, but he could sense the tension humming through her. Just like that, he was hard.

He took the monitor from her and grinned. "They didn't have this kind of stuff when I was a kid."

"Right," she muttered before clearing her throat nervously. "I know you have questions."

"Yeah." He set the monitor down next to his beer and wrapped his arms around her.

Thankfully she snuggled against him, but that tenseness was still there. He didn't like it.

"I'm just going to start from the beginning and feel free to jump in with questions anytime." When he nodded she continued, "When I was being held in the freezer, the guard Grisha killed said something to me about . . . Meghan's baby still being alive."

Selene paused, waiting for him to give her a signal. Since he didn't trust his voice he just nodded again.

"When they took Meghan, they brought her down to Miami since that was Tasev's new base of operations. Grisha gave me enough information that I was able to connect an escort the other guard spent time with to someone who worked at one of the hospitals. From there I was able to track down all the babies taken in the state's system about two years ago. I covered adoptions and those still in foster care. Normally a baby would be adopted quickly but Faith has some medical problems." Selene's voice was hesitant so he squeezed her hand.

"I was going to ask. She's so small. Is that . . . normal?" All kids seemed tiny to him so he didn't know if she was too small for her age or what. And he'd been too afraid to ask.

Selene smiled, the sight taking his breath away. "Oh yeah. She's just a small kid, but she's got some heart issues. Nothing that will stop her from living a full life, but she'll need to make more doctor visits than other kids and she might get more colds than normal. During flu season you'll need to pay more attention to her if she gets a sniffle or fever. I've got her medical files so you'll be able to look at them and talk to her pediatrician whenever you want. You'll need to have her files transferred to wherever you end up . . . living."

He started to comment but she kept going.

"Her parentage has been verified with the DNA you and Meghan had on file so there's no doubt she's yours. Wesley pulled a lot of strings to get her here with me and you'll need to sign some paperwork, but she's legally yours. It took a little longer than I'd hoped, which is why I didn't call you."

Overwhelmed, Levi sat back against the couch. Too many emotions ran through him. He was humbled, awed, and yeah, scared at the thought of being a dad. "Holy shit."

"It's a lot to take in," she said softly.

"Yeah." He was a dad with serious responsibilities now. For the rest of his life. When everything she'd just said registered he turned to face her, pinning her with his stare. "I don't have a place to live right now." He had a lot of money, but no roots anywhere. The few things he'd kept from his former life were in a storage locker.

A ghost of a smile played across her lips. "I know.

You're more than welcome to . . . stay here until you figure some things out. Your life has just changed drastically and I love having Faith here." Multiple emotions flickered across her face, sadness and pain, and the sight was a kick in his gut.

"Why are you sad?" he blurted.

She shook her head. "I'm not sad. I'm . . . I don't know what the hell I am. You have a lot to deal with right now, Levi."

Suddenly he realized what she wasn't saying and a spike of iciness slid through his veins. He tightened his grip around her. "You don't want a ready-made family?" Even if he couldn't blame her, it still sliced him up. Nothing should be able to do that, considering he'd been given the best gift in the world, but he didn't want a life without Selene either. It made him feel hollow to imagine waking up another day without her. She'd filled something inside him he hadn't realized could be filled again.

She blinked in surprise. "Are you kidding me? I love you, Levi. Even all the screwed up parts of you. And I've only known Faith a few days and that kid has completely stolen my heart. I just . . . I know you have a lot of decisions to make. Like, where you'll live. What you'll do for a living. Stuff like that. I didn't think you'd need or want anything else to worry about right now. I'm not going to pressure you to include me in your life."

He cupped her cheek, rubbing his thumb across her soft skin. Her eyes grew heavy lidded for a moment as she watched him. "I'll live wherever you are so that solves the first problem. Preferably in the same house. And I have no idea what I want to do now but I don't need to make that decision for a while. The last few years I've done well for myself and I just want to spend time with my daughter and you. I want to marry you, Selene. When I told you before this wasn't casual, I wasn't kidding. I want a ring on your finger and to wake up to your beautiful face every morning for the next fifty fucking years." He knew it was too soon to say that shit but he didn't care. More than anyone he knew what it was like to lose someone. He wasn't going to waste time because it was too damn precious.

"You're gonna have to start watching that F-bomb around Faith," she whispered.

"I can do that."

"And . . . I think you need counseling. You've been through a lot and—"

"Okay."

She blinked. "What?"

"I agree with you." If anyone had told him a couple of years ago he needed to see a therapist he'd have knocked their head off. But now, he knew he did. If he was going to be a father and husband, he needed help and he wasn't afraid to admit it.

The most breathtaking smile spread across her face as tears filled her eyes.

Heart pounding out of control, he reached for Selene, grabbing her hips and pulling her so that she straddled him. Groaning, he rolled his hips against her, his cock hardening even more at the feel of her on top of him.

"You're also going to have to give me a better proposal than that," she murmured before brushing her lips over his.

He groaned again. The woman tasted like heaven. His woman. She started feathering kisses along his jaw, nipping at his skin and he felt it in every nerve ending. He'd been fantasizing about this for eight straight days.

"I've got to tell you something else." Her breath was hot against his ear.

He didn't want to talk anymore, but . . . "What?" he managed to rasp out.

"Wesley lives not too far from here. We're neighbors." She pulled back to look at him, clearly gauging his expression.

He was surprised, but maybe he shouldn't have been. "Okay."

She bit her bottom lip as she continued to watch him. Finally she spoke again. "I told you my family died when I was young and that's true. They were killed in a home invasion gone wrong. I was fourteen and at the mall of all places when it happened." She swallowed hard and he wrapped his arms around her, pulling her closer. What a shitty thing to have to deal with. He might have lost his parents but at least he'd had a lot of good years with them. "After they were killed the money they left me was put into a trust to be managed by a social worker. She was an idiot and would have mismanaged it before I'd turned eighteen so I transferred the funds into another account and split town. I was always good with computers. Really good."

That being an understatement, considering what he'd seen her do.

"So I managed to live on my own for over a year—renting under an alias. I made friends, but they were all in school during the day—just like I should have been. But since my plan was to live off the radar until I was eighteen, I wasn't enrolled anywhere. And a bored teenager is a very bad thing. I hacked the CIA when I was fifteen sort of as a joke. Mainly just to see if I could do it. After that I had to move and keep moving because I'd stirred up a hornets' nest. I might have been smart but I was still fifteen. I also got on the radar of some very bad people. That's how I ended up in Cartagena. Jimenez had me funneling money for him but he was stupid and gave me personal time on his computer. That's when I contacted Wesley. I didn't know it was him I was contacting but I reached out asking for help and told him I was the one who'd hacked the CIA. I figured the NSA might help since I hadn't hacked them."

Levi rubbed a hand over his face. "That's . . . crazy. I always wondered what happened to that girl. To you."

She smiled at that. "I'm telling you all this because Wesley means a lot to me. We spend all our holidays together and, hell, he's the only family I've had for a really long time." The worried note in her voice clawed at him.

"I have no problem with Wesley." Something he wouldn't have been able to say even a week ago. "I let my rage blind me to a lot of things. I still don't know that I'd go back and change things if I could because everything that happened brought me to you and my daughter. So if Wesley's a part of your life, he's a part of mine." And the truth was, Wesley would probably make a great grandfather.

She started to breathe out a sigh of relief, but Levi

didn't let her. He slanted his mouth over hers, needing to taste and touch her everywhere, to prove to himself that Selene was alive and in his arms and not going anywhere. Rolling over, he pinned her beneath him on the couch, savoring the feel of her arching into him.

When she moaned, he froze and pulled back. "Can we . . . is it okay if we do this out here?" he whispered. What if Faith woke up? He knew pretty much nothing about kids and didn't want to scar her for life if she heard them or something.

To his surprise, Selene let out a loud bark of laughter. She cupped his face in her soft hands. "You have a lot to learn about kids. But I can tell you that yours can sleep through anything. And if for some reason she wakes up we'll hear her on the monitor so we're fine."

Not needing to hear another word, Levi crushed his mouth over Selene's this time, needing to claim and possess her. He couldn't believe how much his life had changed in a few short days. After today it would never be the same again and he couldn't be happier about it. He couldn't wait to start his life with the woman he loved and the daughter he never knew he had. He planned to protect and care for them the rest of his life.

Epilogue

One year later

After navigating around a tricycle and baseball and bat T-ball set, Selene steered her truck into the garage and shut the door behind her. She'd had a long day—scratch that, week—and she needed to see her husband and daughter.

She shrugged out of her jacket as she opened the door into the mud room. She slipped her boots off and headed into the attached kitchen.

A smile lit her face to see Levi at the stove and Faith sitting next to him on the counter intently watching him cook. She wanted to do anything her father did.

When Faith saw Selene her face lit up, those adorable dimples deepening as she threw her arms out and wiggled in place. "Mommy! I hold you, I hold you!"

"Hey, babe," Levi murmured, his lips curling up into a wicked grin that promised she'd enjoy whatever he had planned later tonight.

Hurrying to Faith she lifted her off the counter, soaking up the big hug as her little girl wrapped her arms around her neck and squeezed. The mommy moniker had taken her completely off guard the first time Faith had used it. And if she was honest, the next dozen times, but she loved Faith as if she was her own and she was raising her so she hadn't fought it even though she'd felt a bit like an imposter in the beginning. More than that, she'd worried Levi wouldn't like it. Turns out she was the only one worried.

"How was work?" Levi asked as she made her way to the refrigerator—with Faith attached to her hip— and grabbed a cold bottle of water.

"Exhausting but we wrapped up everything today." It didn't matter that Faith couldn't understand what they were talking about; Selene didn't talk many details about her work in front of their little girl.

Levi just nodded and she knew they'd talk more about the job later once Faith was in bed. She couldn't tell him everything but she still told him a lot about her various missions. It had been something she and Wesley had butted heads about after she and Levi had gotten married, but in the end she'd won. Her job was hard enough and she wasn't going to be one of those people who was forced to compartmentalize everything to the point where her family knew nothing about what she did. Levi understood more than most and he was a good sounding board. Plus Wesley had reinstated his security clearance so Levi was privy to hear certain things.

Even if he'd never return to what he'd done before he still understood what she went through daily. Although now she was strictly an analyst. No more field missions. Not with Faith and Levi to think about. At first she'd thought it would be a sacrifice but the truth was, Selene didn't miss it and her job was interesting and challenging on a daily basis. Sometimes too challenging, as tonight proved. She wanted to go to sleep for a week after the job she'd just finished.

"So . . . talked to Cole earlier today. He knows about a deal on a young Andalusian."

Biting back a smile, Selene peered over his shoulder at what Levi was doing. The cut up avocado, jalapeno, and tomato made her stomach growl because she knew exactly what he was making and it looked like heaven. "The beef on the grill?"

"Not yet. The meat won't take long."

"Yum," she murmured, kissing Faith on the cheek.

She nodded seriously, red curls bouncing. "Yummy, Mommy."

"Can you say carne asada tacos?"

Faith shook her head mainly to be obstinate, not because she couldn't say it. "Yummy in my tummy."

Levi cleared his throat and set his knife down as he turned to look at her. He crossed his mouth-watering arms over his chest. That T-shirt did nothing to hide his raw strength. "Are you going to ignore what I said?"

Selene's lips curved up and she leaned in to him, unable to deny herself any longer, brushing her lips gently over his lips before she pulled back. "We both know you're going to get the horse," she murmured. Cole was a horse-breeder who lived in the area and he and Levi had become good friends in the last few months.

"New horsey!" Faith exclaimed, which further proved

Selene's point that the girl understood far too much already. She always seemed to know what Selene and Levi were talking about, especially when it came to bed or bath time, her two least favorite times of day.

Levi just grinned and took Faith into his arms. Selene grabbed the blade and started dicing the tomato. "Got an interesting e-mail today from Lopez."

Levi chuckled, that sound making her insides melt. A year later and she still couldn't get enough of him. "I think I, or Isaiah, might have gotten the same e-mail."

Selene shook her head and focused on the tomato. "I'm glad they found happiness. It's crazy how stuff works out." Selene Silva, one of her former aliases, had received a wedding invitation to Alexander Lopez's wedding. He was marrying Allison, the woman he'd been so smitten over. Out of the corner of her eye she watched Levi put Faith down, who promptly ran from the kitchen talking about finding her stuffed Elmo.

Levi wrapped his arms around Selene from behind, tugging her back against his chest. Her entire body flared to life as he slid his hands up over her blouse and cupped her breasts. "As soon as she goes to bed, you're mine," he murmured darkly.

She set the blade down and turned in his arms, wrapping her hands around the back of his neck. "I'm going to be yours for the next week." After her last job Wesley had given everyone on it a week off with pay. Some jobs were tougher than others and she wasn't about to argue when she needed the mental break. Not when it meant she got to spend time with her family.

"Good, you can help me mend some of the fences," Levi murmured before nipping her bottom lip playfully.

"Hmm, I don't think so." For their first six months living together he'd been nothing but a doting father and husband, but six months ago he'd started a horse farm. It was small but already growing and she was more than impressed with how much work he put into it. At first she'd been worried he'd miss his former life but Levi seemed incredibly peaceful in a way she'd never imagined. She was certain the counseling had helped too.

"I think you'll find my form of payment very reward-ing," he murmured again, this time nipping her earlobe between his teeth as he rolled his hips against her.

She had no doubt that she would. And she couldn't wait. Settling down and starting a family so early in life had never been in her plans but she'd never been so happy. She couldn't imagine a life without Levi and Faith and was thankful every day for the family they'd made.

ACKNOWLEDGMENTS

I owe a big thanks to my understanding family, who makes sure I remember to eat when I'm on deadline. I'm so grateful to you guys! As always I owe thanks to my fabulous editor, Danielle Perez, for pushing me to make this the best book possible. Christina Brower, for all the behind-the-scenes work you do and the entire team at New American Library: Jessica Brock, Ashley Polikoff, Katie Anderson, thank you. Another big thanks to my agent, Jill Marsal, for all your invaluable help. Thank you to Kari Walker for all your insight and reading the early version of this book. I think I say this in every acknowledgments page, but you know I'd be lost without you. For my wonderful readers, thank you for reading the Deadly Ops series. Lastly, thank you to God.

Don't miss the next book
in the exciting Deadly Ops series by Katie Reus,

EDGE OF DANGER

On sale in November 2015 from Signet Eclipse.

Chapter 1

Wet work: expression for murdering or assassinating
someone ("wet" alluding to the spilling of blood).

Tucker Pankov ran a hand over his buzz cut, the
dampness from his shower already drying. He'd be
glad to grow his hair out again and spend at least a
week at his place in solitude. He lived in a small three-bed-
room home in the Virginia countryside. He'd chosen to
have acres and acres of space between him and his neighbors rather than a larger house in a suburb. He was rarely
there and when he did get downtime, he craved the
quiet.

For his last undercover job, as a psychopathic thug, he'd shaved his head, making himself look more the part of drug-peddling scum. He'd kept his same alias from the job he'd worked before that one with a true psychopath, Tasev. It was a relief to shed both personas.

It was also a fucking relief that bastard Tasev was dead, even if the DEA hadn't been the ones to stop him. He was still surprised that his boss, Deputy Director Max Southers, hadn't been upset when the NSA had brought down Tasev's operation instead of Tucker's elite undercover DEA team.

As he stepped into his bedroom, he turned on the television. Headlines from last week's attack on a political fund-raiser dominated everything.

Tucker should have probably been surprised by the attack, but little could shock him anymore. The drone that had carried out the attack should have never been stolen in the first place. Heads were already rolling over that, and while he cared about the massive loss of life, it had nothing to do with the DEA.

On-screen, Clarence Cochran, a politician who'd just announced his intention to seek the next presidential nomination for his party, was talking about what he viewed as an avoidable death of a man who would have been running against him. Acting as if he cared.

Tucker rolled his eyes. For the most part, politicians in Washington only cared about themselves. He actually belonged to the same political party as Cochran, but the guy was too much of an extremist. That was dangerous no matter what side of the political aisle a person stood on. For the next election he'd be voting against his party line if that moron made a play for the presidency. Tucker reached for the remote to turn it off when a breaking report flashed on the screen.

Max Southers, deputy director of the Drug Enforcement Administration, murdered in violent carjacking.

He blinked, ice invading his veins as he stared numbly at the television, before he turned up the volume. Max was dead? No fucking way. He'd just talked to him a couple of hours ago. Someone would have alerted him.

"You need a break, son, and I'm ordering it. Take a week off and just relax." The corners of Max's dark blue eyes had crinkled in concern as he'd watched Tucker from across his desk.

Max had called everyone in their team "son." It should have annoyed Tucker since he had a father, but he loved the man. They all did. Swallowing hard, he sat on the edge of his bed and listened as a somber-looking reporter talked about Max's murder, basically saying nothing at all. The police had no leads, and they didn't know if this was random or related to one of his cases.

Fuck.

Standing, Tucker muted the television and grabbed his phone from his nightstand. He needed to call the rest of the team and Mary, Max's wife. Hell, he needed to verify this was even true. If they'd reported this without telling her first . . . Hell no. He immediately rejected that. The DEA wouldn't have allowed that to happen. Unless the local PD had fucked it up and there'd been a leak. Because why had no one called the team first?

As he started to call Cole, his phone buzzed, his teammate's name appearing on-screen. Still numb, he answered. "You see the news?"

"Yeah." Cole's voice was grim. "Anyone contact you about it first?"

"No."

"I tried Mary and she's not answering."

Tucker's throat tightened as he stared blindly at the muted television. "You believe he's dead?"

"I . . . don't know. I can't imagine them running with the story unless they were positive."

"I'll call in a bit. We'll take care of her if it is true." For the most part, he didn't believe in happily ever after or any of that shit, but Mary and Max could have made a believer out of anyone after being together for forty years. She'd been with Max since his Navy days, enduring long deployments and raising their two kids basically by herself for months on end. Max had been ready to retire in the next two years. Tucker's free hand curled into a fist. "And we're going to find out whoever did this."

"Fuck yeah." Cole's voice was raspy, the edge in the normally laid-back man's voice razor-sharp. "What the . . . Are you still watching the report?"

"Yeah. Hold on." Tucker unmuted the television, frowning as he listened to the reporter's words. Neither he nor Cole spoke the next few minutes as he digested everything the man on the broadcast was saying. The news station had received an anonymous tip that a Shi'a terrorist group was responsible for Max's murder, that it wasn't a carjacking at all.

What. The. Hell.

"It doesn't seem possible," Tucker muttered. "Have you heard from the Leopard recently?" Leopard was their code word for Ali Nazari, an agent they had embedded in a high profile Shi'a terrorist organization. Almost no one knew of his undercover role. Just Max, Tucker, Cole, and two other teammates. It was too dangerous otherwise.

"No. I'll reach out now. We need to make sure the Leopard's files—"

"Max had a fail-safe in place in case something happened to him. I'll tell you about it, but not now." Never over the phone, even if their cells were encrypted. He drew in a breath to continue, when the power suddenly went off, his television and the steady hum of his heater going silent. Dawn was breaking, so he could see well enough without his lamp on, but he didn't often lose power and there wasn't a storm raging. Maybe a breaker had flipped. "Let me call you back in a sec."

"All right."

As they disconnected, Tucker pulled on a pair of jogging pants and grabbed his side arm from his nightstand. Even though he knew it was loaded, he checked the magazine out of habit. Full. Exiting his room, he moved on silent feet down the hallway that led to the living room and kitchen. As he made his way, he passed the keypad for his alarm system and a shot of adrenaline punched through him.

It was off.

The system was wireless and not linked to his power system, and it never went off-line. Not even when he lost power. He traveled most of the year and wanted his house secure even when he was gone, which is why he'd opted for the wireless system. No way had it gone off without help. This was intentional.

His heart rate kicked up a fraction. Ducking into the closest room, his office, he quickly swept it. Empty. He moved to the window and started to pull back the curtains when he heard a creak.

It was quiet, almost imperceptible, but he knew every sound his house made. It had been built in the forties and had real wood floors he'd had refurbished. And Tucker knew exactly where that creak had come from. A board at the beginning of the hallway, right where the kitchen opened up. It had a very distinctive sound.

Weapon in hand, he moved away from the window and crept to the doorway, giving himself enough room to have his pistol out and drawn without the worry of it being taken from him if someone attacked. If someone made a move, they wouldn't be able to make it to him before he emptied a few rounds.

Whoever was in his home had to know that Tucker was aware of his presence. Or at least guess. The house was too silent. Which took away a little of his advantage.

As he waited, everything around him sharpened, his senses going into straight battle mode. Someone could be here to rob him, but his gut told him otherwise.

He lived far enough out that his place wasn't easy to find, and disabling his security system would have taken time and an expertise far beyond your average thief.

Another creak. This one closer.

Tucker tensed, his finger on the trigger. He wasn't just going to blindly shoot, but he was ready.

Another creak. That one next to the guest bathroom door.

Which meant the intruder would be in his path in three, two, *one*.

"Drop your weapon! Put your hands in the air!" Tucker shouted as the hooded man came into view, his own weapon—with a fucking suppressor—drawn. "Now, or I drop you where you stand." His voice was quieter now, his intent clear in each word. All it would take was a bullet to the head.

It was hard to read his facial expression because of the hood, but the man stood at right around six feet, had a solid build. Wearing all black, including rubber-soled boots that made almost no sound, the intruder looked like a pro.

The silenced weapon clattered to the floor, the sound over-pronounced in the quiet of his home, before the man put his hands in the air. When he moved, Tucker could see the bulky outline of a vest. If he had to take a killing shot, it would have to be to the head.

"Kick it away."

The man did as Tucker said.

"On your knees."

Silently, the man started to kneel down, but at the last second leaped forward.

Training kicked in automatically. Tucker fired, hitting the man in his calf as he tried to dive out of Tucker's line of vision.

The hooded man cried out as Tucker swept into the hallway, conscious of his six as he trained his weapon on the guy.

He'd grabbed his fallen pistol.

Shit.

Tucker fired, two shots to the middle of the forehead. Normally he'd take a center-mass shot but there was no point with the guy wearing a vest.

The man stilled, dropping back with a thud as his weapon hand fell loudly against the wooden floor of the hallway. Tucker moved carefully, kicking it away before he checked the man's pulse and took off the hood. By the time he'd pulled it off, there was a slight blue tinge around the other man's eyes, nose, and mouth.

Certain he was dead, Tucker checked his person for any identifiers and found none before he moved on to the rest of his house. Next he cleared his garage and shed. Then he turned his power back on and reconnected the alarm, resetting it so no one could infiltrate his house while he was gone. He swept his property. He found a four-door car with mud smeared on the license plate hidden off the side of the road about a mile away. Unfortunately there weren't any identifying papers inside. He memorized the plate, then raced back to his place.

Careful to avoid the blood pooling in the hallway, he grabbed his cell and found two missed calls. Both from Cole. As he pulled out his fingerprint kit, he called his friend back. He was going to call the police, but he was taking the guy's prints first. It wasn't that he didn't trust the locals, but the DEA had more resources, and this was clearly personal.

Which meant the chances of this being linked to one of his cases was high. He had to know what and whom he was dealing with, and he'd get answers faster than the local PD.

"Someone just tried to kill me," Cole said as way of greeting. "Can't identify him, but he was a professional."

Well, hell. "Me too. You called the cops yet?"

"No. Someone also went after Brooks. This isn't fucking random," he snarled.

"Anyone contacted Kane?" The last member of their elite group.

"Can't get ahold of him."

Tucker reined in a curse. "Get the prints of your guy. Then pack a bag. Can you dispose of the body?"

"Yeah."

"Do it; then we rendezvous at location bravo." Their team had five backup places to meet if the shit ever hit the fan. They were all random and none had ties to any of them. Tucker had picked the second location because it was the first that popped into his mind.

"You sure no cops?"

"You want to alert whoever sent these guys after us that they failed?" Because the moment they did that, they'd become sitting targets. No, they needed to bug out while whoever was gunning for them thought they were dead or about to be. Then they'd regroup and figure this thing out.

"I know. Just feels like we're crossing a line."

Tucker snorted. He'd cross whatever line necessary to keep his men alive. "Bring all your weapons, ammo, passports—real and aliases—any burner phones, and all your electronics if you're sure they're not traceable. We need to figure out who's after us."

"On it. I'll keep trying Kane."

"Me too." After they disconnected, Tucker packed everything he needed, then took care of the body and blood, storing the dead man in the trunk of the car he'd abandoned on the side of the road. It wasn't the first time he'd had to dispose of a body—not with the jobs he'd been assigned to—but it was the first time he'd removed one from his own home and wasn't telling anyone else about it. He cleaned up the blood the best he could, but if pros came in here with luminol, they'd find the evidence.

But if anyone else came out here looking for him, he'd be long gone.

He needed to stay alive. Because whoever had come after his men had made the biggest mistake of his life.

Chapter 2

Six: in military and law enforcement slang, "six" means "back." Phrases like "Watch your six" or "I've got your six" mean "Watch your back" or "I've got your back." In warfare, your six is the most vulnerable position.

"I don't like this." Cole rubbed a hand over his newly cut blond hair. For the Tasev infiltration, he'd kept it shaggy, playing the part of a mindless soldier. Now he looked like his usual deadly self.

"What the fuck else are we gonna do?" Kane demanded from the front passenger seat of the SUV he, Tucker, Cole, and Brooks were in.

Tucker shifted against his seat in the back. He didn't like this plan any more than Cole did, but they had to do something. Their places were all under surveillance—by whom, they hadn't figured out—and they couldn't go into work because it was the first place their enemy would expect them. Plus they didn't know if someone in the DEA had set them up. Their top security clearances had been revoked in the system at work, which was a huge red flag. Could have been a glitch, but it had happened to all four of them.

It wasn't as if a replacement had been named for

Max yet, so they had no one to turn to. No one they trusted, anyway. Because of their undercover jobs, they were insulated from the majority of the people in the office for their safety and everyone else's. In short, they were fucked right now with no way to know if they'd been set up or even if they'd be arrested if they attempted to head into the office.

"It's been two days since Max died," Tucker said quietly.

"And Ali guarantees it's not the Shi'as," Brooks said from the front, never looking back at them as he surveyed the quiet park.

It was before dawn and everything but the sidewalks was covered in a light dusting of snow. The street sweepers had been out about an hour ago to clear and salt everything. This was a well-used park in a nice part of Baltimore where crime was pretty much unheard-of.

Until now.

"Burkhart's not returning my e-mails." Tucker hated every bit of what they were about to do, but they needed an ally. Of course, what they were about to do was just as likely to make them enemies and put them on another hit list. They had nothing to lose at this point. "This will get his attention."

Cole snorted. "And it'll get us bullets in the head."

Maybe. Tucker shook his head. "Max trusted him." Hell, Burkhart was part of Ali's fail-safe plan if the agent ever got hung out to dry or Max died during the middle of an op. He wasn't even with the DEA, but as the deputy director of the NSA and a lifelong friend of their former boss, Burkhart was a man Max had clearly thought had integrity.

Tucker hoped he was right.

"We're running out of time and we need help." Kane's voice was determined, mirroring Tucker's feelings.

"I see a female runner," Brooks said from the front, his voice grim. "Could be her."

"It's go time. Apparently," Cole tacked on, making his agitation clear.

But in the end, they were a team and would act as one cohesive unit. They trusted one another in the field and they'd support one another in this. Even though Cole was pissed, Tucker knew he'd have his back, no matter what.

He just hoped this plan didn't turn around and blow their lives apart. Moving quietly with Cole, Tucker slid out of the vehicle and made his way to a cluster of trees that lined the park. He fucking hated this plan, but forced his doubts away. They had to do this.

Karen Stafford loosened her scarf around her neck as her sneakers pounded against the pavement. Despite the chilly January weather, she'd been jogging for thirty minutes and she'd started to sweat a while ago under all her layers.

Inhaling the fresh air, she savored the quiet of the neighborhood as she made her way to her favorite park. This early, she didn't run through the park, just around it, where she was still visible along main roads. She also didn't run with an MP3 player because she liked the time to be alone with her own thoughts without any outside noise. She rarely got that with her high-pressure job at the NSA. Even if she didn't have the job she had, she still wouldn't have run with noise pumping in her ears. She liked to be aware of her surroundings at all times.

She carried bear spray with her—because no mugger or would-be rapist was going to be able to withstand that kind of pain—and a switchblade. A gift from her brother, Clint, who'd died in Afghanistan seven years ago. Whenever he'd been home he'd always brought her gifts. Usually weapons, because he'd been determined that she protect herself, since he couldn't have been there. As if he could have watched out for her twenty-four/seven if he'd been there anyway, which was a ridiculous concept. But he'd always been so protective. He'd been more like a parent to her than their own damn father had ever been.

Shaking those thoughts away, Karen increased her pace, enjoying the way her muscles burned and stretched. She ran every day, like clockwork. If it rained, she used the treadmill in her condo's gym, but she much preferred being outdoors.

When she came up to a four-way intersection, she slowed and jogged in place as she looked both ways before crossing. There weren't *any* cars or people out this morning, which was a little creepy. Feeling paranoid, she unhooked her bear spray from her hip holster and held it loosely in her hand. Her friends made fun of her for the precautions she took, but she'd seen too much shit at her job to take safety lightly.

As she reached the sidewalk that stretched along the park's small strip of a dozen parking spots, she slowed. A dark SUV with tinted windows sat in one of the spots, the engine running. The exhaust from the tailpipe was visible and, in the quiet, she could hear the distinct hum of the engine. Glancing around, she didn't see anyone else.

Not caring if she was being paranoid, she slowed

and turned back around to avoid going past the vehicle. She'd just take a different route that didn't involve the park.

At the sound of an engine revving, she glanced over her shoulder. The SUV was pulling out of the spot and heading in her direction. Her heart rate kicked up. She knew she was probably acting crazy but didn't care. Veering off the sidewalk, she raced through the park where vehicles couldn't go. As she cleared a cluster of trees without the sound of running feet coming after her, she let out a shaky breath and kept up her pace.

Holy Shit. Risking a glance over her shoulder, she nearly stumbled when she saw a man dressed in all black step out from the trees.

That face.

Recognition slammed into her with the intensity of a battering ram. Since he wore a scarf around his neck and a knit cap on his head, she couldn't spot one of the distinguishing features she'd seen in the file she had on him. But she knew he had a jagged scar around his neck and tended to favor shaving his head.

She knew it was him from his icy blue eyes.

Grisha. A murdering psychopath.

Fear took hold, its unforgiving grip squeezing around her chest like a vise, colder than the winter-morning air.

Though she wanted to run, she stopped and spun around on the sidewalk, pulling up her bear spray with a steady hand. No one could withstand this, and she just wanted the chance to get away. "Get back!" she shouted, her finger steady on the trigger. She was glad she wasn't outwardly shaking. She needed to paint a picture of calm even if she was trembling inside.

To her surprise, he held up his hands and almost

looked apologetic as he watched her. "I don't want to hurt you, Karen."

Holy hell, he knew her name. So this definitely wasn't random. Because why would this guy be in Baltimore of all places, in the same park she ran by almost every day? Did he know whom she worked for? God, he probably wanted to torture her for information. She wasn't going to stand around and ask him a bunch of questions. She was too far away to spray him. The fact that he knew her name and was a violent criminal was enough for her to run for her life.

Turning, she raced down the sidewalk, her heart beating out of control, the sound of her blood rushing in her ears so loud, she couldn't tell how close he was behind her.

She wanted to pull out her phone, but she'd strapped it around her ankle so it would be out of her way. She couldn't risk slowing down. If she could just get somewhere public, maybe she could flag someone for help.

As she moved deeper into the park, she cursed herself for coming this way. As she risked another glance over her shoulder, full-blown panic exploded inside her like fireworks. He was about twenty feet behind her and closing. He moved fast for such a big man. The range on her spray was thirty feet, so she could take him. She'd only get one shot at this so she had to do it right.

His expression was grim and he said something to her, but she couldn't hear anything above the blood rushing in her ears.

She could keep running, but he was going to reach her soon. And she knew without a doubt she'd lose against him in any sort of hand-to-hand combat. She'd seen pictures of what he'd done to someone who'd crossed him. This might be her only chance to get away or at least get help. Drawing in a deep breath, she let out a bloodcurdling scream, hoping someone would hear her, as she stopped and turned to spray him.

Still screaming, she started to press the trigger when a blur of motion out of the corner of her eye made her stumble backward.

A man burst from the trees lining the sidewalk, wearing the same attire as Grisha. There were two of them!

Pressing the trigger, she started spraying wildly as the newcomer tackled her. She flew back against the sidewalk, her head slamming against it as she lost her grip on the bear spray.

"Don't hurt her!" Grisha shouted.

But that couldn't be right. Unless he wanted to be the one to inflict pain. She tried to struggle, but the other man had her in a firm grip and she couldn't stop gasping, her chest terrifyingly tight. She couldn't breathe through the panic suffocating her. Every horrible photo or crime scene she'd ever seen at work crashed in on her at once. She didn't want to be a fucking statistic! She blinked as everything around her became fuzzy. *Stay awake*, she ordered herself as the edges of her vision started to fade.

No, no, *no*. She couldn't be unconscious around these monsters. But she couldn't control her breathing. It was too fast, too panicked. Pins and needles erupted in her hands and feet. Her eyeballs felt like they were bulging. The edges of her vision closed in. Her body refused to listen as darkness swept her under.